Our Small Town Scars

JAK ANGELESCU

Trigger Warnings:
Scenes of PTSD
Minor mentions of alcohol abuse
Death
Vivid, graphic adult content
Minor mentions of suicide
Panic attacks
Phobias mentioned
Fainting

Special Note

To the man who inspired this story.
I guess you could say that this book is my shadow love letter to you. If you
ever read this book, you're a smart man.
You'll probably figure it out.

Dedication

There were so many people that helped make this book as realistic as possible. And I can't thank you all enough.

My best friend, Holly Lingle, for letting me read it to you and helping me with research on military involvement. For helping me keep myself levelheaded and realistic, and for helping me navigate the struggles of a child dealing with divorced parents. Your real-life experiences helped me so much. Thank you for cleaning the apartment and doing the cooking when I was reclusive for two months to write this. Your never-ending support means the world.

Richard Harrison for helping me with diesel terminology and truck help, as well as offering insight on being a father to a daughter. You have been such a great friend on my writing journey and always so supportive.

Rowan Morris for her endless help with hilarious southern expressions to bring a character to life! Girl, you had me ROLLING with some of these! Thank you for your input when I asked for opinions on social media, as well as helping me design the cover! Thank you!

David Eads. Navy veteran for his professional insight on Navy funerals, processions, and attire. You were amazing to meet and chat with. I hope I get to hear more of your stories soon!

Deena Kerschner Johnson for her INSANELY realistic advice on how to handle someone with PTSD. I had this book all wrong until you answered my questions on social media and reached out. This story turned out even better because of you!

Christopher Till. Army veteran and medic. Thank you for the phone call explaining what a PTSD episode can truly feel like in their varying degrees and how you handle it. And thank you for being a great friend for over 20 years.

Corporal Bill Cunningham for letting me write you a hundred times to ask you all sorts of specific police and investigation questions! Writing this book was so much easier because of you. Thank you! You saved me hours of Google research.

Jillian Simmons for being the BEST beta reader I could ever ask for. You helped me so much on this and pointed out some SERIOUS flaws in my book. I'm so glad I could fix it. For the endless chats, laughs, and support. Thank you, girl!

And last but definitely not least...

Cody Hatheway, active Army who guided me into the right direction with my very first question on military funerals. I've been honored to call you a new friend. Thank you for your support on my author work. Proud of you, buddy!

Foreword

I don't even know where to begin. I guess I'll just start from the heart.

This story is based off some real-life experiences. Some things were taken by what men have said and done to me (both the good things and bad), and some events in the book actually happened. When I was sitting in my room one day daydreaming about my crush, I got the idea of writing this book as a way to get out my deepest, innermost feelings and emotions. I've struggled with my relationships with men my whole life. Now, being 38, I've grown tired of trying to find someone. I've never been in a relationship because I've always been used, or they become abusive right out of the gate. I'm a hopeless romantic, let's just be candid for a second. For many years, it's been an absolute destruction in my very soul to never feel loved or even experience it at all. So, this book is my selfish work. I wrote this about myself, my inner struggles, my wants, needs, desires, characteristics, everything. Writing this book was insanely cathartic and quite healing, actually.

It's important to note that while this does take place in Missouri, the actual town names, highway and street names, and restaurant names have been changed.

Also, I feel it very important to mention that certain situations were gathered from some people's personal experiences. So, please keep an open mind when reading this.

Chapter One

The bed was a complete and total mess.

The linens were rolled up in a bunch and shoved into the corner of the wall, making the floral pattern look like the flowers had been trampled on. The sun blasted her dusty farm town and streamed through the window on a hot day in August. The whole room baked with lingering heat. If only the air conditioner worked better.

One stroke of paint, and then another, and then another. The paint roller was dipped into the pan and one more swipe was given to the old smoke-stained walls.

"A-ha!" Evelyn smiled. "No more nasty crap. I finally get to have all the pink I want, all the flowers I want, all the...whatever I want!"

She tried to continue, but her arms and back were tiring. She sighed heavily, laid the roller in the pan, and flopped upon the bed. "I've been slaving away at this all day long. I think I'll go bake some cookies and... Oh! I'm gonna watch *my* favorite movie, because I can!"

She left the room with nothing but a few strokes of paint on the wall, hardly enough to have been slaving away at it for ten minutes, let alone all day long.

A few batches of cookies later, she dropped onto the couch and snacked, trying to let the air-conditioning do what it needed to do. Even though she was thirty-eight years old, she had never been able to do whatever she wanted.

With a new job as a graphic designer after a brief stint in Los Angeles—a terrible mistake that was—she felt like the world was her oyster for the first time. The very, *very* first time.

Her cell phone rang, playing a jingle from The Rolling Stones. It was her grandpa! Rolling her eyes in a smile, she picked it up. "Hey, Grandpa, what's up?"

His gravelly voice came through, "Oh, I was wondering if you were going to take all of your stuff with you or if I can donate the rest of it."

"No," she said as she muted the TV. Grandpa's accent was thick and heavy, like a billowing plume of tobacco mixed with moonshine. Sometimes she could hardly understand him, even though she had previously lived with him for ten years. Growing up in the boot hill did that to him.

There was a bit of a pause, and she chuckled. "Pawpaw, you still there?"

More silence followed.

"Pawpaw?"

Then she heard him gasping.

"Pawpaw?"

"I..." he stammered.

The gasping was getting louder and harder. He sounded like he was going to cry or something worse.

She sprung to her feet and bellowed, "I'm calling an ambulance!"

"N-no," he stammered back.

She listened and then...

He sneezed.

She pulled the phone away from the earth-shattering sound. It was so sudden and bursting that instinctively she wiped the side of her cheek. She could have sworn there was snot spray there.

She held her chest and laughed. "Damn, Pawpaw, don't scare me like that! Take your freaking Allegra."

"Oh, it ain't that, baby, and you know it," he giggled merrily. A cough followed. Then another sneeze riot.

"I think Daddy got the same sneeze orchestra from you."

"He sure did!" he said in a laugh.

"Now, you know I can't come back and forth seven times a day to pick my stuff up. I gotta take time."

"I wanna know why you won't let your old pawpaw help you. I got that ol' Chevy that's been collecting dust for too long."

She crossed that bright and sunny living room, all with its gloriously stained carpets, into the kitchen to clean off her plate. "Yeah, it's got dust *and* rust. You know you can't drive well since your stroke."

"I wanna help you though."

"I know." She smiled again. "But you helped me for like a decade. You've done enough."

He busted out laughing in that old, dried-up tone. "You're making me feel like a calendar."

She put a hand on her hip, and her big brown eyes glistened. "And why's that?"

"'Cause you're all grown up and making me feel dated."

She giggled at the corny joke. "Always keeping me on my toes."

"I can't tell you how much I'm gonna miss having you here."

She reached for her ceramic white tea kettle. It was one that her mother left her before she passed away, a gift from her Swedish great-grandmother. The flowers were all red and blue, and pops of yellow danced in their black stems and leaves. The phrase "a watched pot never boils" was hand-painted in beautiful old English font, but it was written in Swedish.

"I'm gonna miss being there too, but I had to get out on my own. Live my own life. You know?"

"You sure did! And you're going to do great!"

"Did you need anything?"

"Nope," he said while the TV in his background blared the local news station. "Only to hear the sound of your voice. But come get your crap, 'cause I wanna put my pool table in here and need room for a stripper pole."

His humor caught her off-guard again, and she laughed until her face hurt. Their goodbyes followed, and she hung up.

Wait, why am I boiling water for tea? I have my milk and leftover cookies in the living room. She stopped and looked around. "Wait, I finished my cookies." She watched the kettle smoking, and soon it would give its screeching whistle. She shrugged. "Oh well. Tea sounds nice anyway."

She went back into the living room and sat on the couch and looked at her teacup and then her leftover milk in the glass. She dumped the hot tea into the milk and drank.

It was the dumbest idea she'd ever had. It tasted awful.

With the movie over and the dishes done and on the drying rack, she turned and leaned against the counter to take in her pride and joy.

Her new home.

Not any home. It wasn't an apartment or anything.

It was her own house!

Who cared if she had to buy a little baker's rack to put next to that old and dated, small and white stove with its crusted burners so that she could store her microwave, a few bottles of wine, and her favorite coffee cup? Who cared if the walls in that kitchen were sprawling with yellow-tainted wallpaper that had its glorious ears of corn and random sketches of chickens on them? She sure didn't. It also didn't matter if the one cupboard didn't close properly and slightly hung off its hinges either.

It was all hers.

She smiled and walked over to the refrigerator to think about dinner and as usual spoke out loud to herself, not realizing she did so out of loneliness. "It's been a long day, but a casserole is what I need!"

Halfway through the prepping, her body started to hurt and tire. Her back screamed at her for rest. She put the chopped-up onions and prepped chicken in storage containers destined for the fridge and called for pizza.

Later on, she walked into her room and opened the window to enjoy a forgiving summer breeze and the sounds of the frogs that rang like a melodious country choir. She fashioned the pillows to sit upright in bed and relished in the beauty of the fireflies in her back yard. Although it was muggy, the breeze was too cool and cleansing to ignore. She ate her pizza and smiled.

How the humidity of that Missouri air filled her nose with the thick scent of wet grass. It was so fragrant she even believed that if green had a smell, it would be that. It wasn't quite harvesting season. She loved looking out across her front porch to watch the farmers plow the corn and soybean fields at night. For some reason, their little halos of lights and the sound of the machine chunking away far off made her feel like even if she lived in the country, she wasn't alone.

Maybe she missed her pawpaw more than she realized.

She rolled over and cuddled up with that flattened floral pillow, looking out into the peaceful night, where all she could see was the dark tree line thirty feet away from her house. The breeze came again. An owl called outside near her window.

Stillness. Quietness. Her pawpaw was not there to need her anymore, not entirely. She no longer had the hum of his old Western movies to hear while she cooked dinner. She no longer had the dumb jokes to make her laugh even when she wanted to scream. The thoughts tumbled in her spastic brain, and she rolled onto her back. Somehow an hour had gone by. And another.

She turned onto her left side, but her hip pain said otherwise, and so once more she tossed to face the window again.

The small-town woman couldn't help but think of him. No, not her pawpaw. Whoever *he* was. Her thoughts collided with each other.

No woman her age could deny that need. With taking care of her pawpaw for over a decade, and being sickened by low self-esteem, she had begun to give up on finding him.

Him.

Yes, whoever *he* was. He had to be someone out there. Someone who didn't fetishize her for her weight but also respected her. Somewhere there had to be a man who wouldn't try to use her as the *other* girl or a one-night stand. But now that she was older, anytime a decent man came around, she would always see that gut-wrenching thing—a ring. Being a Pisces, she felt she had so much love to give, and not once did any man reciprocate what she offered. For years she chased bad boys or starved herself for the gym rat. She even once lost her own identity falling for a foreigner who ended up stalking her at work, and dare she say it...

She shuddered.

The moment he had insisted on having sex with her, before she even knew him, it turned her off. All those men. *All* of them. If not cheating or lying, they came with heavy baggage and horrible hygiene, not to mention mommy issues.

She groaned. Perhaps she too had her share of baggage. Perhaps she too had let her hygiene slip ever since she started her full-time job, and her manic-depressive episodes left her without showering sometimes for a week. And perhaps she too had her own daddy issues. And mommy issues.

But more than anything, she had *romance* issues. It was something she craved deep within her flesh. Straight down into her blood she ached for that affirming touch of a protective man. Evelyn often imagined his hands would be calloused from a hard day's work, and he would be sweaty and tired, and she would have dinner ready for him. It was such a contrast to the man she used to want. Those men were fantasy characters with flaming onyx hair riding valiantly on black stallions to rush to their maiden's needs.

But the real world hit hard.

And dreams were apparently for children.

But those men in her beloved fiction books taught her something, and that was to never settle for less than feeling loved and protected. It took her only three times to realize she was not to be played with but loved.

She was always used and left in one way or another.

To hell with it all. She curled up and hugged her teddy bear and cried.

"Face it, you're becoming middle-aged, and by now no man is going to want you. You've been told this your whole life." Tears slowly rolled down her face as she whimpered harder into her bear. "Men don't want a woman past her prime. Here in the damn Midwest, no man wants you unless you're thin with blue eyes, blonde hair, tanned, and either a fucking nurse or a teacher."

But she tried to calm herself down before the crushing feeling in her stomach got too obnoxious. Was it anxiety? She wasn't so sure. "I'll be okay," she whispered to herself. "I'm fucked up, but I'll be okay."

The next day, she woke early to collect a few more boxes at Pawpaw's house. And it was once again another hot and muggy day, and everything she put on felt like it was suctioning to her skin. Her hair felt slimy all over her neck, like she had gotten out of the shower. She *could* have blow-dried it, but the heat on her face would have made her want to scream and escape to Antarctica. Once more, she put on a light-pink tank top, pulled up her denim shorts, shimmying her hips to get them up.

When she tried to button them, it felt like she was trying to stuff biscuit dough back into the canister. "Agh!" she wailed as she once more pulled and tried to button them. "I bought these damn things at the thrift store last month! Don't even tell me they're too tight now!"

She kicked her legs out and put her hand to the baggy crotch area and tried to pull it up.

Pulling the waistline and sucking in, she got them fastened.

"There!" She panted in sweat. "Damn, it's so hot. I swear even Satan's sweating today."

She looked at herself in the mirror. Yep. She certainly looked like biscuit dough popping out of the canister. Her dark eyebrows were bushy, and her chin seemed rounder than ever.

"Oh, hell the fuck no to this. I look about as 'well-insulated' as I feel!"

She changed into a cotton wireless bra, a white cotton tank top, and some light-blue cotton lounge shorts.

Then came the jingle of "Honky Tonk Women" on her phone. She fell onto the bed and answered, "Hey, Pawpaw!"

"Hey, baby girl! Could you do me a favor before you come over?"

She snickered, "What makes you think I was gonna come over today?" She was trying to play coy because she wanted to surprise him with muffins from the local café up in her nearby town.

"There are some black-eyed Susans sprouting up alongside Highway 42. Can you pick a few for me?"

She rubbed her face and let out a sigh of frustration. "Pawpaw, taking that highway takes me out of my way to you."

"Okaayyy...fine. I see you don't love your old man no more."

They both cackled. "Your lame pity parties don't get far with me, you know."

His tone was so sweet as he replied, "Yes, they do."

She sat up. "Fine, I'll get your goofy flowers."

"Bring me muffins too."

"Pawpaw!" she cried humorously.

"What? You got that fancy little café in your town now. I want some muffins! I don't got you here to bake me any no more."

"You're ruining my surprise for you!"

"Oh...uh," he moaned as he scratched his head. "I was gonna ask you for something, but I can't remember what. Must be that dementia kicking in. It could have been me asking for muffins, but maybe banana bread?"

She grinned, kicking her feet about on the bed. "You don't have dementia."

"Thank God I don't, or I'd forget my pretty little granddaughter!"

She stayed still for a moment to take in his love. "I love you, Pawpaw. I'll get you your flowers and your muffins."

She hung up and left out the door, down her little broken steps, and across the stone path that was smashed too deep into the wet dirt. She felt the wild tall grasses and flowers lick at her thighs. She really needed to take care of that. The house came like that, but it didn't mean it needed to *stay* like that.

Highway 42 was a two-way road full of winding passes, cornfields, cow pastures, rolling hills that made it nerve-wracking for her to even go the speed limit due to driveways at every bottom, and even this one weird old, dilapidated house that seemed like it caught fire and tried to fall apart but didn't. There was a chain-link fence that sequestered dozens of old cars in absolute disrepair as well as a heap of some sort of debris. Even though no one lived there, she always wanted to explore inside.

She looked for the flowers, keeping her eyes peeled. Even if she did find them, there wasn't much of a shoulder to stop on. She leaned forward and looked up at the brilliant summer blue sky. The clouds were enormous white puffs. They climbed all the way to where she believed heaven could be. They had a bit of a darker lining to them.

"Ah, cumulonimbus clouds! I hope it storms today. I could really go for some of Pawpaw's guitar picking out on his front porch during the rain."

When the yellow floral culprits appeared, she pulled into the drive of some farmer's cornfield. There they grew in the shoulder's trenches. She got out and followed the gravel shoulder back a bit. Using scissors, Evie snipped the flowers in a beautiful bunch and headed back to the car and went to put them in the back so they would be able to stay out of the sun, but the back of her car was a mess with old mail. She groaned and tried to clear room before seeing an advertisement with a cute guy's photo on it.

"Caleb Wright Rustic Renovations. Where your first home grows with you."

She lifted her eyes and saw the photo of the man.

She almost dropped the flowers back on the ground. He had the kindest brown eyes, so deep and sparkling, that he looked vivacious. With tanned skin and dirty-brown hair, it was kept styled naturally, a stark contrast to his sharp suit he wore. His facial hair outlined a softly sculpted jaw structure, and his smile was youthful despite the age that decorated the corners of those eyes. She smirked playfully. His shoulders were matured in their husky, stocky appearance. He had to have been somewhere around her age.

"Now *that* man looks like a good, ol' fashioned Midwest boy."

For a moment, she let herself look at him and lost herself in thinking how cute he was. He was so cute, it hurt! She tossed the ad on the seat, placed the flowers securely, and got back in. She held her steering wheel and sighed in a daydream. She hadn't had a crush since she was twenty-one.

Then it hit her. "Shit!" she yelled as she slammed her hands on the steering wheel. "I forgot Pawpaw's muffins!"

Chapter Two

Evelyn pulled up to that beautiful white ranch. It was the place she often spent time at during her childhood, and she was so thrilled to take in the smells of all the flowers that Pawpaw had blooming along the front railing of the porch.

As she closed the door, he came out with a swing of that creaking screen door. "Baby girl!" he laughed with his arms outstretched. "I see you made it!" When he got a good look at her, he stopped and playfully grew cautious.

"I know," she said, shaking her head. "I forgot your muffins. I'm so sorry. I got so caught up in trying to go and—"

He stopped her with a smile. He had a great way of doing that. His light-blue eyes dazzled with love. She always hated that she never got those same eyes. She had inherited her grandmother's brown eyes. His age spots were more apparent than ever, and his shorter sparse grays looked like herb sprouts in a garden sticking straight up. She chuckled and patted them with her hand.

"C'mere, Pawpaw." They hugged hard.

Once inside, she felt the sweltering and suffocating heat. Sure, the windows were open a smidge, but the front window was flooding the entirety of that room with hot sunshine.

"You should really pull your curtains closed!" she said as she yanked them tight.

"Ah," he said with a toss of his hand and his back turned to her. He was headed for the kitchen. "I love the sunlight and the fresh air! You kids are too pampered these days. It's only eighty in here!"

"Yeah, but like 180 in the sunlight," she said with a laugh.

Together they went to the kitchen, and she trimmed the stems of the flowers and put them in water with a drop of bleach. He sat down at the table and groaned in delight. "Still using that same trick your grandma taught you, eh?"

"Yep! It does the trick. These things will last a lifetime."

Placing them on the table, she noticed he was looking at her. It was easy for her to guess what that meant. Her weight gain was noticeable.

"Please don't talk about my weight, Pawpaw."

He scoffed, "I wasn't gonna!"

"Okay," she said slowly with a smile. "Then what are you staring at?"

She sat down but tried hard not to let her weight make her knees buckle as she did.

He took a breath. "I was thinking how lucky I am to still have you here." He folded his hands together and placed his elbows on the table looking out the gingham-curtained kitchen window. "Your momma's gone. Your daddy's gone. Your brothers don't come around here at all, and I'm lucky to talk to them a few times a year. I'm so grateful you still come around and see me."

Her hand reached across the table to feel his. The skin was so thin and tanned from his hard yard work. "I'm still so lucky to have you too."

He sat up playfully. "Okay, now that the mushy stuff is over with, why don't you have a man yet?"

Evelyn's eyes widened, and she rolled her head and threw up her hands with a smile. "Oh, for Christ's sake, you couldn't help yourself, could you?"

The kitchen twinkled with laughter.

"You're such a beautiful, hardworking woman! Any man would die to have you. You took care of me for over a decade. Believe me, a man is gonna *love* that."

Evie drummed her fingers and then turned easily to be able to reach for the fridge door and pulled out a few cherry sodas.

"That's the problem, Pops. All men want is for a woman to slave over them, worship the ground they walk on. Midwest men are hard. They won't even call you beautiful or say thank you." Her grip tightened around the can, and he continued to watch her.

With eyes wandering off to the left and down, her lips trembled at the thought. "All I want is flowers. All I want is to feel safe. I didn't think that was too much to ask for."

"Baby, you spend too much time on Facebook and Instagram. Not all men are like that. Especially not here in the Midwest. That's a fabricated image. You need to get back into the real world and forget the way you were treated in Los Angeles. You want flowers?"

She went quiet briefly. "I haven't gotten any since Daddy died. Valentine's day was the last day I got flowers. I miss those little gifts from him so much."

Pawpaw immediately got up and left the kitchen. She was alone then.

A squirrel made a racket outside, and it got the neighbor's dog barking.

Pawpaw came back inside with a fragrant bouquet from his front yard. It was the thickest and most beautiful bunch of zinnias and marigolds she ever saw. She gasped, her eyes watering.

"Here. You want flowers, baby girl? I got ya flowers."

Graciously, she took the bouquet and thanked him.

"Hell," he shouted happily, "I'll give you my whole damn garden if you want. You earned it. But let me tell you something..."

She looked at him.

"Somewhere out there, there is a man for you. No, he may not be that Brazilian pool boy desperado you always dreamed about when you were a little girl." She laughed hard in both cringing embarrassment and amusement. "But he'll be a good man. Is there anyone you got your eyes set on in town?"

Her fingers gently touched the petals, and she smelled them. "Do you know who Caleb Wright is?"

He huffed and crossed his arms. "Sure do. That's a military man. Don't go messing around with them."

"But you were in the military, Pawpaw?"

"That was back when pterodactyls were considered fighter pilots."

Once again, she laughed. "But I thought he did some sort of contractor work?"

"He does. But he's Navy too."

"What's wrong with that?"

"A lot! Your generation isn't as loyal as mine was! You wanna talk about the disrespect that men have toward women, wait until you get involved with that guy! No sirree. You probably will take *one good look* at those brown eyes and his damn dimple smile and think he's *so* cute and sweet!"

"And he isn't?"

"No, he ain't. That's Edward Wright's boy. And he's cold. *Real* cold. He's got a temper like a wet chicken. He used to be a realtor, Evie. He's supposed to look sweet, caring, and kind. It's how he sold houses."

"Wait, Edward Wright? You mean the guy who was in Dad's football gang?"

"Yes, ma'am. And your dad was over at Big Ed's house tons of times, and if he were still alive today, he'd be able to tell you what kind of a cold, apathetic nuisance that man is."

"How many years ago was this?"

"Oh, um." He scratched his head. "I think I have dementia."

"Pawpaw," she warned in a grin.

"About six years ago."

She sat up straight. "He's older now. Maybe things are different. I'm not the same woman I was six years ago."

"Okay, but you can't afford a renovation. How'd you expect to get his attention?"

"I could um... I don't know actually."

"I could take a bobcat to it, and we all can party on the insurance money."

"Pawpaw!" she chuckled.

The rest of the time, Pawpaw kept her company while she whipped up the most decent muffins she could muster. Even though they weren't anything to write home about, she enjoyed his company greatly before heading home.

At home, Evie peeled off those damp and sweaty clothes and sat down on the couch to watch some TV. A massive pile of dishes collected stagnant water in the sink. Bills and mail were scattered on the coffee table. While a cooking show played, she looked at her place. Boxes still needed to be unpacked, and now she had *new* boxes to unpack. A hole in the wall needed to be patched, and paint supplies were all over the place.

She ended up spending three cooking episodes long of trying to prioritize her tasks and organize her schedule. "I can work out for thirty minutes in the morning, and by the time I get home from work, I can work on my garden outside. Maybe ten minutes to paint, and I can meal prep on Sundays!"

Nope. She tired herself out, and while watching the fifth episode, she scrolled on her phone until her eyes were sore, and so she went to bed.

Dishes still undone. Three hours gone and no workout in.

But for the first time in years, she looked up at the ceiling and truly smiled. So many wild thoughts flooded her tender mind, things that would make her happy. Things that would make her...

Hot.

So hot. Her chest flushed, and she felt a flutter of emotions and stirring excitement within.

But she was going to have to stop being so immature and straighten up. If Caleb Wright was a military man and had another successful career, there was a good chance he was a go-getter, a hard worker, and had his act together. She on the other hand got overwhelmed by doing a load of dishes, couldn't get a ten-minute workout routine to stick, and didn't even know how to change the oil in her own car or fill up her antifreeze.

* * *

21

For a few months after that, Evie visited Pawpaw's place and got used to her new life as best as she could and would specifically stop for the flowers until they no longer bloomed. She would stop on that little farmhouse drive and gaze at the beautiful, rolling fields.

She sighed. "One day, I could live on a rolling field like that with the beautiful sunshine coming in."

Her house was nowhere near completion. And even into late winter when things were cold, she realized how drafty it was. Her heating bill skyrocketed, and the house still remained in disrepair. The few paint jobs she did were patchy at best, and the new door handles she tried to put on fell off more times than she cared to count.

And then spring came again, and with it came that lovely local tulip festival she adored. She'd drive along her way to work in the city and gaze out her window to take in the seductive views of popping reds, yellows, oranges, blues. And they would all be like children nestled down in the grass's blanket at the feet of a Dutch-inspired windmill, all with its red paint and charming white blades.

Spring melted into summer. The cicadas screamed their desperate song out into the setting sun, and the crickets and frogs were a symphony as she'd sit out on her rundown porch with her a cherry Coke. Evie watched the traffic drift on by far off when it came, and she'd race outside to marvel at any time the Hercules C-130s flew overhead.

But now it was time for flowers again.

She stopped at that side of the highway and walked back gradually to those wild gifts of mother nature. A mosquito tried to bite her, but she slapped the pest away hard, leaving a little blood splat on her arm. The flowers were plucked, snipped, bunched together, and she even spent a little time lifting the petals a bit more and smiled at them, tilting her head to the side. It was hot. It was a sauna outside. Her thighs rubbed together painfully as she limped back to her car. Her knees and back were bothering her, and so were her emotions.

An hour later, she gave those flowers to her beloved pawpaw by placing them on his chest.

A thunderstorm began its first percussive strike outside.

The murmur of people she hadn't seen in months or even years swarmed her hearing like bugs, like mosquitoes that needed to be slapped away. They never came to see Pawpaw when he was laughing, working hard in his yard, needing help.

And now she had guilt.

Crushing guilt.

With fingers curling around the mahogany edges of the casket, Evie cursed herself. She left him. And apparently, he needed her still.

She felt a hand on her shoulder. "I know what you're thinking, baby sis."

She turned and looked at her oldest brother, a tall and dark-haired man with eyes as dark as his hair. He was the successful child. The one who married when he was younger, graduated with high honors, a brainiac, and a whiz with his finances. Her other older brother had gone on to become a successful DJ.

But Evie shook her head and held him hard, crying into his chest. "I'm so glad to see you again, Darren."

He hugged her back with a squeeze so strong and tight it momentarily relieved her back pain. "I'm glad to see you, too. I heard you bought a house. Congratulations. You deserve it. You've worked so hard. Why don't you come sit with us? Daniel cancelled a gig in Florida to come to the funeral and to see you. He's missed you a lot."

Later on, she watched in the rain while the casket was lowered into the grave. Those Midwest thunder skies were always so menacing that time of year. Dark and diabolic. Pawpaw George was laid to rest and given the twenty-one-gun salute, the taps, and a folded flag for Darren to take.

But he insisted that it be given to his baby sister.

"I want you to have it."

"But why?"

"I think you know why. You took care of Pawpaw while I was busy with my business and my new family. I hardly got to see him at all these last three years." He lowered his head shamefully. "Not to mention, Daniel wasn't even here for almost six years."

Being the loving sister she always tried to be, she held his hand. "Don't be so hard on yourself. He was so proud of you and loved you regardless. You and Daniel both."

That didn't stop Evie from having a full-blown breakdown once she got into her home. She stormed in and screamed, throwing her flats against the wall. Slamming the door closed, she hated everything all over again. She was truly alone now. Her brother lived over an hour away, and she had never truly learned how to be a proper adult due to the untimely deaths of her parents. Pawpaw George was all she had.

She cried herself to sleep.

Often, Evie took him flowers from his favorite spot and would eat muffins and talk with him by his grave, even into the cold and frosty autumn when she had to buy flowers at a store.

She was tired, so she dressed herself in dirty leggings, a baggy sweater, house boots, and with greasy hair and unwaxed brows she headed into town to the drugstore where she'd be able to buy medicine for a cold she felt was coming on, some comfort food, and flowers for Pawpaw.

At the store, she walked in and tried to bypass all of the obstacles one would find in an ill-kept but high-favored local drugstore. And way up at the top she saw the medicine she needed. It hadn't been stocked yet and was still in its shipping box.

"Why the hell are you all the way up there?" she mused.

She stood on her toes, reached, winced, and was barely able to graze the box with her fingertip. And then she heard a voice coming from beside her.

"I would ask you if you needed help with that, but that's a question Captain Obvious would ask."

She chuckled without looking, as her focus was still on the box. "Not at all! I hate being short."

"Well," the deep voice said with a thick Midwest accent, "lucky for you, I like being tall."

Tanned, earthy, and muscled hands stretched up to grab the box, and the man plopped it down on another one next to her.

"Thank you!" Evelyn said, turning to the kindhearted stranger. But immediately she had to shift her gaze upward due to his height. Her heart flushed, and redness came into her cheeks.

He was cute alright. And perhaps if she had felt better and wasn't missing her pawpaw, she may have tried to flirt in some way. But her heart was too heavy for that nonsense.

His handsome dark eyes speckled with kindness, and his face was smooth. He had dimples as he smiled. Her heart simply pooled like a little schoolgirl all over again.

Wearing light-red flannel and washed-out blue jeans, he nodded to her and left, calling over his shoulder, "To let you know, that medicine ain't gonna help much with that fever of yours. You're as red as a tomato."

I'm not flushed from a fever, she thought to herself.

She hurried to get in line after everything was placed in her basket, and she got right behind him, completely unintentionally. She refrained from coughing as he placed his stuff on the register. He *was* tall! He had to be about six-foot-three. Evelyn leaned to the side to try to ease her back pain.

He glanced back at her then turned to get out his wallet. "What are the flowers for?"

"My pawpaw."

"You buy flowers for your grandpa? That's awful sweet. Where's he at?"

She looked away. "At Crest Hill."

He gazed at her in a pause. And then he grabbed her basket and put it up on the counter. "Add this to my bill," he said to the cashier.

"Oh, are you—" Evelyn began but then stopped. "Thank you."

"I'm a soldier myself. Only the finest are buried there. I'm sure he was a damn good man."

"Yes," she said slowly. "He was." After he gave her a brief smile, she thought to ask him his name. But she had to do the dreaded check first.

"I, uh..." She moved to step next to him. Peering out of the corner of her eye, she saw it.

The ring.

Her heart was crushed.

"You what?" He smiled at her.

"I, um, really want to thank you."

He gave her the bag. "Don't mention it. Pay it forward."

Next thing she knew, he was gone and out the door.

She didn't even get to know his name.

Chapter Three

"I don't even have a Christmas tree," she said to herself as she walked in through the door. She rubbed her face in exhaustion. The pain in her body had mounted to a point of needing to lie down, and so she did. She flopped on the couch once more and sulked. There was no lie she could tell herself now. Her mind kept going back to how lonely she felt since Pawpaw passed, and as she basked in her squalor, the horrible encroaching feeling dawned on her. She was destined for a state of disrepair as much as her house was. But the man in the ad from long ago? Too perfect and unattainable. *He would never go for a girl like me.*

Most certainly not. He apparently had his whole life together, and she? Well, she couldn't even fix herself a proper meal those days. And the man at the drugstore? Married, as he should be. But still she rolled her head off to the side with her arms draped carelessly on the couch. The act of kindness he gave her was going to have to suffice.

Evelyn kept staring at the empty corner in her living room. There were still a few unpacked boxes nearby, a dusty end table she was unsure if she'd keep, and a few storage boxes full of clothes that no longer fit her.

She smiled and decided to get rid of it all to make room for a

Christmas tree. Each box of clothing was taken to her sedan so that she could donate it, and soon the table followed. She vowed to herself that she would lose weight for spring, and so all those extra spring clothes were no longer necessary. Before she could slow down, half of the things in her living room were gone. Happiness came over her, exfoliating her dead soul like warm and cleansing sands on achy feet.

With a cup of tea, she sat in front of her computer and opened Facebook. Her mission was clear. She was going to ask if anyone had a spare tree to donate or sell so close to Christmas. Her fingers drummed on the desk. Her brown eyes focused hard. And to her surprise, numerous people responded.

She had her tree, all for free. The people of her small town had pulled through for her. Joshua, her neighbor across the street, was kind enough to go pick it up for her in his flatbed. It was then that Evelyn realized she was going to have to try to reach outside of her introverted shell if she was *ever* going to get along without Pawpaw.

How The Grinch Stole Christmas played on the TV as she decorated the fake tree with a smile. Glee. Joy. Blessed.

Anxious. Afraid. Alone.

Powerful. Strong. Determined.

Sad. Defeated. Melancholy.

Tired.

Weak.

Hurting.

She was hungry. *Starving.* While taking a break from decorating, she had got so preoccupied with scrolling mindlessly on the town's discussion page that she forgot to even think about dinner. And walking into the kitchen? It was an absolute disaster. One more pizza ordered. One more bottle of cherry Coke. Just one more.

While eating a fourth slice, she looked over and noticed Pawpaw's old sunburst Taylor acoustic sitting there against the other couch, waiting for love. It originally belonged to her daddy, but when he passed, Pawpaw took it. So now that he had passed, she took it.

She walked over and picked it up.

Joy.

She tuned the strings.

Happiness.

She strummed a G chord.

No, not that one. She strummed a D chord, her favorite chord and key signature in the whole world.

Perfection.

The little disheveled living room became a breath of unwavering delight. Colorful lights bloomed and sparkled against the muted TV. She kicked up her feet on the old coffee table and slouched back, playing every Christmas song she knew and loved. It healed her nerves in a way she hadn't felt in months. Her voice rose with every high note, longing to feel the magic of the snow on her skin and the innocence of being a little girl in the wilds of Alaska all over again. Back when she was brave. Back before adulthood hit. Back when she believed she could fly and swim with mermaids.

Adulthood was difficult for someone who was never truly taught how to be an adult. And maybe she needed to accept it.

And grow up.

Whatever that meant.

Evelyn Morgan spent that Midwest winter alone, and she discovered how deep and lonesome those winters could be. So lonesome she could cry.

She walked into the kitchen, sat at the table, and held her hands in her hair. Each tear fell on the littered table as she clutched her hair by the roots. The cold draft rushed across her feet to where she always had to wear slippers. But never mind this crying. Evelyn pried herself away from that bondage of depression and simply went to bed. The nips of ice bit at her window, and the smell of someone's wood stove burned in the night air. Perhaps it was Joshua again.

She rolled over.

Who...cares?

Spring came knocking on her door in a few months' time to offer its happy song. Well, it was *trying* to come, but as it would be in the Midwest, it was losing a weather custody battle with winter. Some days it felt like spring, and some days it snowed. Evie would wear a thick wool coat to work in the morning and then need the air conditioner on full blast in the afternoon.

It was March 1st, two days before her 40th birthday, and on this morning the TV played another cooking show. Oatmeal simmered in a pot. A bowl of fresh fruit was directly next to it. The sun shone on the clean kitchen table that was now crowned with a lively bouquet of numerous tulips, irises, and hyacinths. Where disastrous moving boxes were nested and stacked in corners now was a clean space with a decorative floor lamp or some other piece of decoration she'd bought from the local dollar store. One of her newfound addictions, no less. The hair wax pot on her bathroom counter contained watery wax. Her bathroom had rich aromas of rosemary and mint as the shower ran hot and she, inside, was singing.

The tea kettle screamed at her on the stove, and out of the shower Evelyn came and grabbed the towel so fast that she ripped it clean off the bar rack and made it come loose. She scoffed at being torn between the kettle and picking up the screw that fell out. Choosing the tea kettle, she yelled, "I know. I'm coming!" She walked forward and stepped right on that screw, suddenly hissing and hopping while trying to hold up her pink towel wrapped about her.

The stove was turned off, and she sighed and smiled, pouring herself a nice cup. "There we go! That should do it!" She took her oatmeal and fruit into her bedroom, sporadically eating in between picking out what to wear. It was a big day for her. The possibility of a promotion, and she wanted to look her absolute best!

She put a white sundress against her body and looked in the mirror. She grimaced and chucked it to the bed. "I'm not doing senior photos at the lake." Hangers were scooched to the side, and she smirked and then put on a pair of dress slacks, a blazer, and a leopard-print blouse. She cast it away with a repulsed look. "It's springtime, Evie. Get with the program." She sighed and continued as she rummaged deeper.

"No, definitely not," she said. Until then she saw an old storage box. She paused and slowly removed it and put it on the bed. She popped the lid off and saw the dress that Pawpaw got her when she was in her twenties to congratulate her on graduating college. Apprehensively, she pulled it out and let the beautiful fabric fall. It was a lovely shade of celeste, Pawpaw's favorite color. And it was a dressy enough of a material that she could wear it. With soft flowing short sleeves and a tapered waistline, the neckline wasn't too plunged to where it was inappropriate. But this dress was something she wore over fifteen years ago.

Evelyn pushed doubt aside and became eager to put it on. It fell effortlessly around her! Tears welled in her eyes as she touched her stomach and looked at her reflection in the mirror. It fit. Thirty pounds down now. Her full lips smiled widely as she twirled to let the fabric flow and catch the air. The beautiful feeling consumed her entirely. She lifted up her light-brown hair and shook it about playfully.

"I wish you could see this, Pawpaw. Oh, but wait! There *is* someone who can see this!" She turned and grinned. "Teddy!"

The heavy patters of paws came fluttering with clumsy movements, and in came the new fat tabby ginger she adopted, a male rescue named Teddy. "What do you think?"

He rolled over on her foot exposing his sandy-colored belly.

"Oh, a lot of help you are. I'm going for a promotion today, so I gotta look my best!"

Then she smelled wax cooking.

"Ah!" she hollered. She raced frantically into the bathroom and removed the lid to blow it off trying to cool it. "Oh," she said shakingly with a bounce in her body movements. "I keep getting you too hot, then you get too cold!"

There was no time to wait, as she was already running late. She turned off the warmer, packed her tweezers, and headed for the door. She kissed Teddy goodbye and left.

Every step she gave had a dance in it. Joshua smiled and waved at her from across the street. "You got that interview today?"

She opened her car door. "Yes! Wish me luck!"

"Good luck! Maybe before you know it, you'll be designing all the business signs in town!"

She smiled, thanked him, and left. It was a really nice thing to say.

At stop signs, she plucked her brows while looking in the mirror. A car horn honked out of nowhere, and she jumped. "Oh my God!" Before she could even put her foot to the pedal, the truck blazed by her into the oncoming lane and cut her off. She screamed, squeezing the steering wheel. Her heart was in her throat. "Alan Moffet! I hope Hunt gets you on his radar!" She pulled through the intersection. "At least I don't have to worry about your ass tailgating me."

The Chevy truck hit a horrible pothole and almost swerved off the road.

"Serves you right!" She laughed and swerved to the right to miss it but ended up behind a tractor and drummed her fingers, leaning over her steering wheel.

She waited through a construction zone and rocked out to Journey.

Then her tire pressure warning went off. Likely from hitting that pothole too many times.

"Oh, you have *got* to be freaking kidding me right now! Ugh!"

Evelyn looked up and around and saw the only gas station in sight. It was some random one that looked like no one would ever go to unless they were desperate, kind of like her. "Please have air. Please have air. Please have air." She was still breathing heavy from the truck incident.

Circling the parking lot, she saw the one lone air pump and jumped happily, pulling right up to it. But as she got out, her dress immediately caught the wind and whipped about her so fanatically that she had to keep her hands on it. It was horrible! That damn spring wind was ruining her hairstyle and getting strands stuck to her lip gloss. She pulled it away with one hand and tried to lean over to get her pressure checker out, and her panties were almost exposed for the whole world to see in a matter of seconds.

Surely the truckers nearby may like a show, but she wasn't up for that. The busy highway sounds whizzed off the intersection, and she let go of her hair to grab the pressure gauge. And soon enough, she tried to squat down to check the pressure. The wind was everywhere, and so was her dress! "Dammit! It wasn't this windy this morning," she mumbled to herself.

She stood up and tried to configure her dress somewhere between her legs to hold it together with her thighs, but it made squatting nearly impossible, and even when she leaned over, the back end would fly up. Evelyn stood upright and tried to sit down to tuck her dress underneath.

Before she could, a voice called to her, "Ma'am? Would you like some help?" It had a little bit of a snicker in it, as if the person asking the question found her situation humorous. And even to her, it was...now that someone was there to help.

She pulled her dress down and stopped before she ever sat down. "Thank you so much!" she said happily. "I wasn't expecting this wind today and-"

Turning, her breath left her lungs.

The wind blew her hair back behind her with the direction she was facing, and her eyes went amiss with seeing him...*again.*

He chuckled in that boyish smile with those expressive and kind eyes. "There's no need for a lady to be sittin' on the ground in a dress. Here, let me see that gauge."

Evelyn felt her heart racing, pounding harder than it already had been from the truck incident. "I recognize you," she said as she handed him the gauge. "You're the man from the drugstore. You helped me back then. Do you remember?"

He scratched his scruffy cheek and rolled up the sleeves of his blue plaid shirt and grinned. He knelt and felt her tire. "Oh, I remember alright. You're the short girl with the tomato face."

She chuckled. "I had a fever that day, you know."

He felt her tire for wear and tear. He returned the grin, squinting from the sun. "Sure, you did."

Evelyn fumbled her hands to hold her dress down and sucked in her stomach and tried to straighten up her back. But as he worked, he looked at her again and laughed once more. "You straightened up like I was your momma telling you to." Then he stood and towered over her. Even in her full figure, she still felt small next to him. His presence was wonderful, comforting, welcoming, and inviting. She swallowed hard and looked at him again, fumbling to hold her dress and make eye contact. And she never cared to look for the ring again. Her heart was too caught up in the moment to be broken by seeing it. His dimpled smile came again.

"Your tires are bald, and they suck," he declared with a laugh.

The blunt comment rose a laughter from her. She put a hand to her mouth and felt a girlish giggle flood her whole body. The way he kept looking at her, she felt the burning to ask him out regardless of the ring. She could play it off as a gesture of gratitude.

He glanced at her momentarily before pulling away to check the other tires. "It's pretty windy out here. Why don't you sit inside the car, so you don't ruin your hair?"

She followed him around. "It's no biggie. I have about ten pounds of lip gloss stuck in my hair anyway, and I think the wind gods have done all the damage they can."

"Don't say that. You'll challenge Missouri and we'll get a tornado."

"Right?" she giggled. "Or given how bipolar our weather is, it could be another blizzard suddenly even though it's sixty-five degrees."

He laughed. He actually laughed. Evelyn kept her dress held down and said meekly, "Thank you for doing this. I didn't even get your name last time."

The handsome stranger finished the last tire then stood up and ran his hand through his light-brown hair. He gave her the gauge back. When she took it, he shoved his hands in his pockets and smirked. "Now if I tell you that, you gotta promise me you're not gonna get all weird on me."

"Why would I do that?"

"'Cause your pawpaw knew me, and so did your dad."

Her eyes widened.

The ad. The man in the drugstore. It was *him*. How was she so dumb not to put the two faces together? To her credit, he was wearing a suit with a scruffy face in the ad and a flannel shirt and a smooth face at the store.

Wait a minute. How did *he* know who she was? She thought to ask him.

But Evelyn decided against it. She wanted to play naïve. He was obviously nervous about the relation in some way, and so she didn't want to jeopardize anything. "That's what Pawpaw and Daddy knew of you. I don't know who you are."

He outstretched his hand and smiled. "Caleb Wright."

She pulled her hair behind her ear in a nervous grin and extended her hand out to his. The roughness made her feminine skin drip with yearning. His large fingers curled around her plush and soft hand deliberately with a gentle squeeze. It wasn't a rushed handshake and so she felt herself fighting the urge to look, but she had to.

There was no ring on his left ring finger.

Fight it. Don't ask. Be respectful. Don't be nosy. It's none of your business.

She fought for a breath. She could have fallen into his arms then and there, and the loud thrum of the interstate would have been mute and her interview obsolete. It wasn't just a handshake; it was healing to her.

"It's nice to meet you, Caleb."

"And you are?"

"Oh!" she said as she laughed nervously. "I'm sorry. I'm uh…"

He leaned closer to her. "Tomato-faced? Feverish?"

She let out the stupidest laugh she could have ever done. Immediately she tried to shut herself up, because it was a clear sign that giddiness was making her feel dumb, immature, and childish. "Oh, no, um… I'm Evie Morgan."

"Christmas tree girl! I saw your post back in December and I see your posts all the time now. That's how I figured out who your grandpa was. You asked the discussion page how to donate to Crest Hill Cemetery in honor of your grandpa. I thought it was super sweet. Did you ever a tree, though?"

He crossed his arms like he had no intention of leaving. She fumbled to think of a way to keep the conversation going. "I did, thanks! Did you have a good Christmas?"

His eyes rolled. "It could have been better, but maybe in hindsight it was okay."

The separation must've happened then, she thought. Or she hoped it was a separation. She hoped his wife didn't pass away. She knew too well how badly that hurt. "I'm sorry it wasn't better. Maybe this year will be better, right?" she asked tenderly, trying to be the caring person she was.

He scoffed with a smile. "You're kind of new around here, aren't you?"

She nodded with sincerity in her eyes. "I am. I moved here about two years ago."

"Do you like it?"

She shrugged. "It's okay. Do you like it?"

He looked away. "Not really. I live outside town on Highway 42. People in the town can't seem to keep their mouths shut, you know? Everyone's always complainin' about something. Or they're gossiping about someone or something. Or always moanin' about something not being fixed in the town or yelling at each other. That's why I refrain from interacting on the page as much as possible."

"Wait, aren't you a contractor? I think I got your ad in the mail."

He nodded proudly. "Yep! I like to send out pictures with my big ol' fat head for fire tinder."

She leaned over in laughter. They both shared the laughter for a good solid minute before she gasped and wheezed to joke, "If you think you've got a fat head it's a good thing my ass ain't on an advertisement or it'd take up both sides of the paper."

He clapped his hands in the sheer hilariousness, and she placed the back of her hand to her mouth to stifle the laughter.

The humor was a much-needed release for both of them.

A diesel slowly trudged on in and released its air brakes.

She straightened up and tossed her hair away from her neck. "I heard you used to be a realtor. It's a shame I didn't know you prior to buying my house. I could've gotten you a nice-sized commission."

"Oh yeah? Where did you move to?"

She rolled her eyes playfully and sarcastically said, "The white bungalow off of 129 with the dilapidated steps."

He brightened up. "Oh, you traitor. I could've retired on that commission."

"All $3,300 of it?"

"Exactly! I could be rolling off the coast of Kokomo in a yacht right now. But no, you had to be selfish."

She gave a glittering smile. "I can be kind of selfish."

"You don't seem selfish to me," he stated. There was a touch of seriousness in his tone. "I saw the county's post about how you bought cinnamon rolls for the entire sheriff's department for no particular reason."

She looked off in reflection. "Well, it wasn't only to be nice. Deputy Hunt changed my tire for me when it blew out on the side of the interstate, and Deputy Buckley gave me a ride when my car broke down."

He rocked on his heels, grinning. "And that merited $200 worth of cinnamon rolls?"

She looked down at her fumbling hands. Maybe she was a bit ridiculous. "I don't know how to change a car tire, and my pawpaw wasn't in any state to help."

"Wait," he interjected as he held up his hand. At first, he was charmed by her sweet act, but something else crossed his face. "You don't know how to change a car tire?"

"No," Evie replied shamefully.

He spoke again in that smooth Midwestern accent, "That's insanely sweet of you to do that for the department. They all seemed like they loved it." She could have likened his voice to black velvet. Deep, luxurious, smooth, handsome and sexy with the right amount of masculinity.

She smiled and nodded. How badly she wanted to ask him out. Her face rose to meet his gaze. "Thank you, Caleb. I better get going. I've got a job interview to get to."

He cocked his head and shifted his stance, shaking her hand once more. "You're welcome, Evie."

She tingled all over with how he said her name. It was deliberate and succulent, like a ripe peach being slowly bitten into to savor every drop of juice.

He walked to the front door of her car and opened it for her. She paused, smiled, and thanked him before slowly approaching it. His eyes followed her with a soft grin and acute observation, watching her every movement. Once she was in, he placed his hand on the car's roof and leaned over while she buckled her seatbelt. "Oh, and Evie?"

She looked at him, heart pounding in her throat and stomach.

"You don't need to suck in your stomach around me." He winked and closed her door. Walking away, he yelled, "Good luck on your interview!"

Evie quickly rolled down the window and called back, "Thank you, Caleb. Have a great day!"

Although she smiled when she drove off, she nearly cried with both sadness, regret, and happiness at the moment. If only she could have had the courage to ask him out. It was difficult to concentrate on her interview and the long drive home. And once at home, she snuggled up with

36

Teddy on the couch to catch up on the latest drama on the discussion page.

To her surprise, she saw she had a friend request from a man with a t-shirt on, gently muscled arms blanketed with tattoos on one side, and he was leading a quarter horse.

It was Caleb Wright.

Chapter Four

The door of the salon was yanked open wildly and the welcoming bells rang obnoxiously. Everyone turned to stare. An older woman with rollers in her hair sat underneath the dryer while she read a gardening magazine, and the smell of perm was noxious in the air. A few other ladies turned over their shoulders from the nail stands. Their local town sweaters and messy buns and oversized purses gave them a cute and effortless look in Evie's eyes.

She drew in a deep breath with a tight smile and observed the room. Just perfect for spring and her interview, she was rocking a floral print keyhole neckline blouse with paper bag waist belted pants. The outfit was a swarm of blushing pink hues and soft whites, and her high-heel sandals were just the right white to go with it.

Even though they followed her with their eyes that were stacked with heavy mascara, she didn't care. Evie was bursting with so much excitement that she ignored all the peering strangers and sat right down in front of an open nail stand, with one lone nail tech waiting for a client.

"Are you available?" she asked sweetly as she set her purse down. "I've had such an amazing day so far and have to celebrate it and treat myself!"

The lady paused in mid sip of her nutrition shake, made by the local smoothie joint and kept in a locally made tumbler with "Mom Boss" written all over it. Her hair was a deeply dyed red hue and gelled with gentle wisps to accent her short cut. Her age had to be around fifty, and her well-manicured nails were French tipped, and one finger sported a large diamond ring. Her lips were painted in a glossy deep red as well.

She pursed her lips. "Who are you?"

Evie smiled and waved. "Oh, you don't know me. I'm new here. I moved here roughly two years ago and haven't been in here yet. But not only did I have this amazingly cute guy send me a friend request last night, I got a call this morning that I got a promotion at work! So, help a girl celebrate?"

The nearby women snickered and went back to their work and gossiping, still staring at Evie. She looked a bit out of place there.

"Alright, I can do that for ya. What are you wanting?" She put her drink down and began gathering her things.

"Surprise me. I've never done this before. But keep my nails short because I like to play guitar, and I type a lot at work."

The lady looked at this stranger and hesitated for a brief moment before flashing a friendly smile. "You got it, sis. Tell me, what's your name?"

"Evie Morgan. What's yours?"

The tech began cleaning off her old polish. A few moments passed with the aggressive approach. "Myla. Myla Marr."

"That's a pretty name. Far better than mine."

"What's wrong with yours?"

Evie shrugged cutely. "I don't know. It sounds too fanciful."

Although Evie was trying to smile and be friendly, the obvious stares of the nearby women caught her side eye once more. Slowly, she turned and smiled in confusion. The client with the blonde messy bun asked, "And where did you come from?" Her accent was a slight drawl, but nowhere near Caleb's, Myla's or her pawpaw's. The blonde little horror had a voice that was high-pitched yet slow at the same time.

"I lived in Dawson for about seven years."

"Ooooh," she teased with raised eyebrows. A few lines of age and more pronounced cheekbones made Evie believe she was in her early or mid-forties. "You're a cardinal girl, aren't you?"

"Yep! Traded in my feathers for the horseshoes."

"You ever make it to one of the basketball games?"

Evie shook her head. "Um, no." *What a random question to ask.*

"Why not?" the blonde horror said as she sat up more. "All of our town are avid supporters of our school sports." She flexed her long, bony fingers for the technician and looked at them.

Myla stared at Evie. Evie brightly answered, "I don't have kids or anything like that. And I don't really know anyone here. There's really no point in me going. Not that I wouldn't, it's not something I really need to do."

The other woman next to the blonde was a brunette with a body as soft as a natural woman with a tired face and glasses. She was tanned and had those captivating blue eyes framed with a bit of age lines. She leaned over across the blonde's lap. "You don't wanna support our teams because you don't have kids in school? That's a little rude, don't you think?"

Even smiled awkwardly, hiding her annoyance. "I literally got here like, two years ago and just trying to get settled in."

The brunette didn't seem to be swayed. She offered a lackluster response, "Hey, relax. I'm having fun with you." She went back to look at her nails that were now being buffed. "And who's the guy you're into?"

"I'd rather keep that to myself, if that's okay."

"Aw," the blonde jested. "She's one of those quiet, introverted, innocent types."

"No, I'm one of those 'I think he's separated and don't wanna gossip about him' types."

The brunette cackled and stared at the blonde with a stupid grin. "Watch it be Caleb Wright."

The high-pitched, squawky cackling grated in her ears.

"So disgusting. What he did to Ashley was just disgusting."

"Right? What a damn dog. If he'd have been *my* husband, I would have divorced his ass long ago."

Myla softly glanced at Evie. "Ignore them."

Evie straightened up and let her nails be painted. "No, I don't think I will." She turned to the women. "I don't think it's appropriate to be gossiping about someone behind their back."

The blonde quirked a brow. "Listen Miss Cardinal, everyone in town knows Caleb is a jerk. It's only gossip if you're spreading shit no one knows about. It's common talk here."

Evie nervously looked back at Myla, who looked at her expectantly and waited for her to make a comeback.

Evie raised her shoulders and gave a disgusted, twisted face in agitation. "Yeah, but you're both acting like middle school girls. Talking about people isn't cool." The two women glared at her. But Evie continued on, "I can see why you're both friends."

"Oh?" the brunette asked. "Why's that?"

"Flies are always attracted to shit."

Evie couldn't believe what had come out of her mouth. It even surprised her.

Myla coughed quickly in a chuckle, and as the two nasty women stared, the blonde was given a whap on the head suddenly by the old woman with her magazine and it startled her.

"She's right," the old woman said coarsely. "Best to keep your nose outta other people's hog pens, or you'll end up face-first in shit, *Sandy* and *Kelly*."

Evie glanced at both of the women. "Sandy and Kelly? I guess it's nice to meet you two."

Sandy, the blonde, gave her a look. The older woman rubbed Evie's shoulder briefly and said, "Welcome to Laysville. You'll do fine here, city girl."

"But I'm not from the city," Evie said sweetly as she turned to look up at the woman.

The older woman smiled with pressed lips and looked at her. "You're from Dawson, yes, I get it. But no one comes in here lookin' like the prize that you do and comes from a small town. You're the graphic designer from Los Angeles, ain't that right? I see you talkin' on the discussion page all the time."

Evie felt a smile coming on with a friendly conversation. The woman sat in the empty chair next to her, and Evie tried to face her with a loving smile. Evie loved smiling to people. "I am actually! I'm not from there originally, but I moved here from there. Well, sort of. I lived with my pawpaw in Dawson for a long time. But..."

"But what, hun?" the older lady asked.

Evie looked left and right. "He passed away."

The older woman put her hand back on Evie's shoulder. "I'm sorry to hear that, young lady. Must be pretty hard. I'm Margie Atwood. I work at the bank here in town."

Evie greeted her warmly, and they continued to talk. But after a few minutes, Margie asked her with that slow, womanly southern accent, "So is it Caleb?" She lifted her brows in a curious smile. "I couldn't imagine a girl being so giddy over any other man here in town. He's the best damn lookin' piece of real estate this town's ever seen. Every other man in this town looks like he's gotten hit by a semi truck."

Myla popped in, still focusing on Evie's nails, "Yeah and most of 'em need to be."

Evie snickered, amused at the wisecracking older ladies she was with. She lowered her head bashfully. "Well, I'm not anything to shake a stick at either."

Sandy and Kelly kept on as if trying to draw the attention back to Caleb. Their laughter turned into downright insults, like a band of hyenas tripped up on caffeine and cocaine all at once. Her knuckles clenched, but she was nervous and unsure of how to act. She was never one to be rude those days, now that she was older. Evie had changed since she was a younger adult in Los Angeles, and so now fighting and causing problems didn't seem to be the smartest idea in a small town. She wanted to make friends and be civil to people. Being abrasive and defensive was how she survived in Los Angeles and how she had survived so many horrible encounters with men, but in a small town such as this? Saying the wrong thing *once* to anybody could leave her with deep consequences.

Kelly flopped her hand around in her dark hair as she drank coffee from her tumbler. "I'm so glad he moved outta town. I hated seeing that guy anywhere here. He has such a punchable personality. So full of himself!"

Evie's knuckles tightened and her stomach knotted, but she attempted to maintain a cheery demeanor to Myla and Margie.

Myla showed her the color palette. "Which one would you like?"

Evie peeped happily, "Pink!"

"You should get gel," Sandy said. "It'll last forever and help your nails feel stronger."

Evie nodded to Myla and took the pink gel. Worst idea ever.

She learned later that the thickness was so bad that she couldn't properly scratch her back, and it felt clunky to play guitar, open cans, or do anything!

Even that night, Teddy didn't seem to approve of the new sensation of the weird nails on his head. Evie sighed with a smile. "I know, buddy. I'm sorry." She picked up her furry orange friend and plopped him on the new sofa and went to chop up vegetables for dinner. Her cell phone was tuned in to the police scanner app and she sat it down on the counter for comfort.

At once, she heard the dispatch say through minor radio fuzz, "710 May County request for K9 unit."

She smiled, peeling the carrots.

"710, County, show me on duty and en route to 716's location."

It was comforting. Evie softly whispered, "Hi there, Hunt."

The scanner came back on, and she heard the dog howling and barking excitably in the background as Deputy Hunt confirmed the location. Now Evie straight up chuckled heartily.

"Hi there, Atlas."

The very happiness within her was so grand that at times she thought she would cry. Or maybe it was the onions she was now dicing. Regardless, Evie had accepted Caleb's friend request but refrained from shooting her shot straight then and there. He wasn't widowed; he was getting divorced. And in her mind, the memories of Pawpaw came back about warning her about Caleb, that somehow he was no good. But no matter how many times she tried to recall, Pawpaw never truly told her why.

Apparently, some of the local women didn't like him either. None of that mattered to her. She would continue to post her graphic work, her daily motivational things, her workout progress, little clips of her playing guitar, Bible quotes, whatever it would take to show him who she truly was.

Evie tried to be sincere, but sometimes it fell flat.

She sliced her finger. At once she hissed and sucked it, but damn those onions were strong and her eyes watered even more. Running it under cold water, she squeezed a paper towel around the open wound. Then her phone lit up with a notification.

Caleb liked her story. It was a clip of her playing her favorite Garth Brooks song. He had responded, "Dang, girl! You play better than me!"

She yelped and tried to wipe off her wet hands to grab the phone. Yet again, he evoked those sweet little girl feelings in her. The butterflies filled her stomach, and her pulse raced, even though all he did was like her story. It didn't matter. The dopamine rush hit her fragile brain hard, and upon opening Facebook, she saw he liked her post about not only getting the promotion but also her story post about how proud she was of her meal prep and her Zumba class she finally completed.

Wait a minute.

Evie clicked on the little number in the bottom of her story and saw that he had seen every single one.

Even the ones yesterday that were posted prior to him sending her a friend request.

She burst into excitement and jumped up and down, squealing and laughing hard and merrily. Teddy came rushing in and slipped on the old linoleum until he slid into the table with a bonk. She picked him up to kiss his head and held him close, rocking him like a baby to her chest. "Teddy! He's watching my stories *and* liking them and my posts!"

Evie ran through the house until she could find her old Avril Lavigne CD and put it in the DVD player and danced the night away while dinner was cooking, and the wine bottle got more and more empty.

She stayed awake scrolling on her phone that night, feeling the room spinning as if her head was filled with honey and swarming bees fighting each other. All she wanted to do was see if there was anything she could learn about him. She needed to make sure she wasn't lovestruck without reason. Sure, he was cute, but he could've been a crazy asshole. He was clearly watching her stuff, so what difference did it make if she saw his?

As she looked at his profile, his banner was of him and two children. It was a wholesome photo of him alongside a little girl and a boy, who were all sitting on a front porch stoop together. The littlest one, the girl, was on her daddy's lap and had such beautiful blonde curls. She snickered when she saw that he also had a blond boy.

"Poor guy," she joked. "Little blond boys are such rascals."

Her heart saddened. *What went wrong?*

She wasn't about to pry. It was obviously over.

Instead, she reacted to his newest profile photo with a heart, and upon viewing his story saw that he had been leading a horse while his little girl rode, and then there was one of him with his guitar across his lap, selfie-style.

It surely didn't take much for that damn Caleb Wright to kick up her hormone dust.

She reacted to the story and got up the courage to send him a message that read, "I love your guitar!"

The moment she sent it, he saw it.

And she threw her phone across the room and rolled over in drunken embarrassment. Why did wine have to take control like that? She would never have done that had she not drank!

Somewhere buried in the laundry basket, a light glowed, and a little ding followed. She rolled over and paused nervously then nearly tripped getting out of the bed before flopping on the floor to see it. Her hands were shaking.

He loved her message! Evie held her chest and gasped a bit with a smile so wide it hurt her cheeks. Then he was writing.

She was about to swoon. There she lay across the floor to let the cool, spring air wisp in from her window to cool off the alcohol's clammy effect on her skin. The screen's light glowed on her happy face, and his message popped up. "Thanks! I'm not as good as you are, but I can try. I can't flatpick like that to save my life."

He was referencing her cover of a different Garth Brook's song that she posted up when she was sick with that blasted fever in December.

More flutters and smiles. "Thanks," she wrote back. "How come you never post videos of yourself playing? I bet you're good too!"

He responded, "Maybe one time when I've had a few."

The statement made her think. Was he an avid drinker? Weren't most military men drinkers anyway? Hell, wasn't *every man* in the Midwest a drinker?

She playfully went along, trying to match his demeanor and his obvious shared love of country music. "Need a few red solo cups first?"

He responded, "As long as they're half-filled with whiskey."

She wrote back, "Dang, you're brave! If I had whiskey, I'd be face-first in no time. All I've had is wine, and I'm gone. Tripped over nothing getting to the phone!"

It seemed as soon as the honeymoon vibes started, they ended. He gave a few exchanges before Evie decided to leave it alone. Still, she was hopeful. Having a crush on a man in his situation could be very delicate.

The next morning, she texted her oldest brother Darren, who had been in a divorce once already. She wanted to ask Caleb out badly before any other woman got to him. Being such a catch with those rugged blue jeans and perfectly scruffy face and that brooding tall height, he was certain to have a line of hopeful bachelorettes swarming up to his doorstep. And Evie felt she didn't have much to offer like most women her age.

Darren warned her to give him space and time, even though he was excited for her.

For the next few months that ticked on by, Evie watched his stories helplessly and tried to leave as many nice comments as possible about the success of his work, his kids, his life, without leaving too many. After her share of foolish behavior, she was going to be smart about a guy for once.

Growing up meant living her life the best way she could. It meant showing up to work and not checking her phone every five minutes or being worried if Caleb thought she looked good or not. It meant shame-lessly being herself, that kind and caring woman. It meant ignoring the catty women at the salon. Which she frequented still with them being there. It meant tuning out the deafening gossip of the women who frequented the local café. It meant focusing on trying to be happy, despite being still so lonely. It meant wishing Caleb a happy birthday on his birthday but being okay with not receiving it in return. He didn't owe her anything, even though she desired everything.

Evie knew things would go as they were to be expected to go, and she would learn to be okay with it.

Fall came around once more, and once more Evie was sick with that damn flu that was driving everyone wild. The crisp air was cold and damp, and her favorite thing to do in the morning was to sit out on her front porch by the mums and watch the fog consume the nearby cornfield next to Joshua's house. Pumpkins littered his steps and porch, as well as scarecrows being staked out front in the yard that represented his little family. Hearing Joshua's dogs bark used to annoy her, until she started to find them comforting when they chased a coyote off the street. Teddy was an indoor and outdoor cat, and Joshua's dogs knew Teddy well.

They never minded Teddy one bit.

There she sat on her white wicker chair and gazed out in thought. Her exchanges with Caleb had been brief with still the knowing that he was watching nearly every story she posted.

All was peaceful and quiet until the loud muffler of a truck came rattling down that quiet street. She grimaced and leaned over to see that damn white Chevy tearing down the road in a clumsy, maniacal fashion. Joshua screamed at the driver from his side yard where he was busy raking leaves.

"That damn Alan Moffet," Evie cursed. "He's gonna get someone killed someday."

For some strange reason, Caleb popped into her head. She was forty now, and surely no man was going to find her sitting on the front porch in some no-name town. She had to do it, because she couldn't wait any longer.

After work that night, Evie crawled up inside her favorite blanket on the couch with Hocus Pocus humming on the TV.

She picked up her phone. He was active online.

She was going to ask him out.

Her heart rate picked up, and her skin tingled. "Okay," she breathed heavily. "You can do this. If he says no, accept it and move on."

She stared at his name and wrote, "Hey, Caleb! I gotta be honest with you. You're absolutely fucking handsome as hell. I love the fact that you play guitar, work with horses, and you like the same music I do.

You seem like a really nice person too! I'd like to invite you out to dinner sometime or a drink. If not, I totally understand and won't be mad at all. Have a great night!"

And she threw the phone on the adjacent sofa and cried hysterically. Oh, she was so mortified at herself! She wasn't much thinner, and her house was still a wreck. There was no way in *hell* a guy that handsome would ever go for a woman with her body. Not ever. They didn't when she was younger, and she was certain they wouldn't now.

There was no wine to blame this time. The message was sent. The possible damage was done. "Dammit!" she cried. "Why the hell did I do that?" The turmoil within her heart tumbled a storm of regret and anxiousness. What was once confidence immediately was stripped and broken down into self-loathing.

Across the way on the couch, the phone lit up.

With shaking hands, she rolled over to reach for it and slowly looked.

He responded, "Hey, Evie! Damn, I'm flattered you came straight out and asked. Never had a girl do that before! I definitely would love to do that! But I'm in the middle of a divorce right now, as you've probably heard. So, I can't do much more than that. But I really think you're hella sweet. You're a really nice girl. Don't let anyone change that." It ended with a smiley emoji.

Then he added, "It'd be nice to see you when you're not needing help." He topped it off with a winky emoji.

How quickly the tears of embarrassment turned into laughter and little screams of absolute elation.

She let out all of her breath in one long sigh of relief, and her tears turned into a gleaming smile. She wrote back, "Right? You're always there at the right time! And I understand entirely. I hope everything goes okay for you. I couldn't imagine how hard that's gotta be. Well, now you know. So, if you'd like to, let me know when you're ready." She finished with a smiley emoji.

She waited while he saw the response.

And little did she know, he was thinking on the other end. His hand gripped around that whiskey glass, and he looked at his empty house. His kids weren't with him that Friday night, and what she had said was such a kind and understanding response. Over and over, he watched and read her goofy Facebook posts. She was darling, genuine, understanding, passionate, friendly, and always tried to help people in her community as much as possible. On the occasion, he would laugh at her silly posts and even laughed at the memes she would make.

On the other end, Evie grew sore waiting. She bit her finger.

Then Caleb drew in a breath and wrote back, "Do you really wanna know when I'm ready?" He was about to gamble everything and take one last chance. Maybe if he hadn't been drinking whiskey, he wouldn't have been so careless.

She could have broken her index finger swiping her response so fast. "Of course!"

"I'm ready now."

Chapter Five

Oh...my...God, Evie thought to herself. She couldn't stop staring at the message. Was it really true? Tears welled in her eyes, and she pressed her fingers to her mouth in shock, and gratefulness. As Teddy purred lying against her leg, she began texting back. Brave once again. "Your place or mine?"

Please say yours. Please say yours. My house isn't nearly as nice as yours probably is. But then it hit her. He already knew where she lived. He'd have to be careful walking up her steps and prepare for mild vertigo on the slanted porch.

"Yours," he wrote. "I already know where you live. Can I head that way?"

He sent a smiley emoji.

That stopped Evie straight in her fantasies. All at once, the emotional train of romance and love derailed and flew off the tracks. It was a booty call. It *had* to be. Why else would he want to go to her place so late at night? And why the smiley emoji? She knew men well enough to know that once again, she was going to be either a rebound or the mistress. When she had written "your place or mine," what she had meant was for when they met up. She didn't think that when he said he was ready now that he would have literally meant *right now.*

Her heart sank, and her head dropped with regret.

On the other side, Caleb waited while biting his thumbnail. She had seen it but hadn't responded. What was taking her so long? She had asked him out, and now she was getting all weird and reclusive. Once again, a woman was confusing to him. He feared he had already offended her in some way.

She thought.

He waited.

She cried.

He sighed.

He had enough of waiting. Apparently, she wasn't interested in seeing him that night. Or maybe she was busy. He put the phone on his nightstand and called for his bloodhound Charlie to come on his bed. Caleb pulled the crisp, white cotton sheets over his shirtless body and turned off his lamp to go to sleep. He had to be up early, as most contractors and active military people had to, so he didn't have time to wait around. Let her think and think.

But then the darkness of his closed eyes illuminated with blue light and rolling over, he saw she messaged him.

"I'm sorry. I don't know what's come over me. I don't feel well all of a sudden."

She was getting second thoughts, he presumed. But he asked, although he didn't really like to play games with people. He was giving her the benefit of the doubt. Evie didn't seem like that kind of person on social media or even in real life to him, so perhaps something was truly wrong.

"What's wrong? Are you okay?"

"I don't know. My chest feels weird, I'm having trouble breathing, and I can't stop shaking and my feet are tingly."

He knew exactly what that was. "Don't worry. I'm coming over. You'll be okay."

Evie was gasping for breath. Unlike Pawpaw, this wasn't because of a sneeze. This was because of something else far more frightening and unfamiliar to her. "Please hurry," she wrote. "I don't know what's going on."

He sent her his cell number. "I'm on my way. Call me if you need to. I mean it."

She saved his number and sat up straight in bed. It wasn't clear if she was going to faint or worse. This had never happened before, and she clutched Teddy with her heart pounding hard and fast. The grip on chubby Teddy tightened a little, and her hands violently trembled. "Pawpaw, I'm scared," she whispered out loud.

It was the longest fifteen minutes of her life, but Caleb occasionally checked on her and found out the situation was getting worse. In her living room, Evie paced around, and the unsettled nerves in her stomach weren't helping. Not the most romantic first time. As her hands raked through her hair, her legs felt weak, and she knew she was going to faint.

The lights of a big truck came pulling up her driveway. He was there.

Please hurry.

Caleb ran up the uneven stairs, opened the door and rushed to her without even bothering to close it.

All he saw was Evie reaching out to him, her eyes wet and wide, her face pale and her hands shaking badly. All over she shook like she was being electrocuted.

And then she fell into his arms.

She cried horrendously and pressed her face into his chest. It was warm, soft, strong, and enveloping. Caleb put his hand around the back of her head and squeezed softly around her lower back with his other arm. "It's okay," he hushed deeply. "You're having a panic attack."

Through her sobs, she mumbled, "I am? Is that what this is? It can't be. I feel like I'm going to die. I don't get panic attacks." She felt embarrassed as she choked for air through her cries.

He smiled and rubbed her lower back, gently swaying her left and right in his embrace. "Apparently now you do. It's probably from your grandpa passing away. It happens with sudden trauma."

She opened her emotions and clutched his shirt fabric on his chest. "But that was over a year ago. My mom died suddenly, and my dad died quickly. I didn't have this problem then."

His chin was on her head. His squeeze now came with both arms, and she melted. "The body can only handle so much. And believe me, sometimes it takes that long for the trauma to set in."

That thick accent. That deep voice.

But her heart suddenly felt like it was going to burst, and the rise came again. She whimpered his name and said, "I think I need an ambulance!"

He removed his arms from around her and led her to the beige couch, tossed the throw pillows aside, and sat next to her. He held her hands. "Listen to me, you're having a panic attack. The tingling in your hands and feet is because of the disruption of carbon dioxide and oxygen. You're hyperventilating."

Caleb flicked on the nearby end table lamp and looked back to her. "Breathe in deeply with me. Smell the roses and blow out the candles."

Their eyes met. Hers watered and full of fear, his calm and certain of the control he had over the situation.

As they breathed together, they watched each other's shoulders rise and fall. Evie tried to match his pace. Within minutes, the shaky hands he held steadied. Slowly, he reached over and felt her pulse. It was steady. She was steady. The room was quiet.

He smiled. "There. You see? Feel better?"

Evie wiped her eyes. "I can't believe it. How did you know?"

"The military. Always gotta learn the symptoms of certain things and how to handle them at any given situation."

A soft smile curled onto the corners of her mouth. She glanced down at their hands still holding one another. Then Evie lifted her left hand and softly glided her fingertips across the muscled and veined top of his left hand. They were tanned and looked dry. *I can't imagine how a man who could do such kind things...could be bad.*

"Are you okay?" she asked quietly.

"Me?"

"Yes, you."

Their voices were delicate and deep with one another. "Oh, I'm fine. You're the one with the trauma and the panic right now."

She held that hand a bit tighter and leaned forward to look up into his eyes more. "Don't all military people still have trauma and panic?"

He laughed. "Nah. I'm good. We learn to take it one day at a time and live with it."

She shook her head. "Why would you want to live with it?"

"Well," he said as he stood to close the front door. Before he did, he swatted out a few bugs that had flown in. Then he came back, sat down, and leaned against the couch, staring at the ceiling. "It's not that I *want* to live with it. I don't have a choice. What you went through, I can guarantee it'll happen again. And it's scary at first, but then you start to accept that it's a part of life now."

Evie stood up immediately and went to her bedroom. He watched her leave, and then he placed his arm across the top of his head in a slouched, relaxed position. He called to her in a brief chuckle, "Where are you going?" Then he sarcastically joked in a voice too low for her to hear, "Did I scare you off?"

Caleb examined the living room. The carpet was stained and old, but it smelled and felt like it was freshly cleaned. The walls were painted with a petal-pink tone with white trim and crown molding. Either she tried to add the crown molding and did a terrible job, or it needed to be replaced. Right across from him was a beat-up looking antique coffee table that was doubling as an entertainment stand and a bookshelf. There was an old TV, a DVD player, and numerous classic books by authors like Charles Dickens, Sir Arthur Conan Doyle, and even Stephen King. Apparently, she was a Stephen King fan most of all.

How in the hell does a girl who's so obsessed with flowers and pink love Stephen King? he thought to himself.

A few watercolor paintings of flowers were framed on the walls, and they complemented charming photos of her with a gray furry cat and another one with a fat orange cat. He knew from her Facebook posts that the furry gray cat was her old cat named Phil that had passed away. Then there were photos of her family, her and her pawpaw, photos of her on Hollywood Boulevard wearing a stylish bodycon dress and sunglasses. He smiled.

Out came the thundering fat ginger cat. He beamed, leaning over to pet the kitty, who sniffed his hand and then flopped on his foot. "I can tell you *seem* useless, like a big fat paperweight, but she probably spoils you rotten. I bet you're the infamous Teddy she's always posting pictures of." He found the collar tag. "Yep. You look like a Teddy."

Her voice rang from the bedroom in the back, "You did something nice for me." She came back in and wiggled a bottle of shea butter in her hand. "Now I'm going to do something for you." A perky smile and confidence flashed her face.

"Oh God." He laughed. Caleb sat up straight and rested his elbows on his knees to offer his hands to hers. His back rounded, those handsome muscles showing subtly through his shirt. It was attractive to her, those shadowy arcs on his back.

She stood before him and asked, "It's not too cold outside for you? Where's your sweater?"

He looked down. "I didn't want to bother with it. I wanted to get here as quickly as possible. It ain't too bad outside."

To his surprise, she didn't sit next to him.

She knelt on her knees right in front of him on the floor.

His face changed. As she opened the bottle and squirted the shea butter on her palm, one shoulder cocked playfully, and she smirked at him. It wasn't meant to be sexual, rather endearing and affectionate. His eyes wandered to see how her light-brown hair cascaded down her full breasts that were kept snuggly lifted by a gray lounge bra, and her pink tank top allowed him to see the beauty of her collarbone and the curvature of her narrow shoulders. Even though her belly had a few rolls and hung over her lap, the silhouette of her pear-shaped hips complimented it perfectly.

His ex-wife was a lot thinner than Evie was, and he had never found bigger girls attractive before, but there was something divine and welcoming about her fuller figure. That belly would be an amazing pillow to rest his head on. Her hips would be amazing to hold.

No. To *grab*. Caleb's skin flushed as his pelvis felt hot. Her feminine face was caring with those large, expressive, and deep-brown eyes. There was no hint of aggression or anything. His ex in the recent years had been a notorious monster with being bossy, quick-paced, and cold. If only he could muster up the bravery to kiss her. He would take her down to the floor and completely ravage her. Though it wasn't the time to do it, considering what she just went through.

The skin of his shaft grew tighter, and the head became sensitive. She needed to stop looking at him with those bedroom eyes.

Little did he know she wasn't trying to. That was how Evie always looked when she was trying to be kind. To most people it looked sweet and endearing, but to him it looked seductive.

But Evie was a frequent flyer at the Songbird Café in town, as well as a monthly visitor at the nail salon. He knew those places sang with gossip, all ready to be used as cannon fodder against him. So, he shuffled on his butt and tried to contain the feeling.

Evie began massaging the butter onto his cracked and calloused hands. "I know how you feel. My hands get ridiculous in the fall and winter."

"My hands are ridiculous all the time." The massage wasn't helping his situation.

And the heavy sigh he let escape his lips wasn't helping hers.

"Is it because of your job?"

He smiled, something they did often around each other. "Yeah. It's from all the things. I worked on cars a lot growing up. I like to have fun with my truck. Then there's the never-ending yard work. And the horses."

"What about the Navy? Tell me about your job in the Navy."

He smiled. "I'd rather not at the moment, if that's okay."

She looked back down at her work and started to massage the muscles in between his fingers and wrists. There was pain and ache there he never knew he had. She whispered, "You're okay. I won't pry. But you did something so nice for me, so I at least wanted to do this for you. And if you ever need to talk, you can reach out to me."

"I appreciate it, but you don't know what you're getting into. I told you, I'm fine. I've learned to live with it."

Evie looked at him and protested innocently, "I don't believe it needs to be that way though. I mean, even when we get cut deeply, the scars *still* remain, but doesn't the pain eventually go away? So, when we go through trauma or hurt, we can have scars, but can't the pain be healed?"

He hated to give her a reality check, but it had to be done. "Not always. Physical scars can cause nerve damage and adhesions, and in that case the pain will never go away."

She looked down and then turned his left hand over to massage his palm with both of her thumbs. The ache shot up into his forearm at first until she nurtured it away. He adored her innocence of how cruel life could really be. Well, life *had* been unfair and cruel to her in different ways.

Wait a minute. It dawned on him. He had looked over her entire Facebook profile, and life *had* been rough for her. Homelessness, loss of parents, sexual abuse, familial neglect, mania, body dysmorphia. But there Evie was. So what if she had an anxiety attack? She was still calm, loving, happy, and peaceful. Or so she seemed in his eyes. How the hell did she manage to do it without whiskey and other...things?

He didn't know her until about three or four months ago. She was a lot worse before that.

She finished and sat next to him then. "I guess you're right. I never thought of it that way. But maybe on an emotional or psychological level, we can heal. I think we can." A soft chuckle trickled out of her lips, and she looked down at her fingers. "I know we can."

He looked at her. God, he wanted to dominate her completely. What a dumb thing to think at a time like that, but he couldn't help it.

She smiled again. "If there's anything I can do to thank you for what you did for me tonight, let me know."

A better idea came into his mind. "How about I stay the night, and you can make some of that fabulous French toast you're always posting pictures up online of?"

At once they both laughed, and she nodded in a wide grin. "Yeah, I do post a lot about that, don't I?"

He leaned over and nudged her in a little flirt. "Yeah, you kinda do. And it's unfair I haven't had it yet."

She lifted her chin with a proud smirk. "Then I would be honored to make it for you in the morning."

She led him to her room, and she was incredibly thankful that she had kept it cleaner those days. "I'm sorry about the stuff that's still kind of everywhere." She moved a few boxes to the side. "I need to have some shelves put up or get a bookshelf to get these things out of the boxes."

He grinned with his hands in his pockets. "You're fine. I've been there before. I have kids and understand messes and piles."

They both stared at the bed. It was only a full-sized bed. "If you're uncomfortable, um," she stammered, "I have another room."

He looked about. "I think I'll stay in here with you."

She smiled and held her mouth, for the look he gave her indicated he *knew* she wanted him to sleep by her.

"After all," he added, "sleeping alone sucks after you've had a panic attack."

She crossed her arms filled with giddiness and nervousness. Caleb looked out the window and approached it, leaning over the bed to do so. The bed was tucked into the corner to allow more room. Then Evie's eyes widened in embarrassment. All her stuffed animals were on the bed still! What would he think of a forty-year-old woman having stuffed animals?

While he looked out at the tree line, Evie stealthily grabbed the animals and chucked them into the closet.

"Stephen King *and* stuffed animals?" he asked with a grin. "You're a woman of many hobbies, Miss Morgan."

She turned to face him, rubbed her hips and took in a breath. "I'll be in the bathroom changing and-"

He pulled away and approached her. Her heart started to pound again. Luckily this time it wasn't because of panic. In the amber light of that room, in the still of the night, his eyes met hers.

It made her heart beg for a kiss; her body beg to be held. Her lower lip visibly trembled. She could not compose herself at all around him!

"Don't worry about it. I'll go out and you can change."

A few minutes later, she was lying in bed, and he came in after a knock wearing nothing but his boxers. Immediately, her eyes peeled back to the ceiling to avoid staring at him like a horny lecher. She swallowed hard. His tall presence could be *felt* in that room with every slow step and every gentle breath.

Lifting the covers, the bed creaked as he slid in next to her. *Right* up next to her. The warmth of his body graced her cool skin. His feet hung off a bit, and it was hilarious to him. "I think we've got a bit of a problem here."

She leaned her head up to look then laid back down chuckling. "I'm sorry."

He heaved a loud groan and rolled over to face her. "It's okay. I can do this." He bent his knees, but they were still prodding into Evie's legs.

She glanced at him. The moonlight bathed the softness of her face, casting dark shadows around her eyes. Her throat was bare and tempting to him.

She joked, "That's probably not any better, is it?"

The air was hushed around them. He softly blinked before whispering, "It would be if you turned to face the wall." He was trying to hint that he wanted to hold her from behind. When he first came into the house and hugged her, her body was pleasantly plush, and it made him realize how much he longed for that sensation again. How he could curl his fingers deeper and grasp her like hell.

Her throat clenched, and the sensation rolled downward to her chest, then her stomach, then her pelvis and then even deeper within. But that wasn't what she wanted. She had thought about this man for over a year, and looking into his eyes she found some sort of solace she didn't expect to find. That was the peace she longed for. So instead of doing what he asked, she turned to face him and tucked her knees enough into her stomach so that it gave him a little more leg room.

His brow quirked lightheartedly. "That's literally the opposite of what I told you to do." The room filled with soft giggles between them. When he was with her, he found himself smiling and laughing more than usual.

She was going to confess something that probably was dramatic and dumb, but it was in Evie's spirit to be as affectionate and tender as possible, so she confessed it shamelessly, "But I want to see your face. You have such pretty eyes."

He responded with a rolling drone from his stout chest, "I don't know if I can do that."

She laughed sweetly. "Do what?"

"Face you."

"But why?"

A smile crossed his face. He spoke so softly, like a faint whisper barely heard, "Because with the way you look right now, I don't know if

I can control myself." He smelled her Armani perfume lingering softly in the room, her hair smelling like rosemary mint.

She reached out and cautiously touched his unshaven face, being cautious in case he had some serious boundaries. Immediately, her breath quickened while she stroked his jawline. The roughness pricked her palm wildly and perfectly. His masculine and rugged features drove her completely fucking insane. Then she trembled breathlessly and asked, "Why wait?"

The moon's glow faded and within minutes the only light in her room was from the amber back porch light. The autumn rain came in soft patters against those windows causing black dripping shadows on their faces. It was cold that night, and his body was so warm in the bed.

Please at least kiss me, she thought.

"Evie," he began regretfully, "I'm technically still married. I'll hopefully be signing the divorce papers early next year, but...I'm sorry. I can't."

That could have been a deal breaker for some, but it wasn't for her. Yes, her hormones were crushed, but even though Caleb was separated, he was still loyal and faithful enough to a marriage not to cheat on his legal wife.

Evie realized that without him even knowing it, he had prevented her from becoming something she didn't want to be: a one-night stand or a mistress.

"I respect you so much for that. You're a hell of a good man, Caleb." Then she did as he had asked her before and rolled over to face the window.

He scooted up to her and placed his heavy arm around her waist and held her close. Their embrace was natural, warming, and soothing to them both. The protection he gave her at that moment was everything she needed and craved. It was difficult for her not to cry like an emotional Pisces right on the spot.

He let out a long sigh of relaxation as he felt the cushy warmth of her belly. The scent of her hair filled his senses with each breath, and the rain was lulling and steady.

You're a hell of a good man, Caleb Wright.

Evie had never fallen asleep so fast since before her parents died.

Usually, her mind was a never-ending to-do list of goals missed, impractical schedules trying to make up for the time her depression sucked from her and being alone always making her feel on edge. But within a few minutes with him, he had to lift his head to see if she really was already softly snoring. He smiled, because she was. Caleb laid his head back down and thought in the still of the night. The wind howled its bitter song outside. He never felt like closing his eyes. He didn't want to. Within that moment, he succumbed to the pleasure of rest.

He let his mind wander, looking out at the dark trees that swayed. *Don't get feelings for her.*

Chapter Six

That following autumn morning danced with little drops of rain. The birds sang in a myriad of sounds and calls while the trees rustled in the breeze. Outside, the grass of her backyard needed to be mowed up to the tree line, and small pools of rainwater gathered within them like little water worlds. The rabbits were still out eating their early breakfast in the yard, and they were accompanied by the bluejays that were also on the hunt for the early worm. The mums that swept alongside the front stoop reflected the dewy offerings of the day.

Caleb's warm breath brushed the back of her neck as her eyes opened. Normally, she would rush to the bathroom first thing in the morning, but this morning was different. His arm was still around her, and the stillness of his slumber made her feel snuggly and safe.

She'd hoped she hadn't snored that night like a monster with a sinus infection, as her last roommate warned that she did. What a wonderful thing it would be to serve him breakfast right as he woke, but she couldn't risk waking him. What would it be like to wake someone in the military? Would he jump out of bed and begin doing pushups? Would he randomly tell her how to make her bed? Or perhaps he'd be in a bad mood? Her mind toyed with every outcome.

That stupid muffler roared as the Chevy truck blasted past her driveway with loud music rumbling in its bass.

Caleb groaned, "I hate that guy."

She chuckled. "Do you know him?"

He rolled over onto his back. Damn. He broke the embrace and magical morning. Caleb lazily rubbed his sleepy eyes. The gray light of that early morning washed his face, making his brown eyes appear more hazel than anything. He seemed like he was staring off at the ceiling in deep contemplation, or recollection.

"Yeah. Alan Moffet. I went to school with him. He's got a big case of the 'look at me's' and a big fat burr up his ass." The last part of his statement caught her off guard, and she laughed again. He smiled at her. "Well, he does!"

"Maybe he missed his flea bath."

Laughter came again. Caleb loved her sense of humor, how she could crown his jokes with a similar taste of fun.

She asked, "Is it true that he yells at people when he drives? I heard that on the discussion page. That he flips people off and even tried to deliberately hit a pedestrian."

"Yeah, he's quite a peach."

"Do you think maybe he's like that because someone's done him wrong? Maybe a bad home life? I mean, no one acts like that for no reason."

He sat up and turned, rising from the bed. "Nah, some people are born assholes. There's nothing wrong with his past. He's a dick. He's drunk all the time too."

"Um, Caleb?" she asked. What she was about to say could ruin everything, but she had to be honest. He turned and looked at her. Now she was able to see his whole physique, but that was no longer on her mind. Evie sat up and rested back on her left hand and fixed her hair. "You kind of joked about liking to drink a lot and how you needed to be drunk to play guitar for people. What's it any different?"

He held his chest and raised his brows. "Am I an asshole? Do I go around flipping people off and trying to hit people with my truck?"

She stuttered nervously, "Um, no. But maybe he deals with it that way. Whereas it seems like you hide things, maybe he acts out in stupid ways."

"I never said I hide anything."

She swallowed and looked down at the bed before meeting his gaze again. He seemed like he was getting angry. "You didn't want to tell me about your job in the Navy last night. Doesn't that kinda count?"

"Evie, look, I don't talk about my job in the Navy because it's difficult for me. People don't understand." His voice grew in firmness and volume a little bit. "Everyone wants to thank me when I wear my uniform. Ashley said she was proud of me. But then when I come home, it's the same shit. The same ol' song and dance. People wanna act like they care, until it's time to truly care."

She said softly, trying to calm him with gentleness, "And so you bottle it up and handle it with drinking?"

He pointed at her angrily. "Don't act like you know me. And don't patronize me."

She got out of the bed quickly and tried to reassure him with a touch, but he pulled away. "Caleb, please."

"Just," he started as he held his hands up and turned from her, "please make breakfast if you still want to. I have places to be today. I've got a lot of work to do."

She let go of him. His back was turned to her, and he rubbed his face. The delicacy of her voice was like silk over his calloused hands, fractured ears and washed-up heart, but he knew better than to trust people outright.

She sighed. "Caleb, please, I wasn't trying to patronize you. I was actually genuinely asking. No, you're not an asshole."

He wasn't so sure about that. That was all he had heard over the last five years of his life.

She continued, "I saw similarities in certain things. And if you say that Alan's an asshole because he was born that way, and that you and he are nothing alike, then what *is* the reason for your drinking?"

He looked back at her and forced a smile. "Evie, some people drink to loosen up and have fun, you know? Just because I like to get drunk and lighten up doesn't mean I come with a shitload of baggage and problems."

The only way she could even stand a chance with him still was to respect...

These boundaries.

It all made sense now. Caleb's boundaries weren't so physical as they were emotional. Or maybe they were. She wasn't certain. Whatever the case was, Evie nodded to him to end the discussion. It didn't matter what walls he had up. She was going to tear them down brick by brick with her bare hands if need be. It pained her how a man who was so kind to her numerous times could possibly be hurting in any way shape or form. Hell, there was *no way* a recently separated man didn't have some sort of grief he was dealing with, and especially one in the military who had been deployed several times.

And what about his children?

Evie had witnessed how horrible it was for Darren to try to juggle his own divorce while trying to still be the good guy in the eyes of his children. It about wrecked her poor brother. And Caleb had posted about his children so often in such positive ways that she figured there had to be some sort of entanglement there.

She reached out and held his hand. Her lips curled in a smile as she softly looked up to him. He was looking down, and so she lifted his chin a bit to try to redirect his gaze to her eyes. How confident she was to touch him baffled him, but Evie didn't know any better. She didn't know it could be considered rude to touch a service member who was struggling with a morning temper. It was astonishing to him how she knew exactly how to touch him, what to touch, and at the perfect time.

"I'm sorry I pressed you."

His fingers ran through her hair, and he watched her facial expression melt into bliss while she rested her cheek against his palm. She smiled more than anyone else he ever knew other than his daughter, Olivia. He paused his actions and thoughts to simply take her in. The beautiful daylight haloed her completely, and once again he saw the sparkling natural blonde highlights her hair had. She was angelic. His breath rose in his chest, and his stomach tightened. With parted lips, he watched her nuzzle into his palm.

She held his hand to her face, then turned to kiss his palm.

If only she knew what she was doing to him. His nipples began to feel blood rushing to them, making them more sensitive to the cool breeze coming in. She adored his hand and kissed it a few more times. No woman had ever done *anything* that sensual to him, and Caleb could not wrangle what had come over him. He felt delirious, shaken, aroused and adored perfectly. He looked down and saw her voluptuous breasts still snug in that lounge bra, and her tank top formed a lovely curve in her waist. From his perspective, being about six-foot-three, he had all the best visuals.

Then, she looked up into his eyes and kissed the tender skin on his wrist. Her lips were naturally full and lush, and the tender moment made him imagine how good she would feel all over his body. He was absolutely melting and coming undone.

Evie let go of his hand quietly. "I really want you to know that I only want to help as best as I can. You were like my own personal Robin Hood last night." She broke into a giggle at her own statement, feeling stupid and foolish. "Why the hell did I say that?" She threw her arms up and down, looked away from him, then shook her head while rubbing her forehead. "I'm sorry. I can say some *pretty* dumb things when I—"

He stopped her by placing his hand to her cheek again, rubbing her lips with his thumb. Those large fingers still smelled like warm shea butter, and they framed her face completely due to their size. Evie's head leaned back to look up into his eyes. Anyone would say that Caleb was no fool, in that he could see the longing in her eyes. But he had never seen such eyes before. No woman had ever looked at him that way. Something stirred within his body and soul that he couldn't pin. She whimpered accidentally as he came closer to her lips. His eyes focused on her lips and then back to her eyes again, as if deciphering every action she did. Little did she know, he *was*.

He spoke deeply, "You look like you need to be kissed by someone who knows how."

Caleb's heart felt shattered when he saw her eyes watering. An actual tear streamed down her cheek. What was with this girl? Was she truly so devoid of anything like this in her life that a simple gesture tore her into pieces?

Her lips trembled as she whispered in a broken cry, "Why wait?" *Please, kiss me.*

A sweltering sensation flushed his chest and back that wired every damn nerve in his body. Caleb put his other hand on her face and took in all the forbidden beauty of her expression. Her whole body was trembling. As his breath raced out of his lips, he battled a horrible fight in his mind, *what would happen if I did?*

He drew in a deep breath, then slowly kissed her. Their lips barely pressed against the soft and warm flesh of one another's.

Evie let out a hot breath right after his lips touched hers, and then she tilted her head to the side to take the passion deeper. He had her. Like tinder knowing it was time to succumb to the flames, she fell apart with his kiss, surrendering to his every command. No longer would she hold back her affection. Evie lifted her delicate hands to his bare chest and slipped her right hand down the muscular curves of his left bicep. Caleb shuddered from the touch, as if her touch melted his tattoos in the heat. She took her left hand to stroke lovingly up his strong chest, feeling his handsome skin move and give with every gliding motion.

Her fingers brushed his nipple that was alive with pleasure. His chest was strong and thick, his shoulders rounded and broad. His arms were long and built divinely. His stomach, as she then explored it, was soft and naturally defined. Her fingers traced deliciously down his sides and to the front above his groin.

Caleb groaned deeply within his chest and tilted his head to the side, still cradling her face passionately. He kissed her harder, breathing heavier. She let him decide how far to take it, and so when his tongue felt hers, she welcomed it. It became faster, wilder, and then one of his arms went around her lower back to pull her tight against him. She touched his cheek again, furrowing her brows from the emotional turmoil that ended within her. As she held his waist and then swept her hand across his upper back, she imagined him pushing her down to the bed to crawl on top of her. Hell, if he were to actually *do* that, she didn't know if she'd make it out alive. She pulled away from his kisses to gasp with closed eyes, but it only left him kissing her cheek maddeningly.

He brought the fucking woman out of her.

She reached through his light brownish blond hair and pulled him down harder. The kissing grew in temperature, completely unbridled and savage. His hand gripped her hair by the roots, and Evie leaned her head to the side. Caleb knew exactly what She wanted, and he gave it to her. The moment his hot lips graced her neck with burning desire, she gave an audible cry of pleasure and gasped. He opened his mouth to gently bite right where she wanted him to. Her pelvis began to swell, and she felt herself dripping. Pulling his face deeper into her biggest erogenous zone left his carnal wishes aching to be satisfied. Everything she did was furiously passionate, tender and submissive.

He slipped his tongue against hers again and groaned hard. All around her, her body danced with his heat, muscles, height, and she could *feel* his husky moans coming deep from within his chest. She kissed him hard before gasping, their foreheads touching, "You have no fucking idea what you're doing to me." Both of her hands grasped his hair.

He proved her wrong. Caleb leaned down, grabbed her butt and hoisted her into the air. Out of absolute panic, thinking she was going to break his back, she grabbed his shoulders and tried to hold herself up. She didn't know how military men were trained to be able to do such things. He quickly slammed her down on the bed, releasing a yelp of excitement from her, and crawled on top of her.

His eyes met hers, and he fiercely said, "I know *exactly* what I'm fucking doing to you." He hotly kissed her again. "That's why I'm doing it."

Save me, he thought. *Get me out of this. It's all wrong.*

Her legs wrapped around his waist, and he began grinding against her, holding himself above her with his taut arms. She adored how the bed around her head sunk from his massive hands pressing down into it, completely caging her in his lust in which she would faithfully be his songbird. He felt his back muscles become alive with her digging into them, holding them, massaging his waist with long and loving strokes. Her nails clawed at his shoulder tattoo, and it felt like she could peel it off.

They couldn't stop their passionate kissing.

He was going to burst. Within a single minute, Caleb found his redemption in her passion. He could breathe new air, and have those nails rip his memories clean from his mind.

Save me.

Subtle glistening of sweat formed on his temples while her fingers ran through his hair, sending electrifying jitters down his spine. As the kissing grew in fervor, Caleb leaned his chest onto hers and pressed their bodies together in mounting pleasure. The bare skin of his chest was hot against hers, and everything about him felt heavy.

His cell phone rang in his jeans pocket with an Avril Lavigne song.

He stopped, and she paused. Evie's eyes looked to the side as they were still in mid-kiss.

Caleb groaned and got up. "I'm sorry. That's my daughter calling me."

He got up and hurried to find his jeans before she rolled over and picked them up off the ottoman at the end of her bed. He thanked her and dug furiously to answer the call. "Hey baby girl! What's up?" He turned his back to talk.

Evie finally caught her breath and had to practically peel herself up off the bed. She exhaled and wiped her face, fanning herself. She wrenched the window open a bit more. As he talked, she could easily tell he wasn't talking to another adult woman, and even if he did, it wasn't her business. That kiss and the last twelve hours of her life was the best thing she had ever had. Besides, he didn't belong to her. He had a life outside of her, and she was damn certain she would respect that.

Yet what Pawpaw said came back to her, and so did what Sandy and Kelly said. Jealousy was an ugly, nasty thing. She shook her head out. How dare she even judge him like that to think he could be playing around with someone else? What the hell was she thinking? She had no right to butt into his business. It could have been his daughter, and it probably was. Thinking anything else would've made her no better than the catty broads at the salon. But she did listen.

The conversation mentioned something about horseback riding lessons needing to be moved to that day due to the instructor having to leave town early.

He hung up the phone and looked at her with sorrowful eyes.

She smirked and patted the bed to encourage him to sit. He did. "Don't worry about it. It's okay! I think it's cute you have an Avril Lavigne song for your daughter. That's so freaking cool that you're not embarrassed of it."

He let out a huff in a smile while looking down. "Oh, hell no. I'm a fan myself. Yeah. She's only four, but I let my kids share a phone because their mom insists on them having one. So, Olivia got to choose the ring-tone for the week." He gave her that friendly little flirt nudge again. "I know you're a fan as well with the videos you post. She's coming in to concert next summer. If my divorce is finalized, we should go together."

Evie brightly answered, "I would love that! I've never seen her in concert before."

Caleb's demeanor changed abruptly. "Hey, uh, listen. About all this..."

She patted his lap. "Don't worry about it. I won't tell anyone. I want you to trust me, and that's the stupidest thing I could do right now."

"Promise? Because I really can't afford anymore fucking drama in my life. I really appreciate that." He stood and began putting on his clothes. "For what it's worth," he began as he zipped up his jeans, "you're a hell of a kisser."

She smiled and stood to give him a hug. Then she fondly looked up into his eyes again. "You're a hell of a man. But you know that already."

However, the truth of it was that he actually didn't know it. Not until he met her.

She asked, "Still want French toast?" She playfully shouldered him. "To go with that delicious French kiss?"

He chuckled and kissed her again. "You know it."

After breakfast, Caleb put his shoes on, and she walked him out to his truck. His belly and heart felt full, even though his groin was screaming in heat and sensitivity. And it was no different for her. He had to leave to take his daughter to horseback lessons, and so she had no choice but to be okay with it. She really didn't *want* to be any other way, for being any other way would have been completely selfish and cruel.

It was now softly misting.

At the driver's door, Caleb looked to her. "You gonna be okay? I know last night was rough."

She nodded. "I think after this morning, nothing can bring me down."

He grinned. "I'm glad, Evie. I'd kiss you again if you didn't have neighbors across the road."

She shook her head lightly. "Don't worry about it."

He opened his door and as he climbed in, they let their eyes meet once more.

An eternity seemed to pass between them.

He smiled again. "Call me or text me if you need me."

"I will," she said. Then she winked. "Stud muffin."

That raised a laughter from him for sure! "You're a dork. But don't you dare change." He put on his sunglasses and looked around out his back window. He beckoned her with his finger. She came closer, and he pulled her gently for a sneaky kiss out of sight. The only neighbor she had was Joshua and his wife Sarah, and none of them would be able to see anything if she had leant her head in far enough.

Caleb stroked her hair. "Take care, gorgeous. And I'll come back out and take care of your yard. It looks like shit."

"Joshua usually helps me with that, but I'd rather have you do it," she kindly replied. They said their farewells to one another. He closed the door and took off down the driveway.

All that day, he had something within him he had needed for so long. If only he had had that love when he came home from deployment, when he lost a sale as a realtor, when he was sick and overwhelmed with the kids and the constant bombardment of being told he was a failure as a husband and a father.

A *father.*

As he drove down the road heading for the highway home, he thought back to a horrid memory of Ashley screaming at him, *how dare you drink in front of our kids? What kind of a lousy father are you? If you actually took your therapy sessions seriously!*

Take a man's dignity by any other means necessary and he could live with that. But being told he was a failure as a father never escaped him. And then every time he went to the bar, it was guaranteed someone with good intentions would come up to him and ask, "Coping?" Just because he was having a beer.

Later, while he watched his daughter canter on a cute plucky horse, the instructor's husband, Jeff, asked him outright, "You look like you're in the best mood of your life, Caleb."

"Yeah, I've been working on some stuff."

Jeff grinned, taking a drag of his cigarette. "I bet you got another girl in your life already. What's her name?"

He shook his head and moaned in a slightly agitated smile. "No, I don't have another girl in my life, Jeff. I've straightened some things out."

"A divorce will do that to you. That shit straightens everything out. But I know that look. Come on, what's her name?"

Caleb laughed. "I don't have a girl in my life, Jeff."

"That's a shame."

Every time evening came around, it was a wonderful thing. It was when the day was over for him and he could watch his kids play outside while he sat on the porch and watched the sun set. That is, when he had his kids. It was his special moment, especially when he got them on the weekends. To sip a beer, a fine glass of whiskey on ice, play his guitar, watch Charlie scamper in the yard. Then when supper was served to his kids and they were tucked away, he texted Evie to see if she was okay.

While he waited for her reply, he checked her active Facebook story and saw that she had a successful workout at the gym. Her selfie was cute in her obnoxious pink leopard print leggings and her hot-pink tank top. But he smiled while the screen glowed against his face, and he loved it anyway and responded, "Your gym outfits are always so loud. Great job today!"

Evie was in the middle of trying to research how many gallons of paint she'd need to redo that awful bubblegum-pink color in the bathroom. She loved pink, but not *that* much nor in that color. Her phone lit up, and as she looked at it, she jumped out of her chair to see it was him. There was no one around to call her childish for acting so giddy, but the reason for her giddiness was clear. He actually cared and kept up with her. He didn't ignore her and move on, leaving her suffocating with confusion or worry.

She responded, "What can I say? I'm a pretty fashionably loud kinda gal!" She topped it off with a winky emoji. She asked about Olivia's horseback riding, and it made his heart swell that she even cared to ask about his kids. He loved talking about them to her. After talking about Olivia's riding lessons and Zack's love of football, Caleb asked her what she was doing. The texting carried on with him telling her he already knew exactly how much paint to get and that one gallon would be sufficient.

It relieved him how she didn't act like a know-it-all.

And it relieved her how much he didn't talk to her like she was stupid. Evie's father wasn't exactly Mr. Fix-it. He worked in finances, and so she had been left in the dark about certain things. Their texting lasted for hours. He stayed awake texting her until she needed to go to bed. Now the only thing to keep him company was his acoustic guitar. He picked it up and walked out to the garage to let his kids sleep easily, and he sat down in his workshop with a truck still in stages of repair. He tuned it and put a capo on the second fret. After a few strums, he began to sing.

Dad? Daaad? I'm here.

"Dad?"

Caleb turned around and saw Zack staring at him. Zack was only nine, but he wasn't naïve to what had happened. Caleb swallowed. "What is it, bud? Have a bad dream?"

Zack walked over and leaned in for a hug. His dad put the guitar down and hugged him close. "What's up, bud? What are you doing outta bed?"

"Are you okay?"

Caleb paused. "I am. What's up?" He combed his son's hair back with his fingers.

"You were crying."

"I was?"

It happened. Again.

"Yeah, Dad. Are you okay?"

Caleb kissed his boy's head and patted his back. "I stubbed my toe really hard but thank you for checking on me. That's awful nice of you."

"Promise?"

Caleb shut the doors of his heart hard to stay strong for his son and for himself. He smiled. "Cross my heart."

Chapter Seven

Evie was on her way to work, driving down that interstate with the crisp autumn air blowing through her hair. She let her hand fly out the window, lifting it up and down like a plane taking flight. She turned up the volume on her car's radio, remembering his kiss.

Once at work, she waited patiently for the electronic double glass doors to open. She took off her sunglasses and strutted in with the biggest smile she could muster. Everyone she saw, she greeted in a chipper tone and even stopped to exchange other pleasantries. No, she and Caleb didn't make love yesterday morning like she wanted to, but it didn't matter. It was practically sealed for her that if she could be patient and understanding, that once those divorce papers were signed, he'd be all hers.

And she'd be all his.

Hopefully. Evie was a very hopeful and dreaming woman.

She was a graphic designer for an entertainment company that ran the most influential events throughout the entire Midwest, Jamboree. The name may have seemed very childish and immature for some, and their name was actually snubbed by potential clients until Evie came around and rebranded their logo and stylized their font differently. Now Jamboree looked as influential and mainstream as a company could hope, offering anything from hosting drag show competitions, to fashion shows, weddings, and all in between. They even threw a party for the Kansas City Chiefs football team when they won the Super Bowl.

Now *those* were wild times for her. As in, stressful times. She hadn't been to a football game since then nearly five years ago. Nowadays, she didn't care much for noisy crowds.

Today was another day to present her project to the project manager to see if she'd approve of her new marketing design for an upcoming commercial that was supposed to air.

Evie put her bag and her purse on her desk while trying to simultaneously juggle her water bottle and her lunch bag. She heaved it all on the desk in one breath and leaned over. As her light-brown hair hung in stylish waves to the side of her face, she winced again as her back started to ache all over once more. Losing thirty-five pounds and going from 250 pounds down to 215 helped with her back pain a lot, but nothing near as to what she had hoped for. There was always this deep ache that screamed between her shoulders right where her bra band would go. And even though it felt amazing to be relieved at the chiropractor's, it never felt like it went away.

She sighed and rearranged the goods on her desk. "It comes with getting older."

A thin woman suddenly approached her. It was her former best friend and coworker, Missy. "Hey, Evie! You look nice this morning."

Evie cocked her head and smiled. "Aw, thank you, Missy!"

Missy studied her for a moment. "You're wearing a floral blouse again?"

"Of course! How could I deny my signature pattern?"

"You know this isn't Los Angeles, right? You don't always have to dress up. You used to come here more relaxed and chill. What happened to you? Ever since you lost weight, you're all like..."

Evie pulled her hair out of her face and put her hand on her hip. "Like what? You literally just said I look nice."

Missy waved her hand around in front of Evie and grimaced. "I dunno. Like, different."

"I think what you mean to say is I'm coming in here now looking like I actually care. You know, I was really messed up and depressed for a long time after my pawpaw passed away." She threw her hand to the side and looked that way as well. She said irritably, "And at that time, I would come in here with dirty leggings and unwashed hair, and not *once* did anyone think to check on me. But apparently, I now know why." She grabbed her water bottle and walked to the water dispenser, shoving past Missy. "You thought it was normal for people to look that way."

Missy turned and rolled her eyes. She tried hard to keep up with Evie as she protested with her hands out, "I'm saying you were stressed to try to impress everyone in Los Angeles and don't need to do that here. Perry loves you!"

The water filled to the top, and Evie turned and looked at Missy, who was wearing a gray sweatshirt from college and yoga pants with tennis shoes. Her hair was kept up in a lazy high ponytail, eyebrows needing to be plucked, and her soft freckles dabbled her pale skin all crowned by her black hair.

Evie shifted her hip to the side and pursed her lips. "I could tell you to put some weight on, but I don't. I could tell you to pluck your eyebrows and wash your hair, but I don't. This is how I've always loved to dress, but I never could due to money or my weight."

Then she pushed past Missy once more. "You knew that about me in high school."

Missy looked at her friend walking away. They used to be best friends in high school. *Used* to be. But that all changed when Missy got a boyfriend out of nowhere and completely ditched Evie in every moment she needed her best friend. When Evie's father died, Missy was out having sex with her boyfriend somewhere drunk in a McDonald's parking lot and blew her off for a week. When Evie's mother died, Missy had mysteriously ran off to Colorado with her boyfriend and didn't even tell Evie nor answer her phone. That whole week, Evie had thought her best friend was murdered or abducted the same time as her mother's death, and so it was not an easy week for her at all.

At the time, she'd tried to befriend Missy all over again to mend their broken friendship, but it would never last long. Missy teased her for buying a shithole house in a no-named town instead of living it up in a high rise in the city. Evie had her moments of boastful spending when she was younger, but she was an adult now and learned the hard way she had to strangle her finances to keep herself from going under. Sure, she made a healthy salary, but the cost of living had doubled in the last ten years, and so her salary no longer stretched like it used to.

Evie sat at her desk to compose herself. With her face in her hands, the mounting feeling of guilt lingered with the grudge that she felt she still held onto.

She pushed the thought aside and prepped for her presentation that was due in less than thirty minutes. She popped a vitamin into her mouth and washed it down with water. Then her phone lit up on the desk with Caleb's name with a message alert! Well, it technically came up as "Contractor," because she didn't want anyone to see her phone if she wasn't around. Evie took every precaution imaginable to protect his identity.

She smiled and opened it. He sent her a selfie, and she glanced around to make sure no one was looking. It was a photo of him smiling in his truck with his baseball hat on backward. The message read, "I hope your day is off to a great start!"

The little gesture amused her. It was simply wonderful to have a man who made effort to show he was interested or at least cared about her. She outstretched her hand, gave a peace sign, and smiled for the camera. Her lashes were thick and done well, and her lips were done up with a dusty pink that matched her cheeks. The whipped avocado color of her blazer really made her pink floral blouse pop. It didn't matter if it was fall, she loved those spring colors.

She snapped the photo and sent it with a message that read, "I'm great! You look so handsome today! I'm getting ready to present my marketing design and templates for the team. I'm a little nervous but excited!" She speckled numerous emojis everywhere.

He was typing back. She stared for a ridiculously long amount of time at the screen. Either he was a slow typer, or she was impatient. He loved her picture and wrote back, "That's amazing! Ain't no way in hell I could speak in front of people. But I'm also not as cute as you are." He wrote a tongue sticking out emoji.

She reacted with a laughing face. "And you think you're not cute?"

Caleb wrote back, "Not like you."

She responded, "You're a guy. You're not supposed to be cute like me." She ended it with a winky emoji. "You're supposed to be rugged and handsome, like you already are."

On the other side, Caleb was stuck at a red light and was on his way back to his job site from picking up more materials at the hardware store. When he saw her text, he giggled for a moment. He typed back, "So you're saying I wouldn't look good in a floral blouse?" There was a sad emoji at the end of it.

Evie cracked up. She leaned back and held her lips in laughter. The sad emoji at the end was the cherry on top.

"You could try on one of mine and see," she said back.

"It's a date! When can I come over?"

Evie snickered again, rousing attention from some of her nearby coworkers. She should have been preparing for her presentation, and he should have been paying attention to the red light and the traffic.

"How about tomorrow?"

He was confused why she wanted him to wait so long. At least, it was a long time for him. It made no sense. She had been hot for him for two days, and their possible coupling was interrupted. As Caleb scratched his scruffy face, he thought and then wrote, "Why tomorrow?" It was yesterday that he almost had her, that lush body for him to take.

No.

For him to *escape* into.

When Evie saw the message, her heart skipped a beat. She wrote, "I was trying to be respectful. I didn't know how soon you'd want to come over again." She thought. Then wrote, "I thought you had your kids during the week? I know it seems like you occasionally get custody on the weekends but...is everything okay?"

"Yep!" he responded. "They asked if they could stay with their grandma, my mom, tonight for Christmas shopping and present wrapping. She's taking them to school tomorrow."

She smiled and wrote, "That sounds like fun! But are you sure about this? It's not too soon for you?"

He wrote back with a winky face, "Why wait?"

Reading that text filled her body with a scorching heat. Immediately a whirring sensation filled her head, and she had to blink a few times to compose herself. Her imagination flew off into the clouds with the memory of how he held her down to the bed not long ago. That strong military back was all hers to hold and dig into. For his neck to be bitten like she was a blood-thirsty seductress.

What she loved the most about Caleb's body is that it was natural like hers. It was obvious he went to the gym and kept a healthy weight especially for his height, but he wasn't some chiseled and cut body-builder. His muscular frame was just right. He had every part on a man that mattered to her. Strong and large hands with perfectly matched fingers, sturdy and strong rounded shoulders, great bone structure, supple lips, kind eyes, firm and developed chest muscles. And that full head of hair? She adored the way it popped back up after she'd run her hands through it.

It actually amazed Evie that every man she met gave some poor excuse as to why he couldn't maintain simple hygiene, let alone *styling* himself. But Caleb was living proof that a man could still care about his appearance. He had two jobs, two kids, a lot of land to manage and still kept his facial hair neat and trimmed, his hair styled in that fashionable military cut with the right length on the top, and he also always smelled *so* good! He also knew how to style it right.

And his *feet*.

Evie openly admitted to some of her acquaintances and friends that she had a thing for men's feet. It was actually downright gross to everyone she met, leaving her embarrassed and ashamed to talk about it. But Caleb's feet had the same veins and muscle structure as his hands did. They were large and beautiful. If she'd had the time, she would have massaged his feet as well with the shea butter and suckled off every bit.

She shuddered. That very thought made her swell. She squeezed her legs together.

Wait. Don't get too caught up. He's too perfect for you. You're nothing like him.

Shut up! Be brave and bold! He's totally into you! You don't need to be like him, you need to be like you!

She shook her head out.

He had been waiting and saw she read it, but she had left him on read. He wrote again, fearing he crossed one of *her* boundaries, "I'm sorry if that was stupid."

Evie snapped out of her fantasy turned inner turmoil and decided to be brazen with it. She wrote, "Oh no, not at all! I was daydreaming about how I wanted to massage your feet and suckle on your toes that night you came over."

But before she sent it, she deleted it.

It was the most difficult thing to do, but she had thrown herself at men so much in the past, and it never got her anything worthwhile in return. This time, it had to be different. Instead, she sent him a simple text, "If you truly mean what you say, I'll be yours entirely." It ended with a smiley emoji.

Caleb fell back into the seat of his truck and was pissed that the light changed. It was now his turn to go. The light had changed off and on during their exchange, but the line was so backed up that he could still text and pay attention. But not now. The tension filled his body like embers from a raging fire, floating away to the sky like how he longed to take her.

The rough denim of his jeans pricked against his sensitive head; the sensation being mounted from the other fabric of his cotton boxers. His cock felt tighter against the swelling of the skin. What an exhilarating feeling it was to have a woman submit to him so easily. Unlike Ashley, in which he felt like he was playing Russian Roulette with their intimate life. A lump came into his dry throat, and he took a swig of Diet Coke, and he had no choice but to put his truck in gear and drive through.

Therefore, leaving her on read.

Evie's emotions came crumbling down as she assumed he was turned off by her comment.

Stupid idiot. That's what you get for wearing your hormones AND your heart on your sleeve. She never knew how to talk to men unless it was absolute sexual subjection. That was the only way she could get men to pay attention to her, and that was why she had deleted the prior text. It had to be different this time. But now she was left unsure as to whether that message was too romantic, too clingy, too desperate sounding. Anything.

Missy tugged at her arm and jerked her out of the moment. "We're ready for you."

Evie sighed and looked once more at the phone. Nothing. Regretfully, she shoved it into her pocket and followed Missy to the conference room to deliver the presentation.

She stood tall in front of the room of about fifteen people, all with their laptops glowing, coffee cups decorating the table, stacks of papers and pens, and in the middle was a big plate of muffins she mentally refused upon entering. She was proud of that moment. Everyone stared at her. Pens clicked, and outside the window was the scenery of downtown with its art-deco style of buildings. The Municipal Auditorium was not far from her work in the Power and Light District. Rain could be heard once again.

However, across the tables to the right sat Mr. Perry, the actual CEO and president of the company. It wasn't the project manager overseeing the presentation! She gulped hard, as Mr. Perry was a rigid man with a strict opinion. He was great at what he did, and he was a fine CEO that was loved by all of his employees, but still he was a hard shell to crack. He glared at her through his glasses, leaning on his elbow and clicking a pen. His blond hair was recently cut again and styled richly, but he chose a more relaxed attire of sweatpants and a hoodie that day.

Maybe he was in a good mood.

She drew in a breath and began, "Alright. Good morning, everyone!" She turned on the projector and then began passing out numerous folders. "Let's dive into the visual strategy I've created for the prospective marketing campaign." At that moment, her soul dropped into her feet as her cell phone never went off again. The hurtful thought snapped into her head, and she longed to escape it but couldn't.

What if she was a simple rebound? What if she had thrown herself too hard at him?

Her thigh vibrated suddenly from her phone's buzz. It was a text; one she couldn't read.

She tossed her hair behind her back, attempting to fight it. She lifted her head and announced, "I think you will all find it fashionable and buzzworthy! Since Jamboree is becoming a more inclusive company and always reaching to expand its market, I've designed a campaign using an inclusive color palette that reflects different races and sexual orientations. I took the liberty of designing the typography by hand and utilizing asymmetry to keep it modern and fresh."

What could the text possibly say? It could have been anything. It could have been him calling her weird and calling it off. It could have been him changing the conversation, which would have made her feel awkward and self-conscious all over again. She had to fight it. She gritted her teeth and released the death grip she had on the projector's remote.

Mr. Perry spoke up after looking at the folder, "Is that why you took so long to prepare this? You did this by hand?"

Evie boasted, "I did, sir."

"Evie," he calmly said as other people looked at their folders, "we have AI now. You could have done this exact thing in an hour instead of five days."

At once, she felt backed into a wall. All over, her coworkers seemed to jeer at her, and they turned to one another and mumbled under their breaths. Before her heart rate could elevate, she drew in a deep breath through her nose and let it fall out heavily. To some, it could have seemed like she was irritated, but she was only calming herself down the way Caleb taught her. It was true. Anxiety was now her new loathed friend.

"I'm sorry, sir, but you gave me a raise because of my design skills, not because of my knowledge of AI prompts, right?"

"Yes, but I could have had you working on another concept by now. I wanted you to come up with numerous options we could look at." He kept his elbow on the table, still holding his pen up in that hand. "You only gave us one."

She shook her head. The phone buzzed again in her pocket. "I'm sorry, sir. You didn't tell me you wanted me to have multiple things prepared. I apologize. I can have more done in a few days."

"Well, I need like two others, and I doubt you can have it done in three days."

Missy crossed her arms and leaned back. "He's right, Evie. When are you going to embrace that AI is here? We're going to fall behind schedule because of you."

"But," she recounted, "ever since I've been here for the last five years, the clients and customers have come to know my artistic style. It's what we've kind of rebranded ourselves with. I can't replicate that with AI."

Mr. Perry ordered all the folders to be given back to her.

The phone buzzed again, and she jerked nervously. He could be going off on her now.

Mr. Perry stated with a smile, "It's here, Evie. Try to learn how to get AI to replicate your style. Jason Mathers can help you. He's our AI guy here now."

She collected the folders sorrowfully.

He knuckled the table. "We'll reconvene in three days."

Evie nodded, smiled, and thanked everyone as they walked by her to leave.

Then she ran out of the room, slammed the folders on her desk, and darted into the bathroom out in the hall. Her escape was the bathroom stalls, where she locked herself in and cried hysterically. She absolutely fell apart. She had been working tirelessly on those designs, and it wasn't enough. The mascara trickled down her rosy cheeks in an onyx river of despair, and she choked on her sobs while leaning against the door.

The phone buzzed again.

Please, let this be good and happy news.

Boy was...it...*ever.*

Caleb reacted to her last text with a shocked face emoji. The series of texts read, "Why did you have to text me that while driving and on the job? I'm not going to be able to get away for at least another five hours! I would love that. I would love to feel that beautiful body in my arms where you belong. But you should know..."

She waited anxiously.

He had *originally* texted, "My cock got insanely hard reading that text. You deserve it in return. That night, I wanted to lick, suckle and obsess over every inch of you. I wanna hold your legs open against my arms and lick you until you don't even know your own name. I don't want to make you cum just once, I want to wake you with it, give it to you constantly throughout the day. I'd get on my knees and worship every inch with my hands and mouth, and you only fall asleep because I've exhausted you with pleasure. And even as you slept, I would continue it. You don't know how fucking crazy you make me."

But he too, deleted it before he sent it. He needed to get his act together and not be so aggressive with her. Evie was something to be treasured and appreciated, not objectified. He knew she had had enough of that in her life already.

He actually wrote, "I enjoy spending time with you. I've always loved how open and honest you are on your Facebook page and how giving you are to the community even when they don't deserve it, and I can't thank you enough for letting me help you. I get so sick of this 'tough independent woman' thing going around. I get there's a time and a place for that, but if a woman doesn't need me for anything, I'm not gonna stick around."

Her heart pounded, and her muscles clenched. A breathless gasp came from her lips, and she sat on the floor in the larger stall and cried happily.

It went on, "You do something to me that I've never felt before in my whole life. I can't explain it, but you do. It's gotta be either you or the bottle tonight, Evie. I feel happy when I'm around you."

That was enough for her. He was the most amazing thing that had ever happened to her. Then a thought came. Caleb was a military man, and even though he was pouring his heart out to her, she knew there was going to be some rigidity in him, and she was going to have to learn to contain her emotions a bit not to seem overly emotional or too sensitive. She wiped her eyes and smiled with a sigh of finally being through the crying fest and composed herself.

She wrote back, "I'm sorry you haven't felt like that in a long time. But this couldn't have come at a better time. I don't think I could be an 'independent woman' if I tried. I've never felt safe on my own. But I want you to know, that ever since I've known you and have seen how you push through life through, I'm assuming PTSD, and handling two kids and a divorce, not to mention taking care of all of the land you own, and having two jobs? You inspire me to be a better woman."

Now the phone buzzed in his jeans. He walked away from his workers for a moment. When he saw it, he loved her message and wrote back, "You wanna hear one more thing?"

She felt stable in everything. Calmness filled her heart and soul with a tender touch. This was what it was like speaking to a man like an equal woman. "Yes, please." Her heart thumped in her neck as she shifted a bit on her rear.

He smirked. It was a bit out of his nature to write was he was going to write, but he wanted to make her happy. He combed his memory of all the times he'd seen her post about the way men had treated her, and how she longed to be treated right. He wrote, "I know you've been fucked around with. So, I wanna take you on a date first. Is that cool? We can go someplace outside of town where no one really knows us."

Absolute euphoria.

Evie had never been on a date in her whole life. Not once. Leaning back against the wall, she refrained from crying again. It was like Caleb had used those calloused hands to lasso every emotion she had built up within her tender heart and ripped them straight from her chest. To taste the whiskey on his lips again. To feel those rough and strong hands around her petal-soft neck. Once again, he was left on read and he put a knuckle to his mouth, waiting for her response.

And Evie was taken back in time with Pawpaw when he said, "That man is nothing but trouble."

But here he had helped her through a panic attack, stayed with her, kissed her passionately, respected his children, sent her messages to check on her, helped her get medicine on the top shelf, aired up her tires, offered to take care of her grass.

I don't understand how a man who does such kind things...could be bad.

It was such a mystery to her. And then the women at the salon. What the hell was that all about? And what did he do to Ashley that was apparently so bad?

Well, she wasn't Ashley, so it didn't matter. Caleb had a clean slate in her heart.

But here was the *real* test. One of the reasons why Evie had never been on a date was because every time she tried to pursue a man online or whatever, there were so many beige flags that she never even got to the date. Men would say, "I don't care. You pick." It was absolutely frustrating and exhausting trying to plan everything. She wrote happily in a quick test, "I would absolutely LOVE that! Is there a place in mind that you'd like to go?"

He grinned and wrote, "I really love O'Malley's up in Freeton. Have you been there?"

"A few times, I actually adore that place!"

He wrote a smiley emoji and said, "I'll pick you up at five."

The presentations. "Shit!" she hissed out loud. She replied, "I actually don't get off work until five and won't even be home until six. Wanna meet me there?"

"It's a date," he said with a smiley.

She clutched the phone to her chest and felt the absolute dreamy sensation of being in puppy love. Her brown eyes glittered up to the white ceiling of that bathroom.

Her phone buzzed again. She read it.

"Wear your Armani perfume." It ended with a kissy face.

She giggled and wrote back, "Don't shave." It too had a kissy face.

That rose quite a giggle from him! So much that his workers stared at him from across the large living room. He put his phone back into his pocket. "Alright," he ordered and clapped his hands, "let's get back to work, y'all. Enough dickin' around."

Evie was lost in dreamland until the main door of the ladies' room came swinging open. She mumbled under breath, "Shit, shit, shit!" She stood up.

"Evie?" Missy's voice came. "Are you in here?"

Evie flushed the toilet for no reason at all other than to appear like she needed the bathroom. She came out and fixed her blazer. "I'm fine. What do you need?"

Missy stared up and down to examine her. Evie folded her arms and tapped her heel in a smug fashion. "Well, what is it? It's not like a girl can't have a moment to herself in the bathroom."

"What were you doing?"

Evie pushed by her. "Cracking the Da Vinci Code."

Chapter Eight

O'Malley's was a stunning restaurant that boasted glamorous dark-wood counters, black chairs, white tablecloths, and the most sparkling bar display she had ever seen. It was the sort of place where the staff wore black pants or skirts, white Oxford shirts, and ties. The menu changed seasonally, and the most delicious thing to her was the triple chocolate cake that far surpassed any she had ever had. Although she loved the baked goods at Songbird Café in town, they never really made anything sinfully chocolatey, which was Evie's weakness.

The host greeted her warmly and escorted her to a cozy table for two in the darker corner of the back of the dining area. It was up a small set of stairs to a more intimate area where wine bottles were on display and the TVs were a little quieter, if heard at all. She thanked the host as he handed her the menu, and after he left, she began reading to prepare her order.

Music played on the local radio station softly overhead, and she stopped reading to listen closer. The little girl within her called her back to happier days while she heard the lyrics. She closed her eyes and imagined her delicately pink-painted fingertips stroking his rugged face.

In a pickup truck not too far away, Caleb was hearing the same song on the radio and lowly sang along. He sighed miserably. He thought out loud, "Sometimes I feel like she's the closest thing to heaven I'll ever get."

He had to forget it. Forget it all.

He had to forget what happened overseas.

The steering wheel was gripped harder.

He had to forget what he *did*.

She rested her chin on her hand and smiled, drowning in a sea of joy. To let those waves crush her and the rip current pull her further from reality to a place she longed for.

She sprayed herself with Sì by Armani.

He arrived and parked in a spot, then checked his five o'clock shadow in the mirror. "Alright, don't let me down tonight. You gotta be extra rugged. Like Chuck Norris rugged. Like 'houses demolish themselves for reconstruction when I walk in' kinda rugged." He then reached over and grabbed the two dozen roses on the passenger seat and got out. *This chick loves flowers as much as she loves her cat. If I want any chance in hell to start over, I gotta make the right moves.*

And if he ever wanted to truly shake what he'd done, he was going to have to work hard for her.

No woman in her right mind would love a man who did what he did.

She felt a bit shaky, so she shook out her hands and took a deep breath. *Okay, Evie. He's got kids and a respectable role in society. Don't fuck this up. Grow up. Get your emotions in order. Don't be too sensitive. This is your chance.*

Surveying the room, she saw him come in. She rose to her feet, and a smile could not stay off her face when she saw the roses he carried. The nervousness blew away the moment she saw his familiar face. But she also couldn't help but be stunned at what he was wearing. She held her chest from the flutters. Somehow, even while on the job in such a field, he was wearing dark-blue jeans and an ironed white Oxford shirt tucked neatly into a black belt. The shirt framed his shoulders and biceps lusciously, and his hair was gelled in the way she recognized. On his feet were cowboy boots. She couldn't believe he didn't have a coat of some sort! It was downright chilly that evening.

He bounded up the steps to leave the host behind. Her heart raced as she clapped her mouth.

His eyes never left hers. Immediately, he swooped her into his arms and kissed her tender lips while his right hand held the roses behind her back. How he had yearned for that moment all day since he had left her. Her breath swayed with his, feeling his rough hand embracing her silky face. Evie's hands ran over his chest firmly up to his shoulders and then pulled his kiss deeper.

They pulled apart. He grinned, looking deeply into her eyes. "You smell amazing and look insanely sexy." He chuckled to hide his nervousness. With his large hand delicately placed around her lower jaw, he tilted her head to savor the scent against her skin. His nose gently brushed behind her ear.

Evie's head was cocked back due to his height, and she moaned in adoration. "Thank you. How the hell did you get dressed like this so fast?"

He sat down with her at the table and put the roses in his lap. "I'm military. I know how to be prepared. I went home quickly to grab some things on a break and got ready at QuikTrip."

She laughed and asked in surprise, "You changed in a gas station bathroom?"

"Is that bad?"

She chuckled and shook her head. "No, not at all. I can't believe you went through all that extra trouble when every other man I know wouldn't even comb his hair."

He leaned back and playfully knuckled on the table. "Most men my age are losing hair anyway, so..."

She snickered again. He knew he was making her laugh, so he went on with it, "Besides, I'm on a date with a freaking graphic designer. If I showed up in shitty clothes, I'd bomb this interview."

She paused. "Interview?"

Caleb flashed his eyes around the room, still leaning back. "I mean, yeah. Isn't that what all dates are like? Asking, 'What do you like?' 'What do you bring to the table?' You know, that sorta thing?"

She smiled and shook her head out again with a laugh. "Good question! I've never been on a date, so I wouldn't know."

He returned his eyes to her with a smile and finally leaned forward, handing her the flowers. "Here."

She took them lovingly. Two dozen long-stemmed roses were speckled with baby's breath and wrapped in clear wrapping. Their fragrance was a nice break from the roasting garlic that lingered in the air. Evie gazed at the roses and nearly cradled them like a baby.

Caleb looked at her. Her eyes were sparkling, and she was smiling softly. The roses were gently held against her chest. It was so difficult not to let her eyes water. She tried, but a tear rolled down her cheek. She had gotten her flowers. "Thank you."

He put his knuckles against his lip again and bounced his knee under the table. "You really get that worked up from flowers?"

She realized that she was being overly emotional again but couldn't help it. "You don't know what this means to me." He didn't. All those years, she had wanted flowers from a man other than her dad and Pawpaw. She should have felt lucky to have ever gotten that, but this hit in a different way.

As he looked at her, it dawned on him that this woman was definitely on the ardent side, and he was unsure if it was too much for his unbending outlook and way of life. He recalled telling his own father he was sorry he didn't show more affection to him before he went off to war. But he also felt like no matter what he did to show love, it never landed right. Caleb always had a hard time expressing emotions.

Wait.

He swallowed hard as he kept staring at her. Evie *did* influence his confessions of emotions. He confessed nearly all of it in texts earlier. And it damn sure felt good. He could have written an entire five-page-long text about what she moved in him, how her hands gliding across his deltoids made him feel cherished.

He smiled and leaned forward to reach for her hand. "I'm glad. You deserve it."

Her hand was in his on the table, and she felt his strong thumb gliding across it. Their eyes met. Evie then set the roses on the table and reached out to grab his other hand. Even when the waitress came, he never let go and would only make eye contact to give his order, and Evie did the same thing. Before the waitress left, Caleb informed her that it would all be on one check. Then he called out, "Oh, and save a piece of the triple chocolate cake for my girl right here!"

The waitress smiled and nodded. Evie giggled and shrunk down in her seat.

"Thank you," Evie said sheepishly.

"You're welcome. So how was your day?"

She stammered a bit, "You know, we usually talk about me when you're around. Why don't we talk about you?"

"You know a lot about me through Facebook already."

She laughed, looking to the side. "Caleb, you post like twice a month and only upload to your stories once a week, if that. And it's usually about your kids. Not that that's bad or anything."

He smirked. "Well, then what does that tell you?"

She thought then smiled in a soft laugh. "That your kids are your life."

"Yep, that's right."

An awkward silence came.

Caleb looked off somewhere. "I'm not really sure what we're supposed to talk about. I've not been on a date with a new girl at all in almost twenty years."

She leaned forward. "Is that how long you were with Ashley?"

He paused and got caught in memory. Evie could easily see he was hurting. The way his eyes looked down and to the right, still slouched back with one leg proper but the other stretched far out under the table, it was clear as day he hadn't fully recovered from whatever happened.

"Caleb, I still want to know more about you. I don't think you know how fascinating you are. I see what things you do on Facebook. Tell me about those things. I'd love to hear! I see you love the outdoors, and we can talk about the Mojave Desert! I know that's your favorite place." She sat upright cutely. "I love deserts, and your photos are so cool. I miss living in Los Angeles. So, you could tell me about that. Or, even if we talk about your kids, which honestly over texts it seems to be all you talk about." She smiled, trying to cheer him up. "Since they make you so happy you can tell me things I don't know about them. Like your favorite memories with them, their favorite foods, anything. I'll listen."

He sat forward and smiled, brushing her arm with his hand. "You told me you had a shitty day at work. What happened?"

"Oh," she muttered, shaking her head. Without thinking, she stroked the top of his hand that was touching her left one. His presence soothed her. It made her feel stable. "I didn't know I was supposed to have three marketing campaign designs done, and I only did one. My boss wants me to embrace AI and—"

"Fuck AI."

"Right? Like, I get that it has a place for some things like enemy motion in video games or even like tailored learning on apps, but damn. I felt so expendable."

"It's because you are in your boss's eyes. Somewhere else there'll be another pretty woman like you strolling along to make her next big move, but you have a brain and can think for yourself."

Evie ruminated on the remark.

"Maybe you can do freelance work and build yourself up as a free-lance designer? Fuck those people who tell you to use AI. It literally eradicates your decades of hard work and building your own style."

"I wouldn't even know where to begin."

"You're well-known in the community now with all your little chari-table acts and candid posts. And I know Joey is looking for a new design for her menu at the café."

"She is?" Evie said with a piqued look. "I just saw her new menu on Facebook the other day."

"Yeah, and it looks like shit. She needs a new design." He smiled spiritedly.

Evie busted out laughing and he chuckled with her.

She nodded slowly in agreement, trying to come out of the laugh but it wasn't easy to do. Evie loved his blatant honesty.

Then Caleb gave his dimpled smile. "You're the professional. Tell me what you think of her new digital menu. If you're going to ask me about *my* profession, I'm going to ask about yours."

Evie smirked. "Yeah, but you haven't told me anything about your profession."

"Okay, I shoot guns and fix houses. Your move." He smiled again, knowing he was a rascal.

It was unimaginable how many times he got her to laugh. She sat back and put the back of her hand to her mouth, feeling tears of laughter coming to her eyes. Through her laughter, she said, "I already know that. Tell me something I don't know."

He shrugged, smiled, and played along. "Alright. I shoot many different guns, and I fix many different houses. Your move."

"You're an asshole, you know that?" she said through their robust laughter.

The food finally came, and they began eating. Evie ordered a grilled chicken salad with an unsweetened iced tea, and Caleb ordered the avocado bacon burger with fries. She watched him eat like nothing. "Ugh, if I ate like that, I'd be all the way back up to 250 in no time."

"If I had a desk job too, I'd have to eat like you."

She shrugged with a grin, stabbing her salad. "You know, that's a fair point."

People came in and dined. Families left, and tables were wiped down. Occasionally Caleb would glance up at the TVs around to see what the scores were for the games, and he would make comments about them. Evie never understood the obsession with sports, but then again, she knew people didn't really understand her obsession with her cat or flowers. Even though small talk was made, Evie grew frustrated with still not knowing much about him, despite being in contact with him for several months. Was it even logical to be upset with that? Was that a reasonable amount of time? That was a question she had no answer for.

She tried again, but this time she was far more direct. "I know you're probably going to get upset with me, and I'm sorry, but..."

He looked at her.

"I really wish you would talk about yourself more."

He sighed. "Evie, I don't think it's appropriate to do this right now."

"Do what? I thought dates were supposed to be about getting to know about each other." She smiled to reassure him and opened her hands. "You can tell me anything at all you'd like."

"What's so important for you to know? You know I'm divorced. I have two kids. I'm in the Navy. And I run my own contracting business."

She shook her head out and narrowed her eyes. "Yeah, but I'm sure there's more to you than that. Like, what's your favorite food? How did you meet Ashley? What are some of your favorite memories? Ever get hurt on a horse?"

He groaned in agitation then leaned his elbows on the table. "Just be honest, Evie. You want to know why we got divorced."

She stared at him in shock. "But that's not the case at all. It's really none of my business."

"But how she and I met is?"

She was pissed. She could no longer hide it. She had been nothing but nice to him since she had met him, and if all he was going to do was be condescending, then she would get up and forget it. Angrily, she grabbed her purse, and Caleb looked as she stood up.

"You're leaving, I take it?"

Oh, his tone was *vile*! What was she supposed to do?

She answered, "Yes, I am leaving, because—"

She hesitated. The room felt like it froze, and she glanced at the floor, looking at her soft beige suede boots. Then she turned and looked at him. All she saw was him sitting casually at the table, with his elbows on the table, hands folded, and him rubbing his mouth against his hands looking at her.

I will tear down those walls brick by brick with my bare hands if I have to.

She let herself sink in the idiocy of what she was about to do. Was she *really* going to leave over the fact he didn't open up to her after only truly knowing her for only a few days? The seasons had come and gone, yes, but not only were they just getting to know each other, he wasn't obligated to her. And she decided to remember that.

Her purse strap slowly slid off her shoulder as if she was going to hold it but never did. As their eyes met, the nasty and undeniable truth came into her heart. Caleb Wright had to be hiding something absolutely dreadful to be pushing her out of his private life like that. But how was she going to be involved with someone who wouldn't let her in? Was she being too pushy? Was she trying to move too fast, too soon?

How the hell was she supposed to know what to do? The cluelessness of handling a situation like that left her with nothing but a frustrated heart and a confused purpose.

"I'm sorry I got up so quickly. I think I, um, it's a woman thing. So, I need to go to the bathroom."

"Will you...be back?" he asked slowly.

She turned and paused with a weak smile. "Yes, I will always come back."

But in the bathroom once more, Evie found her solace and cried. This was going to be significantly harder than she thought. Love was not the thing she had imagined growing up. She dreamed about her valiant knight as a child, and it was supposed to be perfect. Her hero was supposed to be perfect, not hard to decipher. Military men were different than fairytales. Real life was different.

Everything was wrong. It wasn't like how it was in movies or books, where a service member swept the lady off her feet and was all heroic and shit. No. Their trust had to be *earned* and earned patiently. It wouldn't take any effort at all for her to tell him anything he wanted to know. Why did it have to be so hard for him? Her chest felt clenched from the sadness and despair, and as another woman came in, she silenced her cries. Love was supposed to be effortless, at least in her eyes. Evie never understood why people made things so complicated.

For her, you either loved somebody or didn't. And if you loved somebody, it shouldn't be hard to open up to them. Little did she know she was too childish to realize the very thought indicated she wanted him to love her already.

That was stupid.

She had to get her racing thoughts under control before they crashed into one another and she did something stupid.

He had texted her so many times saying she had no idea what she did to him, how he couldn't wait to see her, and all these other sweet things. Wasn't that love? Or was it?

Caleb paid the bill, and when she came out, she picked up the flowers, and together they walked to her car. He carried her little box of chocolate cake. But she was slow and resistant in her motions. The sunset was coming in the busy shopping district, and once more she pulled her hair from her face as the wind blew. She shivered.

Their eyes met.

Their hearts yearned for something neither one of them could confess.

Evie softly asked in worry, "Will I hear from you again?"

Caleb grinned and lifted her chin to kiss her. Slowly she took his kiss in, basking in the beauty of his lips and his body against hers. Caleb put the box on top of her car, grabbed her hips and pushed her against the car, making her gasp. The crispness of his Oxford shirt was pure luxury against the soft skin of her hands and chest, and even on her throat when he leaned over to kiss her neck.

"Caleb," she moaned.

He grabbed her hair and let her perfume destroy the wrecked feeling he had.

"Caleb," she groaned again a bit louder, trying to get his attention.

And then she pushed him off.

He stepped back, completely stunned. "What the hell? What's this all about?"

"Listen, don't be mad at me, okay? But if you're not going to open up to me about anything, then I'm sorry, but I can't do this."

"So, you *were* pissed off about what I said earlier. And you *were* going to leave. Why couldn't you be honest?"

A deep-seeded hurt rooted in her heart, and she snapped back, "It wouldn't've mattered anyway! Besides, I can't go on with this feeling like all I'm going to be is a booty call!"

"Hey!" he shot back. "You're the one who tried to make the moves on *me* the night of your anxiety attack. I was trying to be a good man and not put that on you, and you came on to me. Now I'm trying to pursue you that way and now you feel like a booty call? That doesn't make any fucking sense!"

Oh shit, Evie thought. Her hands ran through her hair and then over her mouth. Immediately, she tried to pull his hand before he left. She couldn't lose him now. "Caleb, please!"

"What?" he shot back as he turned to her abruptly.

Her lips trembled and she lifted her hands to talk and motion with them, but they were shaking as badly as she was. "Look, I'm so sorry. You're absolutely right. You *are* a good man, but I want to know more about you. Because honestly, I think you need something deeper than a sexual release or being at the bottom of the fucking bottle again. And you won't let me help you!"

He put his hands on his hips. He couldn't believe what came out of her mouth. "Evie, not everyone needs saving. Not everyone needs help. And don't you dare presume to know me!"

Here it came. It knotted in her fists as much as her stomach. Her spine felt hot and cramped. It was coming, and this time Evie would not hold it back. She grabbed him and turned him around before he walked away. "Listen to me. *Everyone* needs help. No one bottles things up like this, hides their life, and drinks like you do unless they're hurting!" She touched his chest with burning desire, an insatiable craving. "You were there for me in every way I needed before I hardly even knew you. You took such a chance on a stranger and helped them. Why can't I take a chance on a stranger and help you?"

Evelyn Morgan had finally broke. All her life, she was never able to tell people how she felt except for the times in Los Angeles where it meant her safety. But this man wasn't some thug trying to sexually assault her or stalk her. This was the man she cared deeply for. Always with a passive and submissive voice in her thirties, she had finally felt confident enough to be open and firm in her stance. Caleb Wright was hurting, somehow, and badly. She made a promise to herself that she would break down those walls. He was worth it.

Caleb was moved. All sorts of emotions blurred into his mind and body, and together they tangled themselves in knots that distorted his reality. He pulled her in hard to kiss her, and even though it hurt her to receive it, it would pain her more to pull away. "I can't thank you enough for how sweet you are." He held his fingers in her hair and spoke passionately to her. "You are insanely selfless, kind, giving, and so beautiful."

He tightened his lips. "Try not to let *anyone* change that."

She smiled and snuggled her face into his hand. "I won't."

"Thank you for the date." He kissed her again.

"Of course, thank you for paying. But you should get going. I know you have to be up early."

One more kiss, and then another. The sun set delicately over the shopping center, igniting a hot orange and fiery pink hue across the glass windows, the cars, the beautiful partly clouded sky. It burned like the infernal lust between them both, and yet both had so much to say but said nothing.

Evie slowly ceased the rapturous kissing into a gentle caress, and Caleb's lips were still grazing hers. "Please," she begged. "Tell me something to turn me off before I beg to go home with you."

Like an unwavering spirit possessing her body, Caleb's right hand slid up underneath her blazer and blouse to stroke her lower back. She curved her lower back to him, adoring the way the mass of it dipped and curved into every inch of her skin. Goosebumps broke out like a virus of yearning and desire all over her; one that could be seen by all but only felt by him. His warm hand rubbed firmly back alongside her hip before slipping underneath her pants, where he finally touched the soft curves of her hip.

He crushed her into the side of the car and placed his hand on the roof, slightly entrapping her. And there she would willingly stay a victim to his passion as long as he had the key to her chains.

The kissing continued, and as he groaned, his hormones overtook his common sense, and he blurted out, "Ashley *never* fucking kissed me like this."

She slipped her hands up on his waist. Since his shirt was buttoned and tucked in with a belt, there was no way she was going to be able to deliver the same succulent touch as he did. She could have pulled it out, but that would look too obvious to any passerby. Even still, her touch made his abs tighten, his muscles contract, and his breathing quicken.

He held her throat and kissed her neck. She shuddered hard with pleasure. And as he did, Evie's eyes closed, and she whispered, "God, I love it when you kiss my neck."

"I know you do," he said softly.

She closed her eyes tighter and opened her mouth to moan quietly, "Why are you doing this right now when we can't be alone?"

He broke away. "I'm so stupid. Sorry, I completely forgot where we were."

"Are you okay?"

"Yeah," he sighed while looking down at the ground. "I was worried you were gonna stay pissed at me in there."

Evie looked away in thought. She thought about everything that had happened. Truthfully, she was in no position to be getting pissed off at someone for being who they were. She simply held him close. She held him *hard*. It caused him, the tired, the lonely, the secretive, and calloused man that he was, to feel the best relief once more. The sun felt like not only was it setting on the day, but it was setting for a lot of hurt he still carried within the rucksack of his heart.

Slowly, Caleb wrapped his arms around her. "Why are we like this with each other? We hardly know each other."

She snuggled into his chest, finding the loud traffic off in the intersection to be nothing of a bother to her. Evie's eyes closed in that affectionate moment. "Let's not analyze it. Let's just live it."

Caleb said, "I'm sorry. I know we both need to be up. We should probably go now."

She grinned up to him. "Would it kill you to skip a shower once in exchange for some rest and relaxation?"

He chuckled and combed his fingers through her hair. His eyes never left hers. "I can tell you right now that resting and relaxing with you is the last thing I'd do."

"I'm serious, Mr. Wright." It suddenly made her nearly die inside with laughter realizing that he was practically named after the infamous joke of finding "Mr. Right." She'd keep it to herself, not wanting to sound corny. Instead, she pressed on with her concern about his never-ending workload. "I respect that you're military, and I'm sure it's hard to shut off. But don't you think maybe once instead of constantly being on the go like you are, you can rest a second?"

"I do rest, actually," he said with a smile. She was being so cute to him!

This was her chance to get him to possibly open up, just a bit. "Oh yeah? Like what?"

"Well," he looked around and said easily, "I like taking Zack and Olivia to the lake and go hiking."

She laughed. "No, I mean like true relaxation."

"But...that *is* relaxation for me."

"Is it really?" she asked, genuinely curious.

"Yep."

"Do you ever just, lay on the couch and watch your favorite movie or something?"

"Not really. I do for their birthdays or like holidays. But not really." Then he asked, "What about you?"

"Oh, I love snuggling up in my pjs, basking with some homemade brownies, enjoying a few good movies, or listening to a good album!"

"Even with all that work you gotta do around your house? How do you ever really sit and rest knowing there's so much to be done?"

Evie rubbed his chest. Their ravenous makeout session had run its course, and they were both apparently okay with that. "I keep trying to fix things, and it's overwhelming. I keep watching YouTube videos, but it's so hard to understand, and everything is so different. I need to mow my lawn properly, but I don't even know where to start because it's kinda big."

He smirked. "It's barely two acres."

"That's big!" she laughed.

"Darling, you're in Missouri. Like eight hours isn't a long drive, two acres isn't a big yard."

"It's a lot when you don't have a riding lawn mower."

Caleb thought curiously and looked at her. He remembered what he had offered a few days ago.

They had said their warm goodbyes with hugs and went home. Evie was definitely going to need to devour that chocolate cake after what just happened.

That night, they texted each other nearly nonstop. Evie listened to the scanner and was trying one more damn time to fix the hinge on her cupboard. The whole door fell off, making her jump and growl into the air with frustration. Teddy came in and lay on it.

She lifted him off and cuddled him sweetly.

Caleb texted her a selfie, and she opened it. A warmness befell her heart, and she smiled with a light in her eyes. He was snuggled up in bed with his kids watching a movie. The text read, "I asked them what movie they wanted to watch. They got so excited to pop up the corn and have snacks in bed. Olivia wanted *Frozen*, and Zack wanted *Shrek*. So, we're watching them both."

"Caleb!" she wrote back enthusiastically. "This is so darling! Look how happy they are. But I'm confused. I thought they were going to stay at their grandma's tonight?"

He wrote back, "I asked them if they'd rather stay with Grandma or watch movies in bed with me. They chose this without hesitation." He ended it with a smiley emoji.

Evie's heart grew so warm. She held her chest and wrote back, "All bundled up by their daddy and smiling at the TV. I'm so happy for you. See, isn't it wonderful? And I'm proud of you. You even allowed snacks in the bed!"

He reacted with a laughing emoji. And reacted again whenever she sent the picture of the cupboard door on the floor and told him what happened. He wrote, "Your hinge is rusted and old. You need new ones. I've got some around here I can bring over sometime."

The texting continued after he put his children to bed, and she made her way to bed for the night. Teddy purred by her stomach. He was now alone in his own bed. They would roll over to a different position and talk the night away until 2:00 a.m. Even though she didn't get to know a lot about him, she was thankful he was interested in her life. And that would be good enough for her.

Friday came. Coming home from work, Evie pulled up and saw his truck in her driveway with a trailer hitched to it. The sound of a lawn-mower hummed in the side yard, and there he came with a big can of Diet Coke in his hand, his baseball hat on forward with the Chiefs' logo on it, sunglasses, and a boyish smile. She folded her arms and shook her head in a grin. He called out to her with his can raised.

Evie approached him, and he shut off the motor. Then he twisted to rest his arm on the front. "Hey, sugar momma. Wanna take a ride on the wild side?"

"With the way my yard looked, that *would* be on the wild side! You are the coolest person ever! I can't thank you enough for this!"

He looked around suspiciously. "Well, it ain't gonna come for free." He winked. "You're gonna owe me something."

"Oh yeah?" She smiled and leaned into him. "What is it?"

His look said it all. The deal was set.

Caleb continued to mow her yard and inside, she watched through the kitchen window while she made the brownies he had requested. Watching all of those baking shows had finally paid off. On the TV screen, one of the Batman movies was queued up and ready to go upon his request. And last but not least, he had brought his overnight bag.

He was going to stay the night and learn how to relax.

Chapter Nine

Caleb came trudging in through the front door with his gray company shirt all smudged with grass stains, dirt, sweat, and for some reason a weird brown smudge on the upper back area. The chilly air had left him cold and damp feeling. He could smell the brownies and their enticing fragrance hovering in the air, and he felt drawn to it like a cartoon character when a pie cooled in the windowsill.

Politely, he removed his work boots and placed them on the shoe mat next to the door and smiled down at the pink tennis shoes, the pink beach sandals, the pink fancy sandals, and for something *extra* different, pink tennis shoes with leopard spots.

He chuckled. Teddy came hurrying over and flopped on his feet. As Caleb leaned over to pet him, it was a purring symphony, but it quickly turned into death play. Caleb yanked back. "Ow! You little bastard!" He scooped the cat up into his arms and planted kisses all over his head. "You think you can handle me, huh? You think you got it all figured out?" Then, Caleb wildly kissed the cat and began baby talking, "You're such a fuzzy little bag of boo boos. You're momma's favorite little wookie smookie."

Teddy responded favorably. But Evie was standing in the doorway that led to the dining room with a plate of brownies in her hand.

Caleb noticed her and immediately cleared his throat, put the cat down, and brushed the orange fur off his chest. "I uh, um," he stuttered. "I know you like talking to him like that, so I was trying to bond with him."

Evie smirked cutely with brows raised high. "Oh, is *that* what that was? For a second there, I thought I was seeing a different side of you."

He leaned over and whispered harshly to Teddy, "You're gonna get me in trouble!" The cat just looked up at him.

Caleb approached her and held her arms gently and planted a kiss on her forehead. Evie welcomed its presence with her eyes softly closed. He kept kissing her tenderly on the face but then started to glide his hands down her upper arms, rousing her goosebumps once more. He had a delectable way of touching her. Next, his hands curled around her elbows, making a subtle sensation to her forearms, down her wrists, her hands...to the brownie plate.

She started giggling with her eyes still closed, finally sensing what he really wanted. It was absolutely adorable to her.

He took the plate away. "Thank you!"

"Sir, you could take my paycheck straight from my hands if you did it like that."

He smugly took a bite of one. "Lucky for you, I don't need your paycheck."

While he ate, holding the plate in one hand and a brownie in the other, Evie lifted up that dirty shirt and stroked his stomach. He stopped eating at once. Her hands possessed the finest texture of silk, delicate and gentle, but then the sturdiness of cotton, plush and warming.

Her hands trailed underneath his shirt up his sternum and trapped his lust within her fingers as she glided them outwards across his nipples. They were hard and sensitive with little tuffs of hair around them, as well as other tinier little bumps of erotic nerves waking up. She stroked back inward and felt a little bit on his chest closer to his sternum. Their gaze was locked and hot.

"You know what I want from you, Mr. Wright?"

He swallowed and spoke, "What's that?"

Evie smiled and drew closer to him with her fingers now gliding down to his jeans. She stepped back and put her hair up in a ponytail. Caleb's heart fucking roared when he saw those bedroom eyes siphoning his soul straight from his body.

Then she took the brownie plate from his hand and walked away. "I want a glass of milk to go with these brownies. Want one?"

He stared. Brownie still in one hand, smudges of chocolate on his lip and his cheeks puffed out in confusion. He glanced down at Teddy who was staring up at him, seemingly to mock him. "Your mom is terrible."

But he had a better way to get back at her. He hurried in through the living room, past the doorway to the dining room with its cozy four-seater white wooden table by the bay window and its cushioned seating, her grandmother's china hutch that displayed all sorts of china from Japan and Sweden. He tried to move cautiously so he didn't topple the little pictures in their frames within the hutch, since he could be heavy-footed at times. He entered the fragrant kitchen and saw her little Swedish kitchen towels all nicely hanging from the racks.

It was the first time he had seen her kitchen in its entirety, as when he ate the French toast, they dined in the dining room, and now he knew why. At first, he was going to rush inside and pin her against the sink only to just wash his hands. She seemed to respond favorably to being trapped by the car, so he was going to relive that moment.

Except, being a man, he noticed the stupid cupboard door she kept trying to fix and kept failing at. He noticed the wallpaper of goofy chickens and cornstalks that had been attempted to be peeled off but only left in distressing strips. She had tried to refinish the counter with one of those cheap Dollar Store stick-on graphics that could look great in pictures but looked trashy in person. Her job wasn't done *too* badly, but it still wasn't even or flattened correctly, and some bubbled close to the wall and the sink.

Okay, it was done very badly.

Caleb stroked the horrible wallpaper. "This wallpaper is corny."

Evie busted out laughing. "Oh my God, you *are* a dad!"

He flashed her a smile, brushed his fingers on the cabinets, and checked the cupboard door. It came off the hinge, and he grabbed it before it fell. "Good thing I brought those hinges for ya."

Evie sat at the small kitchen table, only big enough for two. She pushed the toaster aside to make room for her milk and brownie plate. When she saw Caleb examining everything in her kitchen, all the way from bouncing on the floor to knocking on the walls, she sighed terribly.

She said, "I know. I'm sorry."

"Baby," he said, still in examination mode, "it's no wonder why you're overwhelmed. There are things wrong with this house that you can't fix alone. You need to get an inspector out here. I'm worried there might be some structural issues with the floor joists, beams, possible foundation settling." Then he checked the water pressure of the sink. "Who the hell sold you this house? Did you even get an inspection done on it?"

"I didn't."

"Why the hell wouldn't you?" He checked to see if the window would open easily, and it wouldn't. He had remembered their first morning together when she had to fight with the window to open it. And this one was no different. It was too tight.

"Covid made the housing market hell out here with everyone fleeing from Kansas City to the country. And there were so many offers on this house. I was told that if I waved the inspection, especially since one had been done a year ago, that it would make my offer more attractive to the seller."

He put his hands on his hips, being pissed that this sweet woman was so naïve to the world she didn't realize she had been duped. "Let me guess, the seller's agent told you that."

"Well, yeah," she responded meekly.

"Son of a bitch," he huffed while looking around.

"What's wrong with my house, darlin'?" She only called him by the name because he had started to call her "baby," and it gave her a sense of familiarity, like she had known him her whole life. Like he wasn't *just* her prospective lover but a dearly cherished friend, one she could trust.

He took his hat off to scratch his scalp and put it back on. He examined every little corner and reached up by the back door frame to feel the little crack. "Seller's agents are supposed to act in the seller's interest, not yours. And while he wasn't exactly wrong in telling you this, it seems you've got a lot of structural damage that needs to be fixed."

He turned and she saw the weird brown smudge on his shirt. She laughed. "What's on the back of your shirt?"

He pulled the fabric on his shoulder hard, twisted, and looked at it. "Oh, I accidentally ran through a wasp's nest that was hanging on one of your lower branches, and so I fell when they came at me. It was muddy in that area!" Then he looked back around and felt the counter. "No doubt the reason for some of the structural damage."

Evie sank in her emotions and stared off blankly while her hands cradled her milk mug. "And I worked so hard for this and was so proud of it."

He came and sat across her, offering reassurance with a smile. "Listen, you *should* be proud. I was here before it sold to you because the owners from about ten years ago wanted me to fix it up, but they didn't give me a price I was happy with. You should be proud. That living room was horrible when I walked in here ten years ago. I just thought the owner you bought it from did some of the work you did."

"No," she said dryly. "That was me. It was in worse shape than this."

He held her hand, comforting her. "It's gonna be okay. The crown molding is a little shoddy. But I can teach you how to do it right. And I know a great a guy who can work with you on getting this structural thing taken care of."

"Isn't that like thirty thousand dollars or something?"

"It can be. But I'm a contractor. I'll do a thorough look around here and get you an inspection done. And I'll pay for it."

"But can't that be expensive?"

"Possibly. But you're worth it and need it. I won't be able to sleep at night thinking you could be getting into a worse condition."

"Can we do half? I know I don't make much money, but I can't possibly ask you to fork out a lot for me. You bought my lunch already."

"I'll go down to your basement. We'll start there, and then if it's below $600, you can take it. I'll cover any differences."

She shook her head. "Why are you being so nice to me?"

He slowly smiled and tilted his head and reached for a brownie.

"You know how you keep saying you want to help me and to know more about me?"

She perked up. "Yes, absolutely."

"Well, you'd be surprised what a pretty face and good company can do for someone. Let's just say that."

By saying so little, Caleb had said a mouthful. There was no way Evie couldn't understand now. Like a sparrow knowing what branch to land on instinctively, which one would hold its weight, Evie knew now her lover was someone who wanted to possibly *forget* certain things in order to feel the wholesomeness of something new. And if she kept bringing up the topic of wanting to learn about him, it could have possibly been opening up a scar each time.

She swallowed hard and steadied her breath. She touched his arm affectionately, which was once again something he wasn't used to. Ashley and he had made love dozens of times. But dozens of times in the span of being together for nearly twenty years wasn't a lot. It wasn't like he never loved Ashley, but the torment of being deployed left a heavy strain on their love life. And then there were other things.

When he came to that thought, he pulled away and led her to the basement. Evie followed and listened to everything he said. She turned on the lights and gave him the pad and pen he'd requested to make the notes he needed. It only took him a few more times before he had to go to his truck to get a few more tools.

She waited in the basement and sat on the rickety steps. It was dank down there, and she had been so afraid of basements ever since her brother teasingly locked her in a dark one once. Therefore she never went into the basement again after the showing. But it was dank, dark, and musty smelling down there. While she sat, she thought about his action and how he pulled away from her. This time, she didn't care. *Let him pull away*, she thought to herself. *Let him do what he must do.* It was all so true. A smile crept upon her lips and was felt in every inch of her body.

She didn't want to reopen those scars. She wanted to heal them. She still believed even the physical, emotional, and psychological pain could all be healed. Some could call her naïve, but she simply believed. And even if they ended up never healing, she believed no one should suffer alone.

So, fuck it. She no longer cared if she could *save* him, if he actually needed saving. But if he did have hurt, she didn't want him to go through it alone.

Something scurried across the floor and caught her eye as Caleb was heard upstairs coming in through the door. Her eyes peered a bit more, and she lifted her chin from resting on her hand. "Caleb!" she called upstairs.

"Yo!"

"Can you bring Teddy down? I have a mouse down here."

He brought the big fat orange cat downstairs all cradled up in his arm with the fat falling over his forearm. "I think you feed this Jabba too much."

She laughed and stood. "Yeah, he keeps sneaking into the cat food."

He plopped Teddy down on the floor and saw the mouse in question far off in a darker corner. It was huddling.

Caleb began his search and saw Teddy being absolutely useless. He joked, "Man, even the male animals in your life can't pull their weight."

Evie crossed her arms. "Oh, he's useful in his own way."

"If you have mice, there's a good chance there are foundation issues. I'll wait until tomorrow when I can come over with all my stuff and do a good thorough check, because if you don't need an inspector, I don't want you paying for one."

Evie thanked Caleb for his work and went upstairs to leave him to it and also to cook dinner. He was staying the night, and so she felt that after all the yard work he did, the least she could do was prepare a good, home-cooked meal. She thumbed through her favorite country cookbook and deliberated which recipe would entice a busy man like him. She settled on pork chops with seared mushroom and olive salad with a good fat pile of mashed potatoes. Something filling, something zesty and new, and something comforting. Before she did any chopping, she went into the only bathroom she had and laid out fresh towels for him on the bathroom sink.

After his work was through, he showered using his own products he had brought, and the faint scent of sandalwood and amber lingered in the air.

Dinner was absolutely splendid in both food and company. Caleb shared a lighthearted fishing story of when his bloodhound seemingly pushed him into the lake. On the heavier side, Evie described being forced against a wall in Los Angeles as a man groped down her pants.

By the time their plates were empty, the sun dipped low in the sky. Caleb looked at her as she refrained from crying. It was a hard thing for her to do now. She didn't want to cry in front of him anymore. She'd done enough of that.

"Why did you let me pin you against the car if you had that trauma?" He sat back and stretched hands on the table. His gray t-shirt had the sleeves ripped off, and his sandy-brown hair was fluffy now that it had dried. "I kinda feel terrible for doing that to you now."

"Please don't. There's a difference between consent and nonconsent. I told that man five times to leave me alone. When I threatened to call the cops if he didn't stop, that's when he slammed me into the wall."

Caleb listened sympathetically, slowly rubbing his lips with his thumbs while his elbows rested on the table. Evie's eyes couldn't resist from watering. Every single touch a man gave her was violent, lecherous, selfish, and immoral. The air was still. Not even the traffic outside down near the road was heard. He could see the hurt building in her eyes.

"Every man who has touched me was either not welcome to do so or was using me. It was never genuine. With you, I know it's genuine. At least...I hope."

Caleb asked, "How is it you've never had a decent boyfriend or a boyfriend at all? Even when you were bigger, you definitely weren't hideous, and you're the most giving and loving person I know. You can't tell me you haven't had *one* decent man come around."

"My daddy, my brothers, and Pawpaw taught me what love from a man was supposed to be. And even then, every guy I was attracted to didn't like me in return. I was overweight nearly my whole life. And in the early 2000s the skinny model trend was all the rage. If you weighed more than 150 pounds, you were considered fat. Now that I am older and the body positivity movement has happened and men are more accepting of bigger girls, they're all married. So once again, I'm simply *lusted* after. Always lusted after and never loved."

Admitting the words stung violently like a cobra's fangs piercing her heart, unleashing the cruel reality of truth's venom into her blood.

Caleb had heard enough. Her vulnerability was a classic beauty to him. He took her by the hand and said, "Come with me. I want to do something with you."

Evie looked up to him as he outstretched his hand.

And all she saw was him.

Slowly, she took his hand, and his grip tightened. Like the leader he was in her life, he led her to the living room where he picked up his phone from his overnight bag and brought up a song. When it started to play, he plopped the phone on the couch. Her nerves shook. Her heart pounded as she jerked to hide the tears back. It was *the* song that made her fall in love with country, "Neon Moon" by Brooks and Dunn. Sure, it was a song about a terrible breakup, but the harmonies, swaying melodies, and smokey vibe were all romantic to her.

She looked at his handsome silhouette, his now smooth face basking in the amber lights of her lamp. As the cold rain came with the warming call of an owl outside, he approached her and took her into his embrace. He gently cradled her head to rest it against his chest.

Evie knew what heaven felt like that very moment.

Caleb wrapped his muscular arm around her lower back and held her right hand with his other hand and whispered, "I know how much this song means to you. And I know how much this exact thing means to you." He smirked. "I've seen enough of your posts on Facebook to know." He slowly led her in a dance.

She giggled with a little blush.

The trembling of her lower lip could not be stopped. God himself could not stop it. Thunder nor rain couldn't stop it either. Her body separated from her mind, and only her heart took control. Evie brushed her cheek affectionately up and down on his strong chest, squeezing her eyes tighter.

He hushed her cries. "It's okay, baby. I can take all your tears. I've got you."

She whimpered and felt the tears roll down her face, "Boy, do you ever."

He smiled. Then Caleb tried to guide her out for a little twirl before bringing her back in. When he did, he tried to dip her in playful romanticism, but Evie freaked and clutched his shoulders, holding herself up. She feared he wouldn't be strong enough to hold her. He snickered, "You underestimate my strength, Catwoman."

She giggled as he pulled her upright again and they continued dancing. "I'm sorry I'm too big for that." Then she smirked up to him. "Batman."

He grinned back down into her eyes, searching them. "I easily picked you up on the bed and threw you down. So, trust me?"

She looked up to him and stammered, "I trust you."

Once again, Caleb guided her out for a twirl, and she whirled back into him. She feared the possible outcome and grew nervous. But he caught her and dipped her effortlessly with one arm, yet she was still holding on to his shirt. "Let me go," he ordered passionately.

Her knuckles were white. Her back was stiff, and her abs were overloaded. But slowly Evie let go.

He did have her.

Her eyes sparkled up to his, and he smiled then, pulling her up. He kissed her and then said, "You owe me French toast in the morning for that."

"I never promised you French toast for nothing," she quipped back cutely.

"Yes, actually you did. I just had you in a love spell, and you don't remember."

She smiled up to him as they moved around the room. "You probably did, Mr. Wright."

The night was filled with comfort on all levels. They cuddled on the couch together in their pjs, ate food they both shouldn't have eaten, and watched a few Batman movies before moving to the bedroom. And there Evie brought Caleb up close to her belly. "Here, lay your head on me for a while. Let me rub your scalp and stuff."

He was hesitant. But she patted her soft belly again. The pink cotton pants of her nightclothes were topped off by a long, white cotton t-shirt that even he had to admit felt soft as hell. He could imagine lying on it and being lulled right off to sleep.

"Come on," she coaxed. "You completely enamored me out there. Let me make you feel comforted."

He was still reluctant for reasons he didn't know. But after a minute, he shrugged with a grin and curled up by her. The moment he felt his head resting on her warm and plush belly, his arm wrapped around her tightly with a mighty squeeze. His hand grabbed her belly a bit and it was comforting to hold. His grip hurt her a little, but she didn't mind. It was the perfect resting place for his weary mind and heart.

The moment her fingers ran through his hair, it was now his turn to feel like he was going to either come alive or come undone. He wasn't sure. Her hand brushed gingerly across his strong back, and it made him sigh deeply and collapse in breath. His whole body melted into the mattress, his head completely cradled by her soft belly.

Thunder sparkled outside across the Midwest sky and they both chuckled. Evie said quietly, "Of course Missouri would randomly get a thunderstorm in the fall."

Caleb just groaned, "Mmmhmm."

The rain echoed out in the trees and could be heard plopping little bloops. Caleb's breath grew steadier every minute. Teddy pushed the door open and came in to join them on the bed. It was a tight fit with Caleb's body being all scrunched up to lay on her. But somehow, they made it work.

The following morning, she had to leave for work, and he did as well, but he didn't leave without getting his French toast and a deep kiss.

They kissed with their hands on each other's faces, tangled within each other's hair, pushing their bodies viciously against each other. Caleb sighed, rubbing her cheek. "I'll be having my kids for the week as you know, so I may be sporadic with replies. Is that okay?"

She moaned in a smile, "Of course it is. You don't have to explain anything to me. I hope you have a good week."

He grinned with raised brows and a nod. "I'm gonna have a great week." Before he turned to leave, he asked, "You really are afraid of guns?"

"Yep. It's the loud, sudden noise."

He winked. "Next weekend, I'll teach you how to shoot."

After one more kiss, they left the house and got in their separate cars. But a strange thing happened.

Evie never heard from him again.

Chapter Ten

Evie felt more than a little misunderstood. All alone in her house, as the months trickled on by, the plants she loved so much began to wither and die in the corner. What was once a beautiful sun dress was traded for sweatpants. A stack of bills sprawled across the kitchen table, and the trash hadn't been taken out in two weeks. She walked along the edge of where sanity met insanity, and on this cold, deep winter day while the snow outside fell, she felt herself dying with the season. The screen door wasn't put on right. And she didn't care.

He never unfriended her, and occasionally he watched her stories. But he stopped interacting, and after he viewed more than a dozen well-meaning messages without responding, she stopped watching his stories and engaging with him directly. Instead, she still tried to support him by leaving good comments on his posts.

On the sofa, her cat kept her company. No one noticed the contrast of what she had become and then what she lost all over again. Everything was crumbling between wrong and right. Through her own heart, she heard her own crying. Another flurry fell outside, and she laid her forehead to her knees that were pulled into her chest.

Around that house, something radiated.

Evie felt like she was walking on a wire in some sideshow circus, not even important enough to be the main attraction. Night after night, she would carve out his name in her heart, feeling her fists clench as she drove herself to maddening tears. With clothes all over her floor, the bed didn't have clean or tidy linens since he turned from her. It could have only been in her head, but this time it wasn't.

She rose from the couch to grab wine from the top of the fridge and ignored her never-ending checklists that never were completed. More schedules that weren't met. But as Evie grabbed the bottle, she looked at it, screamed, then threw it at the wall.

It shattered.

All over, she shook uncontrollably. She had lost time, had lost track of it, and no longer understood it.

She was tired of something.

She was tired of life.

Please, catch me. I'm falling. I can't do this.

Scribbling maniacally away in a journal full of wishes, checklists, goals and dreams used to comfort her. But now all it was doing was driving her further over the edge.

That damn pesky mania.

The serene memories of falling into his arms came, infecting her mind like vines overtaking her life.

Evie hurried outside and felt like a ghost blending into the winter fog that lingered in her yard.

"I don't know. I feel like I'm dying. I can't do this."

The tears may as well have frozen to her cheeks. "I think I'm close to understanding Jesus." She gasped through her sobs and held her chest, ignoring the shivering that permeated straight into her bones. Her mumbling was incoherent, and nothing she said would have made sense to anyone but her.

Teddy gave a meow so loudly she could hear it through the closed front window. She turned and smiled, the tears glittering in her dark eyes that had sweaty hair clinging to them. She quickly turned back inside and grabbed her keys and left the house in a frenzied hurry, peeling off down her gravel driveway in anger. Inside back at home, Teddy meowed all alone.

When Evie came home, she flopped on the sofa and ripped open a brown bag and broke open the whiskey bottle and gulped it as hard as she could. Wine wasn't going to work. It hadn't worked in months. She needed something harder. Her throat burned, and her eyes watered. She stifled her cough and kept going.

Teddy meowed.

She didn't stop.

Her walls were crumbling all around her, and through the autumn rain, she walked alone. Through the winter frost, she wept in isolation.

Teddy jumped onto her lap and meowed.

She kept drinking. Her eyes closed while the tears rolled down her face, and the whiskey dripped down her neck.

Teddy hissed, launched, and bit her face.

She dropped the bottle, and it spilled all over the newer, expensive sofa. "Teddy! What the hell was that all about?" She lazily picked up the bottle and placed it on the coffee table after shuffling a bunch of crap to the side. She then hurried to the kitchen to grab towels, but the alcohol was already taking effect on her. Her foot hit the coffee table, and she fought to regain her balance, but it was a losing battle.

The images blurred and slanted. Her head buzzed wildly, and her skin sweated profusely. Evie fell face-forward into her entertainment stand. Lying on the floor, she held her forehead and saw a little blood on her fingers.

Teddy hurried over and began licking her injury. Once more, her sobs came. Evie rolled over and hugged her cat like she was going to die if she didn't. Her face pressed into his fat belly to soothe her headache.

That night, with an icepack to her forehead, Evie sat cross-legged on her sofa with Teddy purring right next to her. She *could* have gone to the hospital, but she had no choice but to try to be braver. She had no choice but to grow up.

And now she knew *exactly* what that meant.

She muttered to herself, "I bet he started seeing another girl." She sniffled. "I can't believe I was so damn dumb to think someone like me could have ever stood a chance with him." She wiped her face. "I'm fucked up, but I'll be okay."

Wrong. She was simply lying to herself.

She briefly sat upright to twist her back to try to relieve some of that nagging upper back pain. Her chiropractor had chalked it up to just having weak muscles, a weak upper back, and playing guitar hunched over and also being hunched over a laptop for work.

Just like she was going to open her laptop again for work.

She opened her laptop to Facebook and saw that some local businesses had approved of her resume for a few freelance jobs they needed help with and wanted to meet with her in person. A lighthearted chuckle came to her when she noticed Joey wrote her and said, "I'd like to see what you can do for my winter menu!"

She drew in a deep breath. Teddy started purring and stretched out with that little 'mrrp' sound. He tucked himself into a contorted ball. She petted him and lured out his purrs. They were loud and comforting. She wrote back, "Great! I'll see you tomorrow!"

On a whim, she checked her story. Caleb had stopped watching her stories over the last month.

He hadn't seen it.

"Whatever," she growled under her breath. "You were watching my stories for a long time, man. Even still, you obviously were interested in me. But, whatever." She stood up and tossed her laptop on the couch. "I don't fucking need you in my life. I got along fine this long without you. And I'll do it again." She twirled around fancifully to walk to her bedroom.

She went to bed with her cat and listened to the sleet and snow patter against the window. Her foot got caught up in the disarray of the unmade bed, and she kicked the covers up a bit more to pull them over her and Teddy. She went to sleep, praying to Pawpaw and to Jesus, who she felt she needed now more than ever.

The empty bed felt so empty. Her stomach knotted, and she began to weep. She couldn't lie to herself. No amount of temporary manic high could alter what she was truly feeling.

She *did* need him. And she missed him terribly.

Evie rolled onto her back and stared at the ceiling.

Control it.

Don't do it.

Her hands rubbed firmly across her face and her breath quickened.

Breath in, breath out.

Her hands began to tremble. Her throat tightened. Then, her hands slammed down to the bed, and she twisted her sheets with tight fists.

She screamed straight from her very soul and cried loudly. Evie just couldn't make sense of why so many men had done her wrong so many times in her life. The ugly black horse of depression stamped and raged on her heart.

You never deserved him.

To her salvation, Teddy didn't flinch. He had grown comfortable around these outbursts. Instead, he just snuggled up by his Evie's tear-stained face.

That next day, Evie tried to look her best and headed into town to the Songbird Café. It was nestled right up off the main strip of town called Starling Street. The street was lined with decaying old Midwest shops that had been around since the town was founded as a railway town in 1867. Some of the old signs were still painted on the brick sides that flanked decaying alleyways. Her favorite was the old tobacco sign that took up the whole building with a circular graphic of faded yellow and white.

On the old tobacco building, it was a tradition that graduates of the local high school could take a horseshoe stamp to the building and write their initials with their graduation year on it. It was a cute homage to the town's mascot and team name, the Mustangs. As she pulled into the parallel spot in front of the Songbird Café, she noticed she was parked right next to a police cruiser, an SUV labeled number 710.

She closed her car door and grinned. "Hey there, Hunt."

Evie entered the slate-painted café, which was a mix of dark gray and metal sheet siding. The old wooden floors had been refinished to keep their natural distressed and worn look, and overhead through a cased opening there were newspaper articles in picture frames that dated back to the early 1900s to top off the rustic charm and cozy feel. To her left, the wall was decorated with old findings such as authentic and framed photos from the town's glory days, an old farm door with chipped paint, and tin signs that offered eggs for a fictional price of twenty-five cents per dozen.

"Helloooo!" sang a chipper voice through part of the café that was further back. Evie closed the door and smiled. "Hey, Joey! How's business today?"

Joey started frantically igniting the espresso machine with its hissing and gurgling sound. She seemed to have ten arms as she poured home-made syrup from glass bottles. "Oh, another day in the life!"

A big German Shepherd, tail wagging, approached Evie. She patted his belly while he jostled all over her. "Hi there, Atlas! I saw your chariot outside!"

As she approached the counter, Atlas trotted alongside her, and Deputy Hunt said warmly with a raise of his coffee cup, "Mornin', Evie! How've you been?"

She greeted him with a hug and a smile. "Good morning, Dan! I'm good. Excited to be here. Joey wants me to redesign her menu for the rest of winter."

"Good, 'cause it's terrible."

Joey scoffed and laughed, pointing her finger. "Hey! I gave you a free extra shot of espresso! I can take it back. Or burn your bagel."

Dan laughed and replied, "Do that and I'll charge you with assault on a LEO."

Joey was like a skinny sprite that grew into being a mom. She always wore her dark-brown hair up in a messy bun and seemed to always wear athletic clothes that sported the Mustangs' logo. She fixed her glasses on her spray-tanned face and boomed loudly while she fixed another drink, "Another chai latte, Evie?"

"Yep! The usual."

"Alrighty, you got it!" she yelled again for absolutely no reason. "One honey chai latte with oat milk, heavy ice, light syrup, and an every-thing bagel with jalapeño cream cheese coming right up!"

The familiarity was good for Evie's sadness.

Joey, being the character she was, stopped working and got caught up in chatter with Deputy Hunt while the radio played country classics. Brooks and Dunn "Boot Scootin' Boogie" was playing, which lifted Evie's spirits. She looked to Atlas and patted her chest. Atlas jumped up and danced with her. He was as freaking tall as she was.

Joey yelled in play, "Hey now, you're takin' my man!"

"Well, you were too busy chattin' with another," Evie giggled.

"I don't like him. He's ugly."

Hunt laughed at the banter. "What?" He stroked his peppered goatee and fixed his glasses. "I may have lost some hair, but I'm the finest in this town. My badge here says so."

Joey playfully countered with her hand on her hip, "Dan, you can't earn a badge at the Dollar Store toy aisle."

He tightened his lips in play and acted like he was going to throw the hot drink in her face. She jerked with her hand up and laughed loudly. "Hey! I'll kick your ass!"

"Sure, you will," Dan said back with a smile. "Get back to work. Evie's drink's gonna get watered down."

"Oh shit!"

Evie giggled as Joey went back to her work. "It's fine, Joey." She patted Atlas, who finally got down.

Dan looked at Evie. "I think it's great you've been designing some local work. You're really good with it. The school loves the new design you did."

Joey called with her back turned, "Yeah, you can thank that tall, cool glass of water Caleb Wright for putting that bug in her head. Too bad he's a jackass. He's a fine jackass with a fine ass, but he's still a jackass."

Dan looked at Joey and put his hands on his vest straps. "What? Why him?"

Joey slid Evie's order over the counter and raised her brows. "Don't you know? They had a brief stint together."

Evie's feet went absolutely fucking cold.

"Oh *really?*" Dan asked teasingly.

Evie looked around. Her heart pounded. Memories of him were drowned in her blood by the whiskey still. "What are you talking about?"

"Oh, don't play dumb, Evie. The whole town knows."

What?!

Evie thought back. Neither Caleb nor she had posted anything about it. She didn't tell anyone at all. Did *he* tell people? She grabbed her stuff off the counter and asked, "What makes you think Caleb and I had a stint together?"

"Evie, his truck was seen at your house a few months ago like twice. Or three times. I don't remember."

"I recommend *knowing* before *gossiping*. He's a contractor, and that was almost *three* months ago," she explained. "He was fixing stuff at my house. Everyone in town knows where I live and how crappy it is. It's no secret."

Joey raised her brow and put her hand on her hip again. She wasn't buying it. "Uh-huh. He was at your house at midnight on a Friday?"

Evie was infuriated. Who the hell would know that? It was like someone was watching her house!

Dan corrected with a sip of his coffee, "That would technically be Saturday morning."

"Shut up, Dan!" Joey said with a grinning scrunch of her face and rapid little head shake. "I'm trying to get tea, here."

What was Evie going to say? She looked left and right.

Joey said, "Dan, read her face. Is she lying?"

Evie bit into her bagel. Dan smiled and stoutly said, "I'm not gonna disclose that. That's her personal information."

"Oh, you suck, Dan," Joey laughed.

But then Dan turned to Evie with a sharp eye. "I know you support law enforcement a lot. One of our deputies, Jake, recently got back on the market. You'd be good for him. I can hook something up if you'd like. I'd feel a lot better about you going out with Jake than Caleb. I've been dispatched to that house one too many times."

She smiled and winked. "No thanks, Dan, I'm not the cheatin' kind." Evie tried to say the expression to derail Joey from thinking she ever had a stint with Caleb. She planned to play it off like she had been seeing someone else. Even if he ditched her, she still wanted to respect his privacy. It wasn't about her. It was about him and his kids.

"That's horseshit," Joey said again. "You're not involved with him anymore obviously. Why does it matter? Jake's hot as hell."

Evie grinned and shrugged. "Who said I was talking about being involved with Caleb? I got someone else." She raised her brows.

Joey turned. "I hate my customers today."

Everyone laughed, and Atlas barked.

"Alright, let's get to the tables. I wanna see what you designed. I'm so excited for this shit."

Evie stopped them for a moment to ask, "I don't understand. What's everyone's problem with Caleb? My pawpaw said he was bad news but never told me why. What's everyone's beef with him?"

Joey put her hand on her hip and slammed her other hand on the counter. "Because he fucking threw a chair at his wife for one. Then he always screamed at her and then cheated on her. Not to mention he also got kicked out of the bar here in town for fighting with someone. Dude's fucking gone."

Everything Joey said could've made sense, except for the cheating part. That part was a wild card for sure. Caleb was loyal to a marriage that was ending, because he never had sex with her and wouldn't. Evie looked to Dan, hoping he wouldn't say the same thing. Her breath felt uneasy within her chest, but she tried not to make her emotions apparent and refrained from shifting around on her feet.

"Dan? What do you got to say about him?" Evie asked.

Dan Hunt scratched his bald head. "I can't really say legally. Be careful around him, ya hear?"

The remarks didn't steer her the other way in one bit. It could have been a stupid thing to do, but Caleb had been nothing but nice to her until recently. And even then, he wasn't mean to her either. He was just avoiding her.

But why? She suddenly thought, and with the thought crashing her brain, she tilted her head as if the thought itself slapped her in the back of the head. *Maybe he's having a PTSD issue.* Or perhaps the divorce had taken a nasty turn.

Everyone parted ways in a friendly manner. Evie followed Joey to the table, but as she sipped her delicious and creamy drink, she thought deeply. It was a good thing she had made that last comment to deflect the fact that she was still--regrettably and possibly stupidly--holding out for Caleb. She had to play it off like she had someone in her life that wasn't him, and never was him.

How the hell did anyone know about Caleb being at her house? It couldn't have been Joshua who saw and blabbered it off somehow, could it? Or Sarah? Evie's house was too far from the road to really be able to tell that. Or so she thought.

Evie wasn't about to waste any time. As they sat down, she put her stuff up on the table but immediately asked while removing her design folder, "Joey, I need you to be straight with me. Who told you Caleb and I had a stint together?"

Joey shrugged. "What does it matter? You guys did. I don't know why you're denying it. You guys would make a *hot* couple!" She frantically shuffled things aside. "That is, if he could fucking take his meds."

Evie shook her head out in irritation. "Because we didn't. We never did. We're friends on Facebook, and he came over when I was having a panic attack. He recognized what it was and saved me a huge hospital bill. That's why he was over there once, and the second time it was to mow my lawn. If someone was snooping, they should have noticed him mowing my lawn."

They stared at each other. Evie warned, "And you probably shouldn't be telling people he's on meds. That's really private, you know?"

Joey gave a look of suspicious disbelief and slightly turned her head, ignoring the recent comment. "You have almost three hundred chick friends on your list. Why didn't you reach out to them? Why did it have to be Caleb?"

Evie leaned her head back in frustration. "Oh my God, Joey. He plays guitar too, and we were having a conversation about flatpicking technique when my anxiety attack happened!" She began fixing her work. "Not to mention, with the way the women act around here, they would only make my anxiety worse." She rested her hands on the table. "I really need you to tell me who told you."

"It doesn't matter. Let's look at these awesome designs!"

Evie stopped her. She was getting mad. No, she was getting downright *pissed off.* "It *does* matter because if word is going around that he and I are sleeping together, he could fucking lose custody of his kids, dammit!"

Joey blankly stared at her.

"Yeah! You didn't think about that, did you?" She gathered up her purse. "Nor does anyone around here think about anyone else but themselves."

"Where are you going?" Joey asked as she turned in her chair to watch Evie leave.

Evie stopped at the door. "I'm sorry, but I have some serious damage control to do. Feel free to look at the examples I gave you for all I care right now." She shook her head furiously. "I can't believe you won't tell me who told you."

Joey protested, "It's not gonna make a difference if I did! Why do you even care about that guy anyway if you two were never involved?"

"He's a human being, Joey! He's got emotions and hardships just like the rest of us. And he's done a lot of nice things for me, more than anyone else here! Out of all the people who gossiped about this, the only one who doesn't get to know about the gossip is the one everyone's gossiping about! Who the hell are you trying to protect?"

Evie flew out the door and immediately dialed Caleb's number when she was in the car. "Please pick up. Please pick up." He wasn't wrong when he told her that the town never shut up. But this time, it now affected her, and it had gone too far.

It went to voicemail, and she left a message telling him it was urgent. She then texted him, "I know you're not talking to me now, and I can respect that, but this is important. Whatever I did to make you mad, I'm sorry. But this isn't about that."

He wrote back, "I have nothing to say to you."

She nearly broke her phone slamming it on her steering wheel. "Caleb, please, I need to talk to you."

Finally, she was relieved when he called.

He answered, "I've got about five minutes. What do you need?"

She sighed in relief and rubbed her hair out of her face. But all over her body felt like she nearly dodged a head-on collision. She turned her car on to get the heater going. "Did you tell people you and I were sleeping together?"

He paused on the other line.

She waited, drumming her fingers hotly on her lap.

He stammered, "I...thought *you* did?" At his job site, he told his workers he was stepping outside for a moment.

Evie composed herself calmly. "I just got done at the Songbird Café, and Joey told me someone told *her* they saw your truck at my place. Which you were, but I explained to her it was simply because of you helping me through a panic attack and mowing my lawn. But someone told her we had a full-blown stint together. You didn't tell anyone anything?"

"Evie, why would I do that? I'd risk losing my kids in a custody battle if I did."

She threw her hand up. "Right? That's what I keep telling everyone."

Caleb groaned hard and wiped his mouth. "So, you didn't tell anyone?"

At first Evie felt like she wanted to scream at him for not reaching out to her sooner. "Is this why you've been ignoring me? Who's been talking to you?"

He sighed and looked at the traffic going by. "Sandy at the nail salon in town told Ashley you and I were sleeping together. And Ashley blew a gasket with me over nasty texts and went all Danaerys Season 8 on my lawyer." His voice shook a bit, which was odd for him. Caleb was always calm and composed. "You visit the salon frequently, so I assumed it was you. You're always posting up your deep-seeded shit on Facebook, so I assumed you probably got caught up in the moment and told Sandy. I had to give my phone to my lawyer and let him comb through it for a whole week, as well as show my Facebook and social activity."

Evie panicked. "Did they find anything?"

"No, I deleted your contact and all my sexually charged texts with you, as well as messages and all but two phone calls so it wouldn't look so suspicious."

"Oh, thank God."

Caleb sat down on the porch of his worksite and watched the gardeners try to dig up the cold, hard ground. He felt insanely stupid. "I can't believe you're not going off on me right now."

"Why would I? You didn't do anything wrong. I'm so sorry the divorce has taken a horrible turn."

Caleb rubbed his face. "Don't be so nice to me. I essentially blocked you out without consulting you first."

"You answered my call. That's all I care about. The rest of that shit doesn't matter."

"Evie?" he said slowly.

"Yes?"

"I'm sorry. I appreciate your calling and telling me the truth. But I really can't associate with you until after the divorce. This has fucked everything up so badly."

Tingling came into her hands and her chest felt heavy. But not because of what he said, but because her nerves were just worked up, worried that she had caused a lot of unintentional grief for him when she had fought so hard to do the opposite.

He rubbed his face frantically on the other side. "And if you don't want to wait for me, I won't blame you. Ashley's being difficult, and I don't know how long this will go on for."

Evie thought. "I have a question though. Wouldn't you cutting off all ties with me make it look *more* suspicious?"

"It's the advice of my lawyer."

There was nothing she could do. Evie smiled. "It's okay. You're the one in the harder predicament, not me."

"Stop it."

"Stop what?"

"Stop making this harder."

"I'm not trying to."

"Evie, you hardly know me. I have no idea why you treat me like some savior that came strolling along and solved all your problems."

Evie sat straight up. "Listen to me. I'm not doing this because of what you've done for me. I'm being this way because it's the right thing to do, Caleb! You've seen how calm and neutral I am when Richard Bailey flies off the fucking handle at people for no reason on the discussion page. You've seen me try to settle tension down in fights. There's nothing I can do. It's not because you've done some-thing so grand for me, even though you have. It's because it's the right damn thing to do!"

"You're insane. You're being way too nice to someone you hardly know."

"Yeah, and you told me not to let anyone change that. So, I'm not.

That's a mouthful coming from the guy who was going to pay for my house inspection."

Caleb tried to bridle the anger in his tone. "You need to stop acting like this and get over me. It's not gonna work."

Her emotions balled up. "What are you talking about?"

"You're not gonna wanna wait for me. This divorce got worse than I ever could imagine. Don't wait around on me, because you're only getting older, and you could have any guy you want if you—"

She had heard enough. "Shut up! Let *me* talk now, Mr. Don't-Presume-To-Know-Me! I don't want another man goddammit. I want you!" She sat upright and shook all over. "I don't care if your divorce takes a fucking lifetime. You're worth the damn wait. I don't want anyone else. I don't care if you call me childish, stupid, immature, dumb, whatever. Too many people give up on people these days over dumb reasons, and I have gotten too invested in you to walk away. I don't give a shit if I have to wait for my whole life for you!"

He listened and felt his feelings rise.

She went on, rabid in her heartfelt expressions to him, "I don't care about your PTSD or what you did in Iraq or wherever it was you were stationed. None of that matters to me, because all I know is the man who saved me in so many different ways!"

Evie began to cry. Through heavy sobs, she held her face. It had hurt her often how many people told her that she was too emotionally charged, but it was how she was wired. She sniffled and tried to calm down, swallowing hard. "If you like me at all, I will wait for you. Take all the time you need, but please, *please* don't shut me out."

They both went quiet.

He said lowly, "You don't know what you're getting into."

Then Evie laid it all out on the table. It was difficult for her to do, but at this point she felt she had nearly lost him already. It made no difference to tell the entire truth even if it was an embarrassing one. She steadied herself first. "I know you only have a minute left, so I'm going to make this quick."

"Okay, I'm listening. Go ahead."

"You wanna hear why I put up with your anger issues? You wanna know why I kept checking on you when you ignored me? You wanna know why I wanted you to kiss me so badly that night? It was because I have never had an actual boyfriend in my life, Caleb. You know that. Every damn man has been an absolute fucking pig to me. You know that. They take everything from me. They sexually objectify me, they've stalked me, harassed me, and assaulted me. I mean, you've seen my posts. Don't act like you don't know.

"I was never given flowers by a guy until you, save for my dad and pawpaw. I've never had a date other than you. When my daddy and momma died, I had only to look to my oldest brother for guidance. Then he moved over an hour away and got married. Then I had my pawpaw, who passed away too!" Her tears came in irate sobs again. Emotional distress was ravaging in her, and it was becoming more difficult to control. "All I've dreamt of since I was a little girl was to be loved, protected, and held. Maybe this sounds like a stupid, childish fairytale dream. But you came into my life and helped me when I had no one else. You made those dreams come true.

"You reached out to me and taught me how to fill my coolant when I posted on Facebook needing help and no one helped me. Every time I was in a bind, you always managed to show up. You helped me with my anxiety issues and those methods *still* help me to this day. You held me and kissed me like I have dreamt of being kissed forever. You reached out to me and actually took the initiative. And like how you told me that you felt happy around me, well, I feel safe around you. So there, you have it now."

She wiped her eyes and took a deep breath. "This is why I'm stupidly, hopelessly devoted to you. I tried not to be. But I can't help it."

He let her get it all out, but he refused to react emotionally to it. He was practical in that moment; he was trained to be. "Evie, these are all things a basic friend does. They help each other."

"Friends don't kiss friends like that. And once again, it's okay for *you* to be a great friend and help me, but I can't do it for you."

"Because you keep thinking I've got some deep-seeded trauma that stems from my job in the Navy. And it comes with the territory. I still love my job and am proud of it, but I can't go flapping off my personal struggles to someone I hardly know. Maybe you work like that, but I don't."

Boy, what a liar he was. If she were to have been there, she would have seen his eyes flinching. Deputy Hunt would have been able to detect his lies a mile away. He went on, "Evie, just because you want a fairytale love doesn't mean you need to have Stockholm syndrome to do it. Not every romance needs to have the soft and tender woman who lets the man treat her like shit because she wants to change him in order to be a good romance."

She listened. His words were hitting *hard*. They were calm and stable, everything the town said he wasn't.

"Stop subjecting yourself to me. Stop trying to fix me. Some people can't be fixed. Some people are good the way they are. You said it yourself on a Facebook post that we need to look at people's hearts and not their actions, and that some people just need to be loved the way they are." His voice grew in fixed passion, "That's what made me so attracted to you. You just love. If love were to be personified, it would be you. So please, give me that same courtesy and stop thinking I'm this hopeless person of misery and just accept me the way I am."

Evie was at the crossroads of truth and realization. It was as if at that very moment, Caleb had accidentally taught her self-respect. His firm hand was everything she loved and admired him for. The way he was able to take control of every single situation possible was remarkable to her. She conceded.

Her voice was soft like snow flurries on eyelashes. "Thank you, Caleb. I really needed to hear that."

"Yeah, you kinda did. But for what it's worth, I really needed to hear what you told me. It's, um, hard for me to listen to that and believe it."

She sighed heavily once more. "Well, how would you like me to handle this? I want to go to the salon and scream at Sandy, but I don't want to make things worse for you. I really want to know who told someone."

"Yeah, please don't do that. Although I admire your will to do it. Ask Joshua, your neighbor. Maybe he said something."

Evie agreed. "I don't think it's in his nature, but he was my first suspect."

Caleb added, "My only thing is he doesn't get into town much."

Evie realized. "No, but I've seen his wife at the salon before."

Caleb looked about. His workers were calling for him. Evie heard him acknowledge them briefly before returning to the call. "Ask her then. I'm sorry, Evie. I gotta go."

"I understand. Thank you for answering."

He paused. "Give me a few more months maybe."

She smiled. "You told me it could be anytime because Ashley's being difficult."

"I know, but I don't want to upset you."

"You didn't. Like I said, if you want me, I'll be here waiting."

Caleb was growing more and more irritated with his life situations. Now the town was talking, his ex was screaming at him, and he was at risk of losing custody of his kids completely. If people found out too much about the possibility of infidelity, it could also jeopardize his business. But Evie was the kindest and most beautiful thing that had happened to him in a long time, and he didn't want to lose her either.

"Caleb?"

"Yes?"

"Friends?"

He cradled his face in suffering. He had to fight his emotions. "Yes, friends."

Chapter Eleven

Evie hurried back home, and instead of turning left right by her little snowman family at the end of her gravel drive, she turned right and slowly drove up Joshua's drive, being cautious not to hit any of his roaming chickens or the few dogs he had. Both of their cars were home, his wife's and his. She pulled up around to the right and parked in front of their two-door garage that was on the side of the house. The house was a pale shade of yellow with white trim, and immediately she was greeted by the welcoming committee of a proud peacock, two dogs, and a roaming pet pig that also wanted to be a part of the action.

Luckily, as soon as she closed the car door, it roused the attention of Sarah, who came outside in her dingy jeans and Chiefs sweater. Her blonde hair was loosely piled on top of her head in an exhausted bun, which was the go-to hairstyle of nearly every woman Evie knew, and her narrow cheekbones gave way to a smile as she came down the stairs happily.

"Evie! What a pleasant surprise! What can I do for you? Is everything okay?"

Evie took a deep breath to control her emotions. So much time had passed since Caleb had helped her control herself a bit, and she tried to conjure up the things that Hunt had taught her as well. "No, I'm sorry Sarah, but everything is not okay."

Sarah halted, shocked by the statement. She edged her head forward to examine Evie with scrunched brows. "What's wrong? Do you need to come in?"

"That would probably be best, thank you."

Sarah escorted Evie inside and kicked away her kids' shoes, apologizing for the mess. The ladies walked across the beautiful maple flooring and basked in the gray beauty of light that the vaulted skylights let in. They both sat on the large, light-gray sofa. Sarah spoke first, "Okay, I'm all ears. What's going on?"

Evie was *going* to come straight out, but she learned from Hunt that a suspect would never confess to something if you asked it outright. Instead, she had to ask *around* the question and gauge Sarah's reaction. "I haven't been having good experiences at the salon lately. I love Myla, but I don't feel the vibe there is any good. I mean, look at my nails."

She extended her nails and showed how perfect they looked.

"They look fine to me."

Evie pressed on, "That's the problem. Do you ever think it's worth having exceptional service from a place so full of mean-spirited people? I've been doing my own now for a while and they don't look so bad."

Sarah played with her bun in her hair, leaning on her side to the back of the sofa. "You came over here to ask me that?"

"You're at the salon more than I am. And I don't know if I'm being sensitive, if they're simply that way, or what."

"Are you talking about Sandy and Kelly?"

Lightning struck. Now Evie was on the right path. Sandy was the blonde she had a weird encounter with when she first went to the salon last year. She was the one who seemed to get irritated that Evie didn't go to the basketball games. And Kelly was the brunette.

She suggested it was Caleb who sent her the friend request, Evie thought.

Evie's heart raced. Kelly was also the one who boldly said it was absolutely disgusting what Caleb did to Ashley, his ex. It couldn't have been any clearer. This had to be Kelly's doing, perhaps in some sort of chance of ruining Caleb so Ashley could get full custody of her children. Kelly knew Evie had come in to celebrate a cute guy sending her a friend request by wanting a manicure.

Sarah waved in front of Evie, who looked like she had seen a ghost. "Yoohoo, Eeeevviiiieee."

Evie jerked. "Sorry, I remembered I forgot to pay my water bill today."

Sarah laughed. "Still on with that mania issue again? Don't you set your phone reminders still?" Sarah's voice was calm, serene, and sociable. It was how she always talked. There wasn't any indication that the mentioning of the salon and the girls there got her nervous or on guard. A text went off in Sarah's pocket, and when she looked at it, she quickly shoved the phone back in her sweatpants.

Evie sighed, looking off.

Sarah tucked her chin and grinned. "Aw, sweetie. I know that look. You're thinking about that tall hunk o' burning love. Aren't you?"

This was it. She had to play along. If she did, Sarah would eventually mention the name. And if she mentioned Caleb, she would know immediately that somehow Sarah Jackson was in on it. Evie smiled weakly and looked down. "Is it that obvious?"

"I think it's cute," Sarah said as she patted her arm. The rooster outside went absolutely crazy, but it only distracted the ladies for a brief moment.

"You don't think I'm weird?"

"No, not at all." Sarah crossed her legs and reached over to pat Evie's lap. "I mean, we all know how much you support the police. With Hunt being single now, it's no wonder why you're thinking about him all the time."

Evie felt an entire anchor get dropped on her stomach.

Sarah continued, "You should ask him out. He already makes specific rounds in this area now for you. You guys are friends. You've got nothing to lose."

Now what was she supposed to do? She and Hunt had never had anything together at all, and most importantly Evie didn't even *like* him like that. She respected him so much, and she already knew that Hunt was quietly in love with another girl, the receptionist at the daycare. It was a fact she only knew due to Hunt telling her himself. She had kept that secret and would take it to the grave. With this, she couldn't go on letting Sarah believe she liked Hunt, because it could jeopardize Hunt's chances with the receptionist, who had helped Evie land her first free-lance job in town by asking her to design a flyer for their fall specials for childcare.

Ever since then, Evie was a hit all over with the businesses, being even more respected there than with her own boss, Mr. Perry.

She had to. Being at a stalemate again, she had no choice but to weigh the pros and cons. Finally, and possibly regrettably, she spoke, "I'm sorry, Sarah, but that's not the case. I don't have a thing for Hunt. He and I are just friends."

Joshua's UTV was heard roaring up the pasture to the back of the house. Sarah asked, "Is it Jake? Deputy Jake Hawkins?"

Evie snickered lowly, "No, it's not him."

Sarah bounced in surprise. "Well, who is it? It can't be Deputy Martin, because I said a 'tall hunk o' burning love,' and Martin isn't tall."

The women laughed.

Joshua came in through the back, and Sarah called, "Hey, Josh! She admitted it's not Hunt, Martin, or Hawkins. Who else could it be?"

Evie listened astutely.

Joshua kicked his boots off the back door rug and shook the snow off his Carhartt jacket. "Hey, Evie! I'm sorry about her prying."

"Oh no, it's okay."

Joshua grabbed a cold beer and sat down on the adjacent couch and took off his hat to scratch his scalp. He said to his wife, "You need to stop butting your nose into other people's business."

The couple entered into a loving bickering match, and Evie thought about how unlikely it would be for Joshua to be involved. That was not in his nature in any way shape at all. What would he have to gain from it? He was friends with him on Facebook.

Joshua sighed and said, "I see Caleb Wright's been at your house lately. You know, if you ever need help with your lawn, I'd be more than happy to help. I used to do it all the time, so it wouldn't bother me none to do it again. I'd be wary about him being around you alone."

Evie wanted to smack her own face. *Not this again.* Apparently being friends with someone on Facebook didn't mean you actually respected that person. Evie tried to ignore it, but the threshold was getting harder to navigate. For a moment, she held her forehead as if to lasso her own racing thoughts in a physical way. It was useless. It felt like her brain splattered against her skull with the urge to make a list of everything everyone was saying. If she did, she would end up obsessing over that list as if playing detective with no actual clues and no real conclusion.

"Oh, really?" Evie yelped as she clutched her chest, trying to force a front. It really meant a lot to her, at least the offer did. "Thank you so much, Josh. I really could use all the help I can get. I thought I could do it with a push mower, but I was wrong. Caleb was at my house to assess certain things because I'm really in over my head. He was so helpful."

Joshua leaned back. "Yeah, he's a good guy. Has some problems, but I think he can be alright." He looked down at his hands for a second.

Nope. It wasn't Joshua.

Luckily, Evie found another way to sneak into the conversation. She slapped her thigh. "I mean, it's insane though. I hate how he was over at my house to help and now the town thinks we're together. It's weird."

"WHAT?" Sarah nearly choked on her water. Joshua didn't react at all.

It wasn't Sarah either. That, she now knew. The reaction was far too visceral to have been feigned.

"Yeah, isn't it weird? I feel bad for him, because he's at risk of losing his kids now, all because he tried to help someone."

Joshua sighed in frustration and slouched back. "Yeah, seems to be that guy's luck."

Evie asked, "What do you mean?"

"I probably shouldn't say this, but I know you're not the gossiping kind. That's how the divorce happened. He tried to do something nice for someone, and it got blown way out of proportion."

"His wife divorced him because of a simple misunderstanding?" Evie asked, her sympathy for Caleb growing.

"No, Caleb was the one who filed for divorce."

"Can you please tell me what happened?" She couldn't refrain from it any longer.

Joshua looked at his wife, who warned him with her eyes that it may not be the best idea. But regardless, she assured him, "Go ahead." A text came through Sarah's phone again, but she didn't check it.

Joshua began, "Do you know Ed Wright, Caleb's dad?"

"I know his name, but I never met him. He was on my daddy's football gang that used to play for fun every Saturday morning."

"Yep, that's him. Ed and Ashley's dad Tim go way back. That's kind of how Ashley and Caleb got hooked up. Anyway, a few years ago, Tim and Ed were drinking together at a Chiefs' party, one of those big cookout kinda things where there were tons of people there. But Tim, being as he gets when he drinks, got a bit too rambunctious and started shit-talking Ed, who didn't like it at all and tried to ignore Tim for the rest of the night, but Tim followed him everywhere and kept badgering Ed about his health condition and making fun of his wife, Caleb's mom. Now mind you, Anne is a damn good woman. She didn't deserve that kind of disrespect.

"Ed had enough of it and told Tim to shut his mouth. Tim didn't like that at all and pushed Ed to where he almost fell down the stairs. Some people tried to stop the fight, but Tim was a mad bull on his damn beer fix and pushed Ed hard enough to almost knock him down the stairs again. That's when Caleb heard the scuffle from the kitchen and came out. He yanked Tim back so hard and threw him into the wall. Everyone was screaming and trying to get them to stop, but Tim had his sights on Caleb now, and they started fighting. Mind you, it's important to note that Ashley wasn't home when this happened.

"When Tim finally made fun of Ed's health condition for the last time and joked that he and Anne had an affair right on Anne and Ed's bed, Caleb lost his composure and did one of those weird military grappling moves and completely broke Tim's arm and knocked his lights out. Boy, I tell ya. It was a full ground and pound if ever there was one."

Evie hotly interjected, "He had it coming! What was he supposed to do? And I take it no one vouched for Caleb or defended him?"

Joshua shook his head. "Not when it was all Ashley's family and family friends. They thought Caleb acted outta line and took it too far."

"That caused Caleb to sign for divorce? I don't understand."

"It caused Tim to lose a lot of feeling and use of his arm. It jeopardized his ability to play on the football gang and do his job, which was in construction."

"Oh, cry me a fucking river!" Evie snapped.

"You don't understand," Joshua said. He fixed his eyes on her. "That put a lot of stress on the family, and eventually got Tim laid off. And because of that, Ashley was pissed at Caleb, and it caused a strain on their relationship. Caleb wouldn't say sorry and stopped going over to her family's house for anything."

Evie threw her hands up. "Good! He shouldn't. I can't believe no one defended Caleb. I'd have done the same thing had I been in his shoes, but I still don't see how that affected Ashley directly."

"Caleb then went through some times of being physically angry. He composed it well until one day Ashley drove him insane and he got mad, lost his temper, and threw a chair at the wall and scared the hell outta his poor kids."

Evie remembered what Sandy said at the salon a year ago. She had mentioned the chair incident.

Joshua went on, "So Caleb filed for divorce after Ashley told everyone he hit her. It took that poor guy forever to mend his name. But..."

Evie slowly interjected again, "The scar still remains?"

Joshua signed sadly, staring off. "Yep, but like I said..."

Evie lifted her head to look at him.

"Don't go messin' around with that guy. He's got some serious PTSD issues, Evie. You're such a sweet, beautiful, loving, and caring girl. He's not your issue to fix. I don't want you gettin' wrapped up in some head case who can't control his anger."

Evie thanked them both sincerely for their hospitality and conversation. As she got to her car, it was one of those long Midwest goodbyes as Sarah and Joshua hung out at her car as she kept trying to leave. Sure, the company and idle chatter was nice, but she really needed to get home to think, and the cold wind was getting in her car from the window being down. When she was finally able to get home, she collapsed on the bed and gathered herself from all of what happened that day. She had only been up for four hours, but it already felt like twenty-four.

Pawpaw's warning came back to her like the drifting call of a whippoorwill. *He ain't nothin' but trouble.*

She rubbed the sadness from her face and then looked at the ceiling. That could've been what Pawpaw was trying to warn her about, in that Caleb had a temper or could be violent, perhaps? But that seemed to be long ago, way before Ashley and he split. Whatever the case, she needed to figure out who told Sandy, who in turn told Ashley, who in turn confronted Caleb.

But the hardest part was that it wasn't a lie. She and Caleb *had* been seeing each other. No, they never had sex. But they came close to it often. They had been romantic with each other. Someone could easily see that his truck was there, yes. But that could have been for anything, like the contracting work he had started to do for her. But someone, somewhere, somehow *knew* they had been sexual. If they accused him of sleeping with her on the sole notion that his car was there, then they should have done it with Joshua's car being there when he mowed for her, or Hunt's cruiser being there when he paid her a visit just for fun.

As Evie thought, she again considered going to the salon to try and see Sandy there. But it wasn't the day Sandy normally went. She was always there on a Sunday after church, and Sunday wasn't until tomorrow. Evie was tired of being sheepish and not confronting people. And apparently Caleb was someone who stood strong for others, and she yearned to do the same thing for him, to confront someone about their stupidity and childish behavior.

But even if Sandy found out, how did she find out?

She sat up and grabbed her phone to open Facebook. Thankfully, he hadn't unfriended her, and now there was really no need to. She pushed on and checked Sandy's friend list. It was going to take her forever to scroll through over three thousand people, so she typed a name in the search bar.

Ashley Wright.

Ashley's name came up as Ashley Polley Wright. Joshua and Sarah weren't on her friend list, and neither was Hunt or Martin or even Hawkins.

Caleb was not on there. She tried everyone. Hell, she even tried her own brothers' names and all of her family, including her late pawpaw. She even tried her coworkers' names and her boss's name. Nothing was showing up. Kelly was on there of course, Kelly Potts.

Evie was truly stunned and stumped. She rubbed her face and finally let out all her breath. The mystery was building more and more. There was someone who put the bug in Sandy's ear, because Caleb told her that Sandy told Ashley that someone told *her*. It wasn't like Sandy simply told Ashley that they had an affair. No, she'd heard it from someone. It could've been Kelly, but how did Kelly find out?

Instead of waiting until tomorrow, Evie messaged Sandy outright. She wrote, "Hey, Sandy. I wanted to clear the air a bit in case you've been misinformed. Caleb Wright was doing some work for me, and it sparked a gossip chain that he and I were having an affair, and we're not. I'm actually seeing someone in the city." That was a brilliant ending, because it called back to what she had told Hunt at the Songbird Café earlier that she was seeing someone.

She continued writing, "So if someone told you otherwise, you've been misinformed." She ended it with a smiley emoji. "It'd be nice to see you at the salon sometime! I've not been there for a long time. Hope you're well!"

She sent it, keeping it cordial.

Sandy saw it and wrote back, "I appreciate you trying to clear the air, Evie. But someone saw you kissing Caleb like two hormonally-deranged teens about ready to fuck against your car outside O'Malley's in Freeton. This is not about his truck being there. And I think it's low as fuck of you to be macking up with a man who's still legally married. Goes to show Caleb's true colors."

Evie lost her breath. Now someone was absolutely fucking *stalking* her. No longer did she feel like it was Caleb's risk alone. Someone was following her and watching her house. Her chest tightened, and her stomach flipped a bit. She made a mental note to buy a ring camera.

But Sandy went on, "Not to mention they caught you kissing

outside in your driveway. So, nice try. But I ain't fucking buying your innocent act, sweetie."

Evie lost her nerve. "You need to tell me who told you. Because now this isn't just about Caleb's divorce. This is about the fact that apparently, someone is stalking me. And I'm freaking out."

"Oh, stop making it about you. Always fucking playing innocent victim. No one in this town likes you. You piss everyone off on the discussion page with your high and mighty antics. You think people like you because of the work you've done but that's a just few people. Ashley and the kids are the ones hurting right now. Not you. Fuck off with your victim shit. No one's stalking you, Evie. People go places, you're just a slut who makes it obvious to the world. Learn some decency." Sandy twisted the knife. "Jesus would want you to."

With that, Sandy blocked her.

Evie felt her breath quickening with a violent panic attack coming on. It was the worst one she had ever had. She tried to breathe deeply, but it didn't work or help at all. She rushed for her purse and popped a few CBD chews into her mouth, but the escalation happened so instantly that she couldn't contain it. The room began to fade; her legs grew numb. She called helplessly for her cat as she reached for the phone to dial 911. This time, she was truly alone. She couldn't call Caleb.

Alone.

The color dripped from her face with sweat alongside it. Her breath became shallow, and her lips tingled. Teddy came in and rubbed against her frantically, trying to get her attention.

Alone.

Dying.

Alone.

Dying.

Frantically, she dialed and heard the voice say back, "911, what's the location of your emergency?"

Evie stuttered, feeling herself losing consciousness, "6390 Maple-"

She collapsed, unconscious.

"Hello? Ma'am?" the voice on the other line said. "Ma'am?"

Evie was motionless on the floor, and Teddy yowled to the air. He licked his mother's nose, and she didn't move. Once more, he gave out a sad meow and purred against her face, nestling down by her neck. He push-pawed into her neck gently.

Evie didn't get up.

And the snow fell gently outside.

But breaking the sound of the silence, a Chevy truck roared up that road, tearing across and nearly hitting a mailbox after swerving to get back in the correct lane.

Chapter Twelve

"Miss Morgan?" a voice softly called to her.

Evie heard a murmur of voices all around. One was dim in sound to her left and said, "You sure she isn't on any medication?"

"She's told me dozens of times she doesn't take anything."

A pressure came to her shoulder, and it jostled her tenderly. Something was wrapped around her finger and arm. And then there was another motion that she sensed around her. Her head felt like someone smashed it with a hammer.

"Her blood sugar is low. Is she diabetic?"

"No, she's not. But I do know I saw her this morning at Songbird Café. That was way earlier at almost 8:00 a.m. She had a bagel for breakfast, but I don't recall her finishing it. Then again, I left before she probably could."

"Miss Morgan?"

Evie groaned and finally came to. As she gazed about in confusion, a pounding came to her head that she couldn't escape. A familiar voice called to her again, and she looked to the right to see Deputy Hunt by her. She was surrounded by a bunch of paramedics. "Hey there, doll face!" Deputy Hunt chimed. "You took a nasty fall. You okay?"

What a hero to see at a time like that. So badly did she want to sit up and throw her arms around Hunt and hug him, but her energy levels stuck her to the floor.

A paramedic slowly helped her sit up and called for Gatorade, water, and a Snickers bar. Evie was still a little dizzy, but she felt like she could breathe better. She mumbled, "Yeah, I guess I'm okay. I don't know what happened." She placed her hand on Hunt's shoulder and nearly cried. "I'm so glad you're here."

He rubbed her back. "You're alright."

The paramedic opened the Gatorade for her, and she chugged it quickly. She was *dying* of thirst! "Do you remember what you were doing or what you felt before you fainted?" he asked.

"I was um, in the middle of having..." She stopped and rubbed her head. "I had a tense conversation with a nasty woman on Facebook over something stupid. She said a bunch of nasty things to me. I think I'm being stalked and uh..."

"Stalked?" Hunt asked. "By whom?"

"I don't know. It's too much to explain, but I felt myself having a panic attack, so I tried to take some of my CBD chews, but it didn't help. My legs got really tingly. My lips got like...weird feeling, and I fainted. I don't remember anything else."

The paramedic asked, "What have you eaten today?"

Deputy Dan Hunt began to open up his notes to scribble down anything and mostly prepare to ask her about being stalked.

She became alert. "Oh God. I didn't realize, but all I had today was a bagel, and that was over six hours ago. But I didn't finish the bagel, and I didn't eat dinner last night."

The paramedic checked her mouth. "You could also be suffering from dehydration. Even though it's uncommon to faint from not eating unless you have a medical condition, it could've been exacerbated due to dehydration and the stress. Your heart is fine."

"That's good to know."

"Do you want us to take you in?"

"Um, yeah. I'd feel better if you did."

Evie was taken to the hospital and treated for mild dehydration, stress, and low blood sugar. Deputy Hunt sat next to her as the monitors beeped.

He patted her arm. "It's okay. I know you've had a hard day, but I need you to tell me why you think someone is stalking you."

"I... As you know from this morning, people in town think Caleb and I were sleeping together. And neither he nor I told anyone anything close to that. But people are saying it was because they saw us together at O'Malley's in Freeton, which we were. But it was a casual hangout. And then everyone's been seeing his truck at my place, but he's been doing work for me."

"Is there reason you believe this is stalking and not a chance encounter that someone saw you? And also, who told you any of this? I'd be glad to go and talk to them on your behalf."

She relaxed deeply with his kindness. "You know Joey was one of them. If you could actually get Joey to talk, I'd be forever grateful. She wouldn't tell me who told her. But the real culprit is Sandy Stottle-meyer. She's who told Ashley, Caleb's wife."

Hunt jotted down everything. "Anything else?"

Evie continued weakly, "The person who saw everything is telling people a bunch of lies. And it's gonna jeopardize Caleb's custody rights."

Deputy Hunt squinted at her. "Honey, don't you be lyin' to me. You know I can see it a mile away." He got up and closed the door then turned and sat back down with a heavy sigh. He leaned over her bed and held her hand. "We'll set it right. Now, tell me everything."

Evie was about ready to cry again. "I can't," she stammered.

"Evie, if you want me to help you, ya gotta tell me the truth. You know I won't tell a soul. You've kept my secrets, now please trust me to keep yours."

Her tears came and she sobbed a little. "Okay, okay. Caleb and I *did* have a few times where we kissed. He took me out to dinner at O'Mal-ley's, and we kissed a lot by his car. And...we almost had sex a few times."

There went her dignity, right down the fucking drain. But it felt like no matter what she did, she was going to lose. Tell Hunt the truth and break Caleb's promise of their secret love in order to catch someone stalking her, or lie to Hunt and just keep stressing over lie after lie.

As Hunt scribbled, Evie poured her heart out more, "And we kissed in his truck. Well, he was sitting in his truck, and I leaned up inside so no one could see. Joshua's house is too far to be able to see anything, and people are saying they saw us kissing in his truck."

As Hunt wrote, even he nodded. "Yep, even I can attest to that. Sounds like someone may have been on your property or looking from far away with binoculars or something." He sat upright. "Is this why you believe someone is stalking you?"

She slowly nodded in tears. "Please don't tell anyone."

Hunt stood and rubbed her shoulder firmly. "Listen, I ain't gonna tell no one nothing. That's not my job. My job is to protect you. Nothing of what you said earlier today matters at all. Do you have any clue who it may be? Do you feel in danger?"

"I have no idea who it is. I thought it could be Sandy Stottlemeyer, but she found out from someone else. My only true guess right now is Kelly Potts."

"Got it," he replied dutifully. "You'll be okay. I'm gonna leave and see what I can do."

She lowered her head. "Thank you, Hunt. I don't know what I could ever do to thank you enough."

He smiled and stood. "Those cinnamon rolls were preeeettty bangin'. It's been a while since we've gotten any."

She smirked and thumbed her fingers together. "You got it."

He left her to comb the area for any signs of someone stalking her and even went as far as to take a list of other possible suspects down.

She had confessed to the doctor that she hadn't been eating well over the last three months due to heartache, depression, and stress. When he offered her to get a prescription, she declined it. It wasn't like she was clinically depressed, not at all. There were other people out there who were worse than she was and who truly needed such medication to function normally.

She needed to get over Caleb and stop being so dramatic and immature. Or to see him. To see his smile. To feel his cuddly hugs. To see those brown baby eyes that sparkled when he smiled.

She was waiting for her discharge papers when a little knock came outside. "Come in," she called to the nurse.

But it wasn't a nurse or a doctor.

Evie almost flew out of the bed when her heart leapt to the heavens. It was Caleb. There he was again. He came for her, as he always did when she needed him most. His blue jeans were worn with white paint and his company's hoodie smelled a bit like paint and his cologne.

She hadn't seen him in three months. He had a box of her favorite chocolates in his hand, a dozen roses in the other, and tucked into that arm was a plush cat that looked like Teddy.

She clasped her mouth and forgot her pain. All she could do was reach out to him with the mists of love brimming in her eyes. He didn't even hesitate. He hurried to her, dropped the gifts on the bed, sat down, and took her in his arms.

When his strong arms embraced her, she shed all those tears. She trembled immediately with emotional release. She wept into his shoulder. He whispered affectionately, "It's alright. I'm here."

Oh, dear *God*. That deep voice rumbled in his chest and gently vibrated her cheek. That accent, that warm and sweet accent all blushed with protection and kindness. It drenched her soul with relaxation.

She choked in embarrassment, "I'm so sorry. I didn't mean to put this on you!" She clutched his sweater.

He brushed her hair with his palm. Caleb felt that she had lost a considerable amount of weight since he'd last seen her. It concerned him, but she didn't want him to feel responsible at all for her foolishness.

"It's okay," he replied. "You're not a burden. You didn't put anything on me. I'm here on my own accord."

They pulled away from each other, and with it he took every fucking ounce of despair she had and wove it with masterful hands into peace. "Are you okay?" He stroked her face, longing to see her nuzzle into his hand the way she always did.

His heart broke, because she didn't do it.

"Yeah. It's dehydration, low blood sugar, and stress. I'm getting released soon. But how did you know?"

He rubbed her thigh, looking down at it as if it was difficult to look her in the face. Her skin was dry with smudges of makeup and patchy foundation, and her eyes looked bruised and dull. Her thigh was so much thinner, and the reality of it was hard to accept. She had lost almost forty-five pounds in those three months, now weighing 170. He kept brushing her thigh as he spoke, "Sarah saw the paramedics at your place and called me immediately. She knew you and I were friends and thought I should know. I'm glad she did."

"Why do you look so sad?"

The room was quiet and calm save for the random beeping of her monitor and the nurses talking outside. "I um, I don't know. I guess I just can't help but feel bad for what I did to you. You never would have done that to me."

"No, I wouldn't have. But that's not the point. You came, and you didn't have to. I've missed you so much."

Caleb's hand was dry and cracked from outside work and dusted with a few paint splotches. His palm was rough and raw, most likely from handling some of the horses, so she presumed.

Evie added, "I'm not innocent either. I went to talk to Joshua and Sarah to see if I could see if they were the ones who talked, but they weren't." She thought about the cause of the divorce but kept it a secret. She didn't want him to be mad at Joshua. But it caused her a great deal of sorrow for him. Caleb was so misunderstood that it made her want to rip her hair out.

He looked at her. She sighed, going on, "And so after seeing who Sandy's Facebook friends were, I even checked my own family members and coworkers and boss. I had no idea who would've told her. So, I confronted her and tried to clear the air that you and I weren't together, and that I was seeing someone."

He lit up worriedly and asked, "You're seeing someone? I thought you told me you'd wait for me?"

She softly giggled, "No, I'm not. It was a lie to try to deflect them, you know? But Sandy..." She grew dark in consternation. "She told me that the person who told *her* saw us kissing and you pinning me to my car at O'Malley's and even kissing in your truck."

"And you have no idea who it was? Sandy didn't tell you?" He wasn't the least bit angry at her for trying to right a wrong. She had good intentions.

"No. She called me a slew of horrible things and then blocked me." She looked to Caleb. "Is there anyone you may know?"

He thought. "The only person I could possibly think of is if Ashley had Sandy spy on me to try to gain full custody of our kids." He shrugged and laughed sarcastically, feeling a bit crazy by the idea of it all. His thick, Midwest accent came out full throttle with that darling twang she adored. "As goofy as it sounds, that's literally the only thing I can think of. And Sandy is making it up that she heard it from someone."

Evie was released, and Caleb walked her out to his truck and opened the door for her. "Can you get in alright, Miss Morgan?"

She smiled at him. The frigid evening breeze blew through her hair and swept it across her face. He gazed into her eyes, realizing it was a very similar look to when he aired up her tires. That was long ago, before the drama. Before people talked. Before things were hard.

"You sure you should give me a ride home? Won't that look suspicious?"

"Fuck what people think. Get in. I trust my lawyer will handle it. Someone's obviously following me anyway. May as well treat you good."

He helped her inside and was taken aback by how thin she had gotten in such a short time. Not that her weight was unhealthily low at all, but so much in such a short time didn't look healthy either. She had lost some muscle mass, and her eyes looked a bit sunken in. But had been dehydrated. Maybe it was that.

On the ride home, Evie looked out the window to the wild grasses trying to sprout up through the melted snow. They bled along the interstate into the twilight air that dazzled against the icy plains. The window was a bit cracked, and her eyes were softly narrowed looking out. She pulled a stray chunk of blowing hair behind her ear. Caleb looked at her. He too glanced out and saw the darker skies on his side were already filled with stars that danced like little children at play.

The crescent moon was sharp, jagged, and smiling down upon the starry children. It was about a thirty-minute ride home, and so they had plenty of time to talk together or be quiet. Caleb looked nervously at her again and saw she wasn't well.

And by not well, she wasn't looking at him and was quiet. Evie was always smiling, chipper, spunky, lovable. But now she was withdrawn, defeated, and tired.

"Don't let it get to ya," he offered. "Remember what I said? Don't let anyone change that?"

"Do you have horses?" she asked with her eyes still lost in the vast openness of the outside world.

He smiled. "I do. Why do ya ask?"

"I've always loved horses."

"Evie, are you changing the topic on me? I already knew that about you. I know how much you loved the music from Spirit. How you watched Sea Biscuit and Secretariat a hundred times in the theater. How The Black Stallion was where you found your love for them."

She smiled out the window, leaning her head against it. "I wrote that once a long time ago. That's sweet you remembered."

"Why do you ask about horses?"

"Well, if this ever comes to a head and we're still friends, I would love to ride now that I'm small enough to."

He shot a look at her. "What? You've never ridden before?"

"Not since I was a little girl, like four years old. My daddy promised me a horse when we moved to the country finally, but then we never could afford one, and by then I had gone out to Los Angeles. When I came back, daddy died, and my momma sold the house."

He hated to ask but had to. "How did your dad pass away?"

She paused and looked out again. "Colon cancer. It came quick, and by the time he was diagnosed, I moved back and only got two months with him."

"Fuck," he groaned deeply as he looked out his window. "Evie, I'm sorry. What about your momma? How did she die?"

"She was killed by a drunk driver."

He thought about Alan Moffet. "I bet that's why you hate Alan so badly."

"Yeah, I do." Even turned and looked to him. The moon-kissed sky bathed his handsome face. He was stubbly a bit all over again. He looked at her eyes then back at the road again. Then back to her, and back to the road. Then as the nerves built up within, he looked out the window. He knew that face. He could sense the purpose of those sweet eyes.

He sighed. "Ashley and I met in middle school. We shared a class together, and I thought she was the most beautiful thing I'd ever seen.

Of course, being in seventh grade doesn't really amount to much with all I'd seen. But she had this charm about her I couldn't resist. Our dads knew each other through a football gang and so we saw each other a lot."

Evie had her hands folded on her lap and listened respectfully. She was finally getting to hear about him. Even better, he was opening up without her even asking a single question. He shook his head. "We dated, and I finally proposed to her after high school. She knew of my military goals and supported them a lot, which was another reason why I loved her so much. But I guess deployment changes people."

"Did you go to Iraq?"

He hesitated, gripping the wheel harder. He wiped his face before resting that hand on his hip.

"You don't have to tell me."

"No, it's... I haven't told anyone. Not even my own dad or Ashley. So, it's really hard. I'm not sure if a car ride is appropriate for it."

She smiled. "Then don't tell me. It's okay."

He thought and then slowly responded, "Yes. I did go to Iraq, but I'll stop there."

The winter fog came in washes on that dark highway. Regardless of the dark highway and the risk of wildlife crossing and the fog, he maintained a healthy speed and didn't show an ounce of stress or fear. Evie laid her head upon the window and closed her eyes. She adored the rumble of the massive engine below her. She soaked in the scent of his cologne and the smell of the leather seats.

What a magical night.

"Thank you," she solemnly said.

"For what?"

"For everything."

He glanced over to her and saw how peaceful she was, tranquil, at all the perfect moments of the event. He observed her narrowed left shoulder that was drowning in that baggy old sweater she wore last time he saw her. Her light-brown hair hung down to her elbow and was in desperate need of a trim again.

Had he broken her?

He wouldn't be surprised if he did. Apparently, he destroyed every beautiful thing he touched. "Evie, I'm really sorry about all of this. I'm so sorry that I brought you into my life. Maybe I should've just," he shook his head in anger, "stayed out of your life."

"I'd rather die today than live a millennium without knowing you."

What a punch to the stomach that gave him. Caleb reminisced about everything in his life. There was no way a woman like her could love a man like him. "Baby, I still don't understand what you see in me."

With her head still turned and slumped into the window, she mumbled, "Then someone has torn you down so much that you can't see the forest for the trees anymore. And remember what you said? Can't we let people be?"

"No," he said a little more heated but still smiling. "There's a vast difference between someone like you, who loves unconditionally and is always happy and loving, and someone like me who has anger issues and throws things."

"You're pardoned for being human, if that's what you need. But to let you know, you didn't solely cause this, Caleb. I was diagnosed with bipolar mania after my momma died. My manic episodes can run boiling hot with love and a euphoric high all the way to needing to recluse and sleeping all the time and not paying bills."

Evie felt that hand on hers that rested on her lap. *His* hand. The warm and calloused touch softened her broken heart. Hiding away, she cried a little, then she embraced that hand in hers. "You came back," she said through her tears.

"I will always come back, but I know there'll come a time when you see who I am. And Evie, you're not gonna stay."

She slowly turned and looked at him, and he looked back at her. She gripped his hand and her gaze melted from focused to tender. She whispered like a sweet butterfly landing on his torn soul, "Wait."

His eyes grew tight as she felt her fingers on his hand delicately. She whispered again, "Just wait, my darling. I've prayed my whole life for someone like you. So, no matter what your life throws at you, I'm not leaving. Just wait, you'll see."

Her eyes. It was those bedroom eyes again. His heart raced seeing her so soft looking. So docile and beautiful. Her lips almost seemed to pout, but they always naturally looked like that. Her hair framed her face, and with her weight loss, it made her eyes all the bigger and more expressive.

He looked back to the road and saw an emergency turnaround that was used strictly for emergency vehicles or the highway patrol units. Still keeping his eyes focused on the road as he shifted in his seat, he asked, "Is Teddy gonna be okay?"

"Yeah, Joshua and Sarah texted and said they'd feed him tonight and tomorrow if I had to stay overnight."

Caleb downshifted hard and took an aggressive turn into the gravel passthrough. Immediately, they drifted, and Evie yelped hard holding on to the handle above the window. "Caleb, what the hell are you doing?"

"Something I should've done a long time ago."

"No, seriously. Where are we going? Why are we turning around?"

Not too long after, he was going back in the opposite direction and took the exit for Eagle Rock Lake. Still holding on, Evie looked around in panic. "Why are we going to Eagle Rock Lake?"

"I can't tell you. But I promise I'm not gonna hurt you. It's a surprise. Trust me?"

She let go of the handle. "I trust you."

Twenty minutes later, Caleb pulled into the parking lot of the Eagle Rock Inn. It was a secluded motel that was nestled off of the highway and had a pristine view of the lake surrounded by pine trees and some that were nothing but wiry branches. Its little yellow sign lit up to showcase vacancies, boats for rent, and the enticing offer of color TV and cold beer. The moonlight danced like ripples of lost souls on the partially frozen black water. The fog had cleared.

He parked the truck, and in the quiet they both stared forward at the doors of the inn. Then, they slowly looked at one another.

Caleb Wright had had enough of waiting.

After checking in and with the room keycard shoved in his back denim pocket, they walked out on the poorly lit sidewalk to their room. Evie looked up at his rounded shoulders draped snuggly with his company's sweater, his hair fluffy and tempting. She could stand it no longer.

She pulled him by the hand up against her body, and he instinctively followed her passion and took her. Caleb pinned her to the wall and kissed her furiously. As their bodies glided against one another, she reached her weak hands across the strength of his chest, letting his moans come hot to her starved lips. Their breaths escaped once more as Caleb dipped down, grabbed her by the ass, and lifted her to the wall. A river of pleasure flooded her blood and skin, and so she wrapped her legs around him. His hands squeezing hard into her made her cry with excitement. Caleb then leaned over, enshrouding her with his height, and lifted her higher to kiss her throat with unbridled affection.

She wanted to scream and release all of her life's trauma into him. He had broken her chains, then had accidentally broken her heart, then broke her loneliness.

He pushed his strong hips between her thighs, and he felt her curl her hips forward as if already ready to take him. A hard yelp raced from her lips in shock. His cock was already hardening through his rugged denim jeans, and it was easy to feel.

"Caleb," she moaned breathlessly. If she didn't get him that night, she would never be able to live her life normally. The soaring longing to have him was plagued within her very bones to a lethal ache she couldn't escape. His sounds surrounded her, his scent was her oxygen, and his mass was her escape.

His teeth raked against the soft skin of her throat, eager to bite, to kiss, to adore, to cherish. Her hair fell around his face and devoured his senses with that rosemary mint shampoo all over again. It drove him insane. How soft and feathery it was, like billions of fine silk feathers tickling his face and nose. The warmth it gave shielded his face from the icy wind.

He whispered to her lips, "I don't wanna wait for you anymore. I don't care."

She trembled and replied, "Neither do I."

It was so easy for him to hold her now. Even though she was still thicker, Caleb's strength was rough as he pressed her harder to the wall with his chest. She kissed his chest through his sweater, and upon holding his shoulders, she felt that his muscles were tighter, larger, more pleasurable. She gasped, "Damn, boy." Her hands slipped down his deltoids and squeezed hard. "How the *fuck* did you get so jacked?"

He pulled her from the wall and pressed his forehead to hers. She laced her fingers behind his neck and his deep voice came through those rough lips, "Workin' out." That was all he said. Plain, to the point. Caleb wasn't one much for talking when his cock felt like it was going to burst. He pulled her away from the wall and carried her the rest of the way to the door, stumbling a bit with their furious kissing. He tilted his head to the left and let his eyes close to savor her a bit before checking to make sure he'd reached the correct room. Evie hotly kissed his throat, and it rattled his body with desire. Goosebumps shot up all over his back and chest.

With hard force, Caleb pinned her to the door and began fidgeting for his keycard. He looked down to focus a bit and Evie reached up to hold his face and kiss it.

He snarled, fighting with his pocket, "Come on you stupid fucking thing!"

It roused a giggle from Evie. She whispered like that seductress she could be, "Don't worry, baby. You have all night to fuck me as many times as you need."

What a personality flip that was. But she couldn't help it. Evie could be both a longing lover and a sex-starved siren. Caleb was man enough to bring both sides out of her.

"Evie," he said from within his cavernous chest. He looked into her eyes and told her sternly, "I know men have only fucked you in your life." The door was open and holding her now with only one hand tucked under her rear, she wrapped her legs tighter, savoring that embrace with how strong he was. He walked inside and shoved the door closed with his butt. He took her over to the bed and slammed her on it, holding her hands down immediately. He grabbed her face and bore his eyes deep into hers. Hers were watering, wide, expressive, and ready to submit.

"I'm gonna be the first to make love to you."

Her heartbeat was heard in her ears. It was as if time slowed at his absolute command. The confession tore her apart in ways that no words could ever describe, and built her back up with bricks of love, with stones of respect, and a foundation of trust and friendship. It made him happy to see tears pricked at the corner of her eyes, and then one by one they fell, and they fell for him. Everything was for him. Every breath she breathed belonged to him. He leaned over and claimed her lips with his. His thick accent came like beautiful honey, "Go ahead baby, cry. Cry it all out. I wanna bring the woman outta you."

She curled her fingers into his hair, shaking with the way he mounted her. All the things he straightened out of her, all the tough lessons about self-respect he gave her came flooding back in sugary memories. She panted, "You already have."

Caleb felt the skin around his shaft blistering to a breaking point. The head of his cock throbbed with sensitivity against his jeans, but before he could truly take her, he remembered one thing he had texted but deleted it before he sent it. He was going to taste her for as long as he wanted.

Evie reached down to grab his sweater and shirt along with it, and he ducked down so that she could remove them. Now her eyes feasted on his beautiful manscape of a body, with a perfectly rounded chest, rigid nipples, and softly defined abs. His biceps flexed a bit, and his obliques caved when he reached above his head to scratch it.

She sat straight up, grabbed him by his waist, and placed her full lips around his left nipple. He exhaled loudly, "Damn, woman!"

Evie grabbed his back with clawing nails and pulled him back on top of her. His hands crushed the mattress down with its weak and aged springs, and his chest hovered over her. With closed eyes, his lips trembled. She licked his nipple and worshipped the subtle salt of his skin. Over and over again, she blew his mind with how loving she could be, and even Caleb himself never had a woman treat him so fucking *good*. Her hands were felt everywhere.

The lights hadn't even been turned on yet, and they weren't needed. They didn't care about the lights. There was enough coming in from the parking lot. Her tongue's dancing and lips suckling on his nipple were insanely erotic to him, and he wanted her to have it. Within his lust, he needed to give it to her. He slipped down so that they were eye-to-eye and kissed her, holding her throat gently. He needed to be very careful with her, as someone so abused could easily switch. "Stay," he ordered in an airy, deep voice.

Evie looked up as he slid down slowly, each movement causing the mattress to creak and his breath to become louder. "Caleb," she begged, and he knew *exactly* what she was begging for. To have him lick her, kiss her, let her soak the sheets with pleasure. "Oh my God, please!" He hadn't even gotten her sweater lifted to kiss her stomach, and when he did, the soft and plush skin was finally his to devour. He pushed his strong and rugged hands all the way up her sensitive sides, pushing her bra up with it. Evie's breasts were exposed to the air.

He had her sit up, removed her top and her bra quickly, and held her back to guide her down to the bed, kissing her all the way down. Her shoulders shrugged with excitement, and her brows pursed with his kisses. His right hand glided all the way across her left breast, and she nearly screamed when he took her nipple into his mouth. She grabbed his hair and gasped hard. With the ache breaking between her legs, Evie was completely subdued by his pleasure. He kissed lower and began pushing his tanned hand down under her sweatpants and onto her left hip. He was going to pull down her pants but instead stopped to trace his large hand around to the front underneath her panties.

She opened her legs further immediately.

Caleb's hand covered her entirely with a warm and massive presence. She breathed quicker, feeling how large it was on her. He felt her sweltering heat and lips being full and hot. Evie arched her back and twisted her head to the right, and he knew exactly what she wanted when she did that, and he gave it to her. Caleb rose to her face, and his teeth bit down in her erogenous zone on her neck, and the pressure was perfect. His middle finger touched her wet clit.

She screamed.

There was no stopping her hips from grinding against his finger. She wrapped her right arm around his muscled upper back and felt the muscles twitching on his right shoulder from the work he was doing. His moans were muffled into her throat, and her yelps came in rapid pants with tightly closed eyes. Evie dug her other hand's nails into his arm, feeling every twitch and contraction.

Knotting came in her stomach as her hips swelled with pressure, and his finger continued to glide over her clit in perfect rhythm. But then strangely, a thought came to his mind. She was such a people-pleaser and always did everything to make *him* happy. Knowing this, the horrible thought came to him that she could be *faking it*. No woman got that worked up over something so simple. At least, not to his knowledge.

He stopped biting her neck and removed his hand so that he could use it to redirect her attention to him. He then went back to her working her clit, and asked, "Do you like this?"

She gathered herself. "I do."

"You sure?"

"Why wouldn't I be?"

"Because I know how much you like to make people happy. This ain't about me right now, baby. This is about you. Do you like it?"

Evie paused and clutched his arms. "I do, but..."

"But what?" he asked peacefully, keeping his face close to hers. He stopped his finger.

"I'd really like to cum with you licking me out. I've never had it before."

If Caleb could go back in time and punch every fucking man she'd ever had, he would've done it. The thought of nestling his face between those milky and velvety thighs made his breath unstable and his nerves shot. He lovingly kissed her and whispered, "Anything you want."

It then occurred to Evie that she hadn't showered that day, and she hadn't shaved in a month. Her confidence in the situation fell apart and she kept her legs closed tightly, regretting her decision. How embarrassing it would be for him to have her when she wasn't completely fresh, clean, and smooth.

That damn fucking depression.

He swept his hands to take control of hers and guided them above her head to the mattress. Each of his fingers traced slowly down her wrists with electrifying pulses and tickled her inner arm, across her breasts tenderly, then curved down her stomach around her waist, and his mouth kissed everywhere it could. Caleb untied her sweatpants string and with one firm yank, pulled them lower until the unshaven surface of her lush pubic skin was revealed for his eyes to feast on. Evie twisted her hips and then arched her back, feeling his breath so close to pushing her to the edge.

She closed her legs tighter and he grabbed her hips hard. He warned, "Don't you dare."

She tried to sit up. What a horrible battlefield of the mind.

But Caleb pushed her back down and said to her, "I don't give a shit what you're feeling self-conscious about. You're beautiful."

She whimpered, "I haven't bathed today, and I haven't-"

His aggressive kiss immediately silenced her. "I don't care, baby. I really don't care. Lay back and give yourself to me. Let me taste everything."

Just like with his shirt when they danced, and just like the handle in his truck, she let go. She trusted him.

He moved back down and kissed the soft flesh, so warm and luxurious. It smelled like her hair, that intoxicating and feminine rosemary mint. He briefly pressed his nose against her, as if it was a succulent peach that was forbidden for him to eat. In a way, it technically was. Already those sweet juices were glistening when he pulled her pants down farther, and he saw her lips were swollen. Above he heard her spattering breaths as she clenched the sheets. Without removing her pants all the way, he kept his elbows on the bed to lock her legs together with his arms, and he leaned over and licked her clit slowly. Just the tip of his tongue to the tip of her clit first and then the length of his tongue to the underside and glided it back up. He did it again, letting the width of his tongue push her lips apart a bit. It throbbed against his tongue.

Evie clenched the sheets so hard, and she cried while trying to pull her legs apart. She wanted him to completely eat her insane.

Caleb then sat back and smiled, being heatedly turned on by how he fueled her arousal. She wept hard while he removed her pants. He then got down on his stomach and opened her legs to him. Her legs rested against the muscles of his arms, and she was physically jerking and twitching. It was almost amusing how easily she got so turned on. Evie's breath was atmospheric in the room.

The moment her fingers glided through his scalp leaving lovely goosebumps on his back, he took his lips around her clit and kissed her deeply. His arms slipped up her sides until his large fingers could massage her hard nipples.

She burst into uncontrollable tears. Harder, she grabbed his hair, and Evie's legs shook when he licked her. His name could not stay out of her mouth, and quickly she already felt the pressure building inside of her. He heard her toes pop as they curled, and her sexual and sporadic whimpers made it difficult to maintain that pace. He knew that was how she liked it, but the sounds she gave made him want to go harder, faster. He couldn't wait to have his cock in her.

Caleb's cock was pressed uncomfortably into the mattress, and his body was twisted a bit due to his height. But it didn't matter. In her love, he found his escape. While her fingers draped around and cradled his scalp, he was able to forget everything that ever hurt him. Closing his eyes, he savored the moment as he tasted her. He licked her harder, and her hips withdrew into the bed with a jerk.

She was *tender* and apparently didn't like it. He backed off immediately and continued his sensual and gentle approach. Once more, she pressed herself deeper into his mouth.

She moaned vulgarly, "Oh my God! Eat my fucking pussy!"

His brows went up in surprise. *Holy shit! Where the hell did that come from?*

She pulled his face deeper. The cum from her began dripping down, and he stopped to lick up every bit of it. Once more she begged him to, but when he tried to go harder again, once more she withdrew. It didn't make any sense to him! One moment she was pulling him deeper, but then when he tried to go harder, she withdrew. *Oh well. I'll let her take control and keep doing what I'm doing.*

What he didn't know was Evie's mind was being tortured, ruptured, broken, and tossed about in euphoria. She was so out of her mind with love and pleasure that she didn't know what she wanted, but she did know that Caleb had barely started for a little over a minute, and already she was cumming *hard*. It built even more, and her chest and stomach grew heavy.

"Please, don't fucking stop!"

His hands slipped back down and then took a hard squeeze to hold her ass cheeks. He pulled her hips closer and harder into his mouth. She was truly being licked in the deepest way possible.

The primal grasp made Evie feel cherished and worshipped, and so she stroked her own nipples and lifted her head to see him pleasuring her. "Mmm, you make me feel so fucking good."

He looked up and saw her looking at him. Their eyes met, and she watched his mouth completely disappear between her lips, eating and licking, sucking and worshipping. Evie stretched her legs wider and lifted her hips higher. Caleb could've done that all night long. She was sweet tasting, natural, soft, and rolling her clit with his strong tongue was amazing to him.

He kept on with his slow pace. And Evie stifled a scream. And then she broke.

Her cum flooded his lips and tongue, her hips bucking away from him, but he grabbed her thighs with his arms and held her steady.

Her screams were absolutely *deafening.*

He sat up and saw that her whole face was completely drenched with tears, sobbing heavily and uncontrollably. She begged, "Please kiss me."

Her eyes met his, and she looked like she had been brutally tortured, or so he saw it as that. It was as if she was completely inconsolable! Her cries were loud and could've been considered jarring to most, but Caleb treasured those cries. She felt trapped with his eyes to hers, and Evie outstretched her arms in wanting. There was no way in hell anyone could've understood what an emotional release he gave her. His touch had been absolutely perfect and executed just for her. There was no rushing, no stupid, immature dirty talk that was apparent when men watched too much porn.

Even though he was trying to unbuckle his jeans, he stopped to give her exactly what she wanted from him. When Evie saw him lean over to her, she kissed him with every drop of blood in her body. With bridled cries and burning love, Evie gazed into his eyes that hovered above hers and wept, "I love you."

He had to get those fucking pants off. He sensed how badly she needed to be made love to, and so as they together helped shuffle off his jeans, he kissed her quickly.

And then those sacred words caved into her very being. Caleb moaned to her lips, "I love you, Evie."

Her whole soul was practically thrown at him.

The jeans were kicked off aggressively and Evie felt him grip around her legs with those strong arms, and he pulled down further onto the bed with a violent yank. If he had properly gotten onto her before pulling her down, his head would've hit the headboard due to his height. She couldn't stop saying his name. The air was suffocated with sexual sounds from both of them, preparing to possess each other with a life-long desire. Evie stroked his tattoo sleeve on his arm, letting the muscles give way underneath her firm touch.

They kissed hard. Evie wrapped her legs around him, and he crouched a bit to try to meet her with his mouth. With one more final kiss and a beautiful tongue on hers, she felt Caleb grab his cock and guide it against her throbbing pussy. Evie sensed the tip gliding her lips apart, and his name still never left her breath. Nothing could interrupt them now, and Evie was free to cry as loud as she needed to, as loud as he *wanted* her to.

Caleb tilted his head and wrapped that large left arm underneath her neck, cradling her. He took her in a crushing strength, and she danced on the verge of turning insane when his cock teased a bit more. She was unaware he was trying to perfect everything first. With his cock feeling exactly where it needed to be, he removed his hand from it and braced himself on his elbow not to crush her entirely.

Their eyes met. Their hearts raced.

And Evie felt his thrust deep inside of her.

She could've sworn to God she saw stars.

There was no stopping her. Evie opened her jaw so hard that it nearly popped. She couldn't even breathe from the pleasure. Her heart raced harder as Caleb's thickness filled her completely. His hips slammed into hers, causing the mattress to shake and her legs to wave back and forth. They locked around him a little harder, but her mind became numb, and she lost control of her body. He had planned to be slow and steady at first, but that was not what either one of them wanted now.

All she could feel was her jaw stretched painfully wide, unable to even phonate a sound. The sounds of his cock thrusting were loud and glorious, the bed's old mattress creaking with every powerful drive. All over his back, her hands felt stiff. She didn't know what the fuck to do. Then Caleb felt her hands grab a hard hold onto his ass and pull him in deeper. He pulled away from her a moment to lift himself up, allowing her to marvel at his chest muscles and how his tattoo sleeve crept a little onto his pec. He never took his eyes off her.

Caleb's body felt like there were a million fingers worshipping it in every place, every nook, every scape of muscles, and every fiber. One moment she would rub his back wonderfully hard, then grab his taut biceps, then squeeze his ass into her again, then back up to his hair where she scratched deeply. The soaking thick cum she already gave him made his efforts substantially easier, and his cock felt tighter and hotter. They shared a quick kiss before Caleb took her higher. He rested his cheek against her temple, closed his eyes, and went harder.

And harder.

She screamed.

And *harder.*

His mind left his conscious state as she welcomed him in deeper with her cries. Evie told him he could go harder, and it tore his lust in half, fracturing his self-control.

Caleb removed his arm from underneath her and held himself up with both hands. To the left Evie looked and twisted her head to watch his forearm muscles and veins contract. She shifted to lick his arm and kiss it. Nuzzling against it, she held her hands onto his shoulders and tried to calm down, but she couldn't.

A sudden echoing growl rattled from his stout chest, and Caleb's gasps of pleasure were coming.

Evie begged, "Please, cum inside me!"

She needed it. She didn't want him to pull out. And he didn't want to. None of them were thinking at all. And none of them cared.

In that position, Caleb was able to fuck her harder and harder. Evie's hips tightened and the sensation came deep within, a tickling sensation that was mounting and growing, building and scorching.

She dug harder, whispering, "Caleb."

He didn't stop, and neither did her body.

She called his name again, "Caleb!"

Evie arched her entire back but then quickly curved her stomach to sit up a bit, using his shoulders as leverage. Her eyes squeezed hard, and she knew she was having an orgasm. "Oh my God, please don't fucking stop."

He wouldn't. He was almost there if she wanted him to be.

Her absolute mind and soul were purged.

Evie came in heavy flows all over his pulsing cock and she clapped her mouth to prevent her bone-rattling screams from being too obnoxious.

Caleb's moans filled her back up with everything she rid herself of, and then his cock tightened inside of her and shook hard with a quick pulse.

His whole body moved up and down with the full release being met, and as they touched each other's faces, they felt each other had shed tears.

And for the same reasons.

Caleb withdrew and held her tenderly, wiping her face with his thumb.

Her body convulsed. "I'm sorry!"

"Shhh, it's okay!" he laughed sweetly.

But she wouldn't stop apologizing. And sadly, Evie turned a little from him and covered her face. For some strange reason, she burst into a fit of loud weeping.

He stopped touching her because Evie didn't stop crying. She couldn't.

As Caleb watched, Evie screamed her guts out into her palms. The emotional release was incomprehensible to him, and he worried he had hurt her.

He tried to pull her hand away. It was impressively rigid, but he managed. "What's wrong? Are you okay?" he asked, still panting from the heat.

Her hands shook as if telling him to go away, but that wasn't what she was signaling. "I'm sorry!" she cried again.

With his arms gathering her up, Caleb pulled her over on her side with him. The loving embrace warmed her and protected her. Within those strong arms and hot, dominating chest, he cradled her. Magically, she took a deep breath and calmed down, finding solace in nuzzling her face against his hot and damp skin. "I'm sorry. You don't know what you did for me."

He brushed her back and kissed her forehead. "I know exactly what I did for you. That's why I did it. If only you knew what you just did for me."

She giggled softly, for he revisited something he had told her already when they first tried to make love. Back then, it was merely sheer lust. Now, she knew it had grown into love. She couldn't have her insecure mind play tricks on her thinking that when he told her he loved her it was all a lie. But her mind was so stricken with nirvana that never occurred to her.

And it wasn't true. As Caleb kissed her, and she tried to lazily meet his kisses, he did in fact grow to love Evelyn Morgan.

Without a care in the world, Caleb Wright was allowed to sulk in his fully drained body. The mattress was old, and the bed was rickety, but Evie made it feel like home.

She made everything feel like home.

Home.

Caleb fell sound asleep with her locked in his arms. And for once in many years, he had the deepest sleep of his life.

Chapter Thirteen

Caleb's heart rate shot through the roof, and his head felt like it was splitting apart. She wasn't sure what had come over him, but he looked lost, confused, or something different. It was as if he stared right through her but never *at* her. The light coming in was like milk and honey. Dawn had come. She tried to softly get him to talk to her by touching his face. The pricks of his stubble were rough along his jawline, but still Caleb didn't move. He had blanked out completely.

She didn't care. Instead of pushing or prying, Evie lifted her head, tenderly kissed his cheek, and whispered with a breathy voice, "I love you." And then, she simply nuzzled against his face. The jagged roughness of his skin didn't phase her at all. Sure, it burned, but she wanted to feel that fire. She wanted to be closer to him. She wanted to *be* there with him, wherever he went off to. During a recent blizzard when she felt afraid and alone, Hunt had stopped by and chatted with her over coffee. It was then and there she learned what certain signs of PTSD could look like. She was by no means an expert, but she could try.

Caleb's eyes glazed over, and she waited patiently, still stroking his face with one hand and his shoulder with the other. She kept her eyes deadlocked on him at all times. After about five minutes, she lifted his chin and kissed his lips. He didn't respond.

She made her way over to him after closing the door and sang a little chipper good morning to him. He looked up to her and thanked her for the snack and soda. The problem was deep within him. Evie wrapped her arms around his shoulders and licked softly behind his ear. She wasn't making toxic thoughts any less toxic. She kissed his throat, stroked the muscles on his back, and it left him yearning for another escape. Anything to get his mind away from what he was thinking. The PTSD episode had been long gone now, and so that was no longer the weight on his mind. It was what he had said to her last night.

When he said he loved her.

It was the stupidest thing he could have done. But they were both so caught up in the moment that neither of them was thinking. Perhaps Evie did love *him*, because that was how she was. But he hadn't really known her for even two years now, had only had one technical date with her, and so there was no way in hell he should've been so stupid to say such a thing. Especially to a lovesick woman like her. Yet now he knew there was no way in hell he would tell her he didn't mean it. It would surely drive her over the edge if he did.

Fuck it all.

He put his chips and his Coke down on the nightstand, grabbed her, and threw her down on the bed. His mind switched out of that sensible and rational thinking. "I wanna make love to you again."

Evie settled below him willingly and stroked his arm. "Don't even think about that. Whatever you want, whatever you need." She looked up to him. "I'm here."

He shuddered. His nerves ran hot and all over his skin pricked. Evie lifted her beautiful face and kissed him, whispering, "Use me. I'd rather be your little slut than anyone else's girlfriend."

"No," he said sharply. "Don't say that. Look at how you are, even right now. You want me to use you, but you don't know the first thing about really being at the mercy of someone else." His deep voice grew harsh, "Stop succumbing to me. You don't know what you're doing. That's not what you're here for."

She pleaded, "But I want to. I know you wouldn't hurt me. Besides, you just told me last night to give myself to you. So I'm simply doing it again." She raked her fingers through his face and his hair with ravenous desire. "I don't think you understand how much I want you to let it all out in me. I want to be the reason your beautiful mind is freed."

He got off of her and she sat up. He shouted, "Stop saying that!"

Confusion came across her face. "I don't understand. Say what?"

He looked at her and waved his hand away in anger. "That stupid 'beautiful mind' comment. This mind isn't fucking beautiful! Get your head out of your romance books, Evie!"

"Um, I actually don't read romance books. I thought you knew that."

Caleb faced her and once more warned, "Don't ever call my mind beautiful again. You don't know what kind of fucked up shit I have going on in there."

She stood and approached him like a phantom of beauty, cautious and unwavering. He was sweating. This time, she knew not to touch him. "I read Stephen King books," she said as she locked her eyes on him. "Your mind, in all of its chaos and hurt, is beautiful to me."

Like an irate man would, he snapped at her, "That's the stupidest fucking thing I've ever heard you say. Do you know how delusional you sound right now?"

She walked up to him closer and glared at him. Her voice was even, calm, like still waters. "How about the fact that I find your mind beautiful *not* by the mess that's within it but by the love you still give to others despite suffering so deeply?"

Caleb was going to open his mouth to dish out his infamous "I'm not hurting" line, but he immediately clapped it closed.

Evie rose her brows in a smile.

He shut himself up.

But casually, she brushed his shoulder and sighed. "It's okay, Caleb. It's okay to be confused, pissed off, strong, weak. It doesn't matter. But those things you must have seen?" She shook her head out and looked up to him. She wanted him to know that she was meaning every damn word she said. "Any man who can go through what you've obviously gone through, and still love his children, hold two jobs, and still find it in your heart to take care of your property, care for others the way you do...you don't find that beautiful?"

He couldn't answer. There was no comeback he could give. No

matter how hard he would try to tell her that he was okay, Evie now knew he wasn't, since he accidentally confessed it when he mentioned that his mind was fucked up.

"Now," Evie slowly said as she turned around with her back to him. She pressed her body up against his and began sliding down her sweatpants. His cock grew hard inside his boxers as his chest raced with breath. Once she dropped her panties and sweatpants, she removed her bra and top. Grabbing his hands, she firmly placed them on her hips and turned to look up in his eyes. "I want you to use me."

Take her. Fuck her hard. Everything you've ever wanted to do to a woman, do it now.

His hands trembled and clenched around, releasing a sexual breath from her. She reached up and stroked his neck, letting her arm slide back down his chest. "I can feel your cock getting hard. If you don't wanna use me, that's fine. But I'm still gonna give you what you deserve no matter what way you choose. So go ahead and choose."

At once, Evie felt his grip around the back of her neck, and he forced her forward until she fell over the bed. She would be lying if she said she wasn't scared, but she had trusted him with her very life. Caleb pulled down his boxers and Evie felt his hot and muscled body on her from behind. She felt trapped.

No.

She felt...protected.

That was exactly why when Caleb pinned her against the car it turned her on and didn't scare her shitless. He had earned her trust so much that when he took control of her it felt safe and protective, not violent or demeaning.

Suddenly, the grip on the back of her neck got way too tight and she questioned her decisions momentarily, until she realized he had taught her to have a say in things. And so quietly, she whimpered, "Can you lighten your grip a little?"

He immediately did.

She knew she could trust him. Those long fingers then curled around almost to the front of her neck, but he never applied pressure. He knew that was a dangerous thing to do given where his fingers landed.

Her soul was set on fire. Everything he did had such control over it, that she pushed back into his hardening cock, feeling it brush against her thigh. She wanted him to fuck her as hard as he needed to.

Caleb hotly kissed the back of her neck and grabbed his cock to feel for her. "Move your legs apart, baby."

She did.

As he smelled her hair, the goosebumps rose all over her skin with the dancing of his hot breath on her back, and his warm chest pressed onto her back, pinning her down. Then he slipped one arm around her face to let her rest her head on it.

She braced herself as Caleb was moving hot and fast all around her. His breath was unsteady, and his moans were loud and deep. Being as tall as he was, he was easily able to lean over her. His hand guided his cock to her, and then he let go to wrap that arm underneath her.

Evie was thrusted forward when his cock slipped into her pussy, and the bed hit the wall. She lifted up her head with her mouth open, feeling his pleasant rage thrusting harder into her. That was what she wanted. He had done enough for her by being cautious and tender, and so she wanted him to feel like he didn't have to hold back.

Harder, he went deep inside, his beautiful glute muscles flexing with every hard thrust. Evie felt her hips being smashed into the edge of the bed, and she let it happen even though it hurt. Deep inside of her pussy, she felt that glorious cock hitting a spot she never felt before.

All over he kissed her, grabbed her hair by the roots, said things she couldn't understand due to how fast and rambling it was. She didn't care, and neither did he.

Caleb could finally let it go.

Evie's moans started to come more loudly, and when Caleb saw her turn her head and look into his eyes, he knew she was enjoying it.

He took it further and sat up to slap her ass as hard as he could. She whimpered in pleasure, "Again!"

The blood rushed into his cock so rapidly he thought he was going to cum. He had never been able to act like that or do that before. He did it again and again until he finally pulled Evie back *gently* with her hair as to not throttle her cervical spine. "Do you like that?"

She cried in gasps, "I fucking love it!"

He crushed her. He went harder, feeling his absolute release and he came all over inside of her. Their cum together dripped a little down her shaking leg, and she turned her head to look at him. He asked, "Want me to keep going?"

Whatever the hell it was that Caleb brought out of her, she had no idea. Evie threw her head back from pleasure and begged for it. He dug his nails into her ass, her back, bit the back of her neck to hold her steady in his jaw, and finally he felt her cum on his cock. Her head pressed down to the bed in collapsing exhaustion as he then kissed her cheek.

But she wasn't done with him.

Evie got up, turned around, and slipped off the bed and immediately took him in her mouth. She wanted to taste every drop of him and lick every inch.

Caleb let his head go back and he moaned loudly. Ashley never liked sucking him off.

Evie acted like she would die if she didn't.

She looked up at him and then closed her eyes, feeling absolutely honored to take him into her mouth. Her hand started to stroke, and her full lips kissed the under the head of his cock right where his shaft started. She licked the vein and drove him as far back as she could handle.

The loving feeling warmed his whole soul. She wasn't rapid or impatient with it, but slow and deliberate. He finally came again with hot spurts down in her mouth.

Later on, they lay entwined in each other's arms again, their passionate kissing never stopping. Something built within Caleb's heart. Every way she touched him, he couldn't get enough of it. He lowly whispered, "How could I ever thank you?"

It *used* be that he would tell her what happened in his past that made everyone so cautious about him. But she gathered enough from Joshua's stories that perhaps she would finally leave it alone. Everyone thought Caleb Wright was a drunken service member with a bad temper and a tenacity to be abusive. Boy, he was anything *but* that.

"You don't need to thank me," she said in a smile.

He moaned in a grinning delight, "How about breakfast?"

Evie offered to have a proper breakfast at the restaurant in the lobby, but Caleb refused, stating that he'd rather take her to a place a little bit better. Off of Eagle Rock Lake there was the family diner called the Eagle Lodge, and that was where they shared a beautiful breakfast together overlooking the scenic lake. The deepest days of winter were frosty and cold, but it seemed like it was now going to be a mild and quick winter. She sipped her hot chocolate in a way that left her savoring every sip. The surrounding trees sparkled on the rims of the lake. So many maple trees, oak and other ones she didn't know.

Caleb leaned over on his hand with his gigantic breakfast steak with nothing but blood smears on his plate, and he kept watching her eyes stay closed.

"Really enjoying that hot chocolate, are we?"

She almost didn't hear him talking to her because of how lost in a daydream she was.

"It's homemade! You can tell!" she happily replied. Then she looked out the large glass window again. The docks were alive with fisherman bundled up and ready to go out again, all yelling and playfully bickering with each other about how their wives were probably enjoying the peace and quiet away from them. "I love it here. I've never been here before."

"You haven't?" he asked.

"No, I would love to live by the water. I'd love to have horses too. Someday I will."

He offered a toast of his coffee to her hot chocolate. "Someday, you definitely will. You'll live by the water and have all the horses you could ever want."

The morning haze hovered over the dark lake, and she watched a bald eagle splash into the water, catching a hefty fish. The fisherman on the dock yelled, "Why can't we have that kinda luck?"

She laughed.

Once more, Caleb paid the bill, and she thanked him. The long drive home would've been a long drive to anyone else, being forty-five minutes, but to Caleb it was a backroads stroll. He occasionally looked at Evie who was snuggled in his sweater against the window, closing her eyes in happy thought. He reached out and grabbed her hand, causing her attention to come to him. She smiled back and sat up to enjoy the view of the road and that big hand engulfing hers. Their eyes met, and he smiled. "I meant what I said last night."

He really believed he did.

Relief. Evie replied with love in her eyes, "I did too."

Then her playful side came back out as she crawled a bit over to kiss his cheek. He laughed and turned to kiss her quickly. Evie's head rested against his strong bicep like a gentle lamb ready to sleep in a sunlit field. The road hummed underneath them, and she held his hand on the center console.

They came to her house, and before she got out, he pulled her in for a luscious kiss. She snuggled her nose to his chin and closed her eyes. "I have to confess something."

"What's that?"

"My house is an absolute mess due to my depression. I'm sorry."

"Don't be. I don't judge people."

She sweetly teased while touching his chest, "Wanna fuck me again inside?"

He was surprised all over again. He withdrew his head and quirked his brows down to her. "I always painted ya to be the sweet, innocent type. You were so not like that last night. Nor this morning. What gives?"

She brushed his arm with a teasing grin. "I can be, but I feel comfortable around you. I feel like I don't have to be all prim and proper all the time."

He snickered. "You most certainly don't!"

Not even a few minutes later, Caleb was on her again holding her down to bed. She had been like the only drug that ever fixed him, and he was the only therapy she wanted. After their second coupling, Caleb ordered takeout and showered with her, kissing every part of her body and washing her hair. He finally got the best back scratch of his life. They ate, watched movies, made love, cuddled on the couch, on the floor tangled up in the bed sheets. It had been five times they had made love, but even though Caleb was wearing low on his stamina, neither one of them wanted to be done.

That night while he stayed over, she rode him passionately. It was beautiful to be on top of him, to kiss his nipples, massage his chest, and throw her head back as he taught her exactly how to move her hips that felt so good to him.

The cold night sang with the empty branches swaying in the trees. She was cradled by him, snuggled up. Caleb randomly shot up and freaked out. "Evie, I wasn't wearing a condom at any time we had sex!"

Without opening her eyes, she reached into her purse on her nightstand and lifted up her birth control pills, shaking them in play with a smile.

He laughed loudly. "Oh, thank God! Are you always on birth control?"

She rolled over. "I got on it the first time we almost had sex. I went straight to the doctor."

"And you kept taking it even after I blew you off?"

She thought quietly and lovingly looked at him. "A girl can dream, right?"

Evie quickly texted Sarah and told her that she was home, and that caring for Teddy was no longer needed.

The next morning, Caleb helped her haul her trash bags down to the yard and was kind enough to help with her dishes and finally fix that stupid cupboard door. While they listened to the local rock radio station, he taught her exactly how to fix it, and it dawned on her that it actually wasn't that hard. He was a great teacher. Occasionally, they would exchange warm smiles, and once she even playfully poked his butt with the screwdriver. It was alright though. He got her back by spraying her with the sink attachment and smacking her ass. The whole morning was nothing but fun, laughter, kissing, hugs. All the things he had missed out on for so long.

It was all the way she got him to laugh.

He realized how spoiled he was getting with her. That weekend he had stayed every night. The morning hugs, the soft kisses, asking how he slept, getting the best back and scalp scratches ever, the kisses planted all over his body, the food she cooked for him. Everything. But it was now time to turn back to his work, and so he left her that morning and promised that after the week, he would come back and see her. She waved him off as he walked to his truck, and he took off down the driveway.

Suddenly he slammed on his brakes before the end when that damn Alan Moffet tore down the road, swerved up into her driveway a bit, and knocked Evie's mailbox right over!

At once, Evie ran as hard as she could down the long driveway calling his name and almost slipped on thin ice. "Caleb! Are you alright?"

Caleb got out of the truck and looked at her box. "Yeah, I'm fine, but damn!" he scorned as he tried to lift up the post. It was ruined and fell back over. "Don't worry. I'll come by this weekend and fix it."

As Caleb picked up her mail, Sarah called out as she rushed across the road. "Caleb! Oh my God, are you okay?"

"Yeah, I'm fine. The mailbox ain't."

Sarah said with her hands in her hair, "It doesn't matter. As long as you're okay! Evie, are you alright?"

Evie wrapped her pink robe around her a bit more. Not that she was naked underneath, just cold. "I'm shaken up but okay. I'm glad he has good reflexes! With that person stalking me and now this, I probably should get a ring camera."

Sarah gasped, "Someone's stalking you?"

"Yeah," Caleb answered dryly again, putting the post and box in the bed of his truck so that it didn't get further damage. "She doesn't know who, but someone is."

Sarah said, "I have a ring camera. I'll take a look back at the house."

"Thank you, Sarah. That means a lot. I've been meaning to get one, but I keep forgetting."

Caleb hugged Evie quickly as not to cause any weird vibes, as Sarah was staring at them intensely. He said to Evie casually, "Be safe. I'll be back this weekend to fix your basement."

"Thanks, Caleb! And take care!"

When Caleb left and headed right, Sarah took a long hard stare at Evie. Evie shrugged. "What are you looking at? He literally hugged me."

Sarah folded her arms and gave her a look. "Evie, you know he's in the middle of a divorce, and the whole town knows he's the most sought-after eligible bachelor now."

Evie retorted, "That's funny, because I thought everyone hated him. How can he be *so* desired yet so hated at the same time?"

Sarah kept her arms crossed. "Seems like you're not denying it now." "I'm simply responding to what you said, Sarah. There's nothing going on between he and I." Evie was completely trapped. Caleb had told her that he didn't want to wait for her anymore, but she also still didn't want to gamble their secret, either. She had to somehow try to keep it contained as best as she could, but she was losing that battle more and more everyday.

Sarah approached and put her hand on Evie's shoulder and raised her brows, trying to care. "Evie, I don't want you getting hurt. Ashley is on a warpath right now because of him being around you. You told me that everyone's talking about it, and I saw the comments on your Facebook page."

Evie rolled her eyes. "Oh, for God's sake. It literally doesn't matter what I do. People are going to talk. There's literally *nothing* I can do to stop it now, all because of the person who told Sandy."

"You came home with him Saturday morning, in his truck."

Evie glared at her, and then her head turned to the left in a warning look. "He gave me a ride home from the hospital."

"Where did you stay Friday night? I didn't get your text that Teddy was cool until Saturday morning!"

"Why the fuck are you interrogating me? You're not Ashley's lawyer, nor are you my mother!"

Sarah shot back, "Listen! I'm trying to prevent you from getting his kids taken away! You can't keep crying about the town gossiping about you having a fling with him but then pull shit like this! Like coming home with him in his truck after being gone all night! Joshua and I stayed and took care of your cat, and I swear to God, if you were out having a fling that night while we took care of your cat, I'm gonna be pissed! If you don't want the town talking about you two, then stay the fuck away from him!"

Evie grew tepid in her emotions. "Why wouldn't you defend me on social media? Why would you talk to me like this instead of having my back? You don't really think these things, do you?"

Sarah threw her hands up in agitation. "I honestly don't know. I believed you when you went into the hospital. But now with this? I don't know. But I do know that I care about you. And you're going to ruin your business endeavors here in this town if you get your identity from a booty call!"

Evie was on the verge of tears until Joshua appeared from across the street. He only meant to call his wife back for help with the animals. Before she left, she turned and faced Evie to give her one last hard look.

The horrible reality was that as Evie went inside, she realized Sarah wasn't wrong. The more she and Caleb were together, the heavier the chances were. She texted him, "When is the divorce being signed? Do you know?"

Once again, she deleted it in a sigh. She didn't want to ruin a good weekend.

She thumbed through her mail as she sat on the couch by Teddy and thought about who could have told Sandy.

No one else came to her mind until she thought...

The mailbox.

Alan fucking Moffet.

And perhaps somehow Kelly fucking Potts.

She did what any sane woman would do. She first made her profile completely private then unfriended every single person except for Caleb, her brother, Joshua and Sarah, and Deputy Hunt. It had to be a delicate thing, and she tossed over more potentials in her mind. There *were* numerous nasty comments, weird messages, and everything that she had to clear out. But she had taken so many beatings lately that now they didn't even faze her. Then Evie noticed a peculiar friend request popping up. It was Alan Moffet.

And the mutual friend had been Sandy Stottlemeyer, before she had removed her from her friend list and got blocked. Taking a chance, Evie sent him a message. "Hey, Alan! I'm gonna come straight out and ask if you've been telling people about Caleb and I."

She wasn't surprised in the least when he didn't respond or even see the message.

Until 2:00 a.m. She rolled over wide awake now, hoping it was Caleb. Her heart picked up a little bit when she saw Alan wrote back. He said, "I don't give a fuck about Caleb. I have no idea who the fuck you are."

She couldn't help but laugh! She wrote, "You knocked my mailbox over today with your truck. And you sent me a friend request."

The charming Alan wrote back, "So? I'm supposed to be sorry about it?"

Then he blocked her. It was weird how he had sent her a friend request then acted really odd. Perhaps he was on a drunken warpath again.

"Whew," Evie sighed as she petted Teddy. "Caleb wasn't wrong. He *is* a peach!"

But in a mad rush of mania and confusion, Evie pulled the plug on everything and deactivated her entire account. She needed the peace.

Chapter Fourteen

A few days later, Caleb was sitting at home with his guitar across his lap, trying to figure out how to play a certain chord from sheet music he had printed off. The song in question was one Evie always wanted to do a duet with a man, and it was "Need You Now" by Lady A. She had never told him this to his face, but over a year ago when they became friends on Facebook, he had combed through all of her posts and saw a video of her performing it at the local bar's open mic night. It was beautifully done, and the caption mentioned that she longed to do it with a man.

And he was trying pretty damn hard to be that man. But he found himself to be a terrible singer. The chords weren't hard at all, but his singing voice was something to be desired. Not to mention the harmonies he had to figure out were tricky. Over and over, he tried to find his pitch in utter failure, receiving a howl from Charlie. Caleb laughed and sang louder, "Teach me how to sing, ol' boy!"

Together they yowled, and Charlie's drawl turned into barks and woofs. He had little time to practice because his children were going to be coming over in a few minutes and he never focused on anything else but work and his kids when they were around. The cold light pooled across the maple flooring, casting a honey glow on the wooden beams that stretched across the cathedral ceilings. The iron chandelier's faux candles were lit to give a little more warmth to the stark living room that was washed with a series of beiges, maples, honeys, and the occasional pops of soft blues and greens, primarily seen in the area rug and throw pillows.

The fire's crackling was the only sound heard after Caleb and Charlie quieted down. Caleb rose from that comfortable chair and approached the large fireplace and looked to the large round mirror that rested on top of it. With one hand leaning on the wooden mantle, he stared at himself for a long while. The bookcases that flanked the fireplace were ones that he had custom built himself, and they were decorated with his medals, awards, photos of his children, Chiefs' memorabilia and collectables, and a few knickknacks from his travels overseas.

Moving from the fireplace to the large side windows, he pondered if his life had truly come to a peaceful place. He had missed Christmas with her, but with Valentine's Day and Evie's birthday right around the corner, he would make up for it. Those holidays meant the world to Evie, especially Valentine's Day and Christmas. Since both of them were proud Christians, he hoped she would understand. Caleb drew back those lofty curtains to peer outside at his large pond and horses.

Suddenly, his daughter Olivia was pulling at his arm. "Daddy?"

It happened again.

At once, he leaned over and picked her up, hearing his ex-wife had come inside. He kissed Olivia's cherubim face. "Hey there, Munchkin! How'd ya get in here, huh?"

"Momma let us in."

Ashley approached with Zack by her side. There she stood about as tall as Evie. She had deep brown hair that was kept in styled curls down to her shoulders, and her tan was just as dark as every other woman's in town. Thin brows framed her deep blue eyes, and she came in wearing the athleisure style that was just as prevalent in the town. She was stale in her expressions. She began cautiously, "I'm sorry, Caleb. You weren't coming to the door, so I used Zack's key to get in."

"You rang the doorbell?"

"Yep. Let's not make this any weirder than it already is." She took Olivia from him. He tried to resist but didn't want to stir any problems.

Regrettably, he let his daughter go. Ashley kissed her daughter, who was staring off somewhere else.

She put her daughter down then hugged and kissed her children, then left the house.

The cold night air was brisk as later on, Caleb sat up in his bed with his bedroom window cracked a bit. He felt a little claustrophobic, and the fresh air helped. He always wanted to use this time specifically for just him and his children, but the divorce had taken an ugly turn, and he had lost custody of his kids for two weeks out of the month. The court had cited that Caleb's possible affair was detrimental to his children's wellbeing. The weekends and partial weekdays were awfully quiet around there. The large four-bedroom house used to be filled with laughter all the time. Now it was stark and empty more than he had felt comfortable with.

Thank God Ashley had brought them over an hour earlier so that she could attend a meeting. That little extra time was golden to him. It felt good to have them just across the hall, sleeping in their beds, and him close by just in case they needed him.

But what his own children didn't realize, was that he felt he needed *them* more than they needed him.

A little bit of loneliness came, and he reached for his phone to check on Evie. First, he opened his Facebook to see if she had posted any new singing or cute workout photos.

His heart was thrown out of his mouth. It said, "The page you are looking for is either missing or can't be displayed" with the broken thumb icon.

His chest flushed with sweat. She obviously blocked him. He tried to hide it by scrunching his brows, staring at his phone as if stupidly, but inside he was in utter chaos. With one hand behind his head and his naked chest exposed, he called her.

Over on the other side, Evie was taking a hot bubble bath with her favorite Stephen King book in her hands. Candles were lit, a face mask was on, a glass of wine was on the nearby counter, and Teddy was sleeping on the soft, faux-fur bathroom mat. She jumped happily as she reached for the phone and answered it, "Hey there! How are you?"

"I'm fine. How are you?" he asked casually.

"Oh, I'm great! I'm taking a hot bath with a book. What are you doing up this late? It's almost ten."

"I couldn't sleep. I wanted to ask you a question. Did you block me?"

Evie smiled and put her book down on the floor by Teddy, who ended up just using it as a pillow. "No, I didn't block you. I deactivated my profile for a while. It got to be too much."

"Why? Did something happen?"

Evie sighed and took her light-brown hair out of its pin so that she could run her fingers through it. "Not entirely. But I got to thinking. I feel like it was either Kelly Potts who told Sandy or Alan Moffet, or somehow, they're all in it together. And so, I started combing through their Facebook pages, wasting time and worrying about it, when in all reality it doesn't matter anymore. No matter what I say or do, I'm not entirely welcome in this town anymore, you know?"

Yes, he did know.

Evie continued brightly, "And my therapist told me that sometimes social media can be bad for my approval addiction and manic episodes. So, I thought it'd be best if I just let it be and let it go and live my life happily. Whatever that may be."

This woman never ceased to amaze him! He had to tell her, "Evie, all adoration and lust aside, I am really fucking proud of you. It takes a lot to admit that to yourself and shove it out. You're protecting your peace and taking charge of your own self-worth. I'm really, *really* happy for you. And you should feel proud of yourself."

"I have you to thank for that."

He smiled. "Well, I do wanna know why you think it's Alan?"

"Because of how often he drives around here like a maniac. And how he seemed to deliberately hit my box. I know he's an asshole to everyone on the road, but he also works in Freeton. I'm not sure about it anymore though, since I tried to write him on Facebook, and he got all weird and blocked me. He acted like he didn't even know who I was. I don't know why he'd be like that, but I don't care."

And neither did he. Perhaps it was time to truly leave the past in the past. If only forgetting *his* past could be so easy. He changed his thought trajectory and asked, "Would you like to go hiking with me on Saturday after Ashley takes the kids back?"

"Sure! I'm not athletic, but I can try."

He thought and smiled. "Actually, why don't we take a boat out at Eagle Rock? You love the water, and I love fishing. It's supposed to be around sixty-five degrees that day. Sound like a good compromise?"

Evie swirled the water around with a grin. "I'd love that."

"And we can stay at the inn that night."

"Um," she said cautiously, rousing alert from Caleb. "Sarah saw us coming home together, and she said that if I didn't want the town talking about us having a thing, then I shouldn't be coming home with you in your truck like that."

"Is Sarah your mom?"

"No."

"Is the town your mom?"

She giggled. "No."

Then, he asked playfully, "Am I your daddy?"

She laughed. "You most certainly are."

He grew serious again. "What's done is done. People apparently already know I've kissed you, but no one can prove anything. Just because I bring you home in my truck doesn't mean anything. There's nothing in my separation agreement that states I can't bring a friend home in a truck. And Sarah can mind her own damn business. She doesn't own you, and neither does the town. Like Ashley doesn't own me."

Evie paused.

Caleb asked sternly, "You understand me?"

"Yes, I do. Thanks."

He said with a smile, "Goodnight, baby girl."

Their goodnights were over, and Caleb rolled over to go to sleep, daydreaming about being with her. Roughly fifteen miles away, Evie slathered shea butter all over to keep her skin soft for him. It took a bit of extra effort with that damned dry weather. But she would try. As she lay in bed, a negative thought came jousting into her mind. She tried to shove it away, but it was hopeless. Yes, she felt she did have a boyfriend. A secretive one, but eventually it would become whole.

However, she was almost forty-one now, and with the rarity of good men in her life, all of her hope was placed on Caleb with ever staying in love. If he didn't work out, she wasn't sure if she'd ever find someone even half as good as he was. Sadly, Evie would probably give up.

Just wait.

Over on Highway 42, Caleb watched the darkness outside his window creep in as the moon was hidden by the ominous clouds. It was as if the sky was mocking his emotions. Evie stayed through him being divorced. She stayed through him ignoring her. She stayed through his random PTSD episode and all the bullshit going on. But what would happen when he was deployed?

And what would happen if she found out what he did?

All he could do was keep his faith strong in her. But he made a vow to himself that the next time he'd see her, he would try to tell her everything. He couldn't keep it on his chest anymore. The only way he'd ever be able to guarantee she'd never leave him was to tell her what she had wanted to know for almost two years.

And that was why he was trying to escape his shadows.

Chapter Fifteen

January 17th

A week had gone by. It was a day of freezing rain, sheer winds, and graying skies. In that little bungalow Evie was racing around trying to think of what to wear. Even though she had lost a lot of weight, she hadn't really gotten out much to buy new clothes due to her depression that lasted for nearly four months. She mostly had two types of clothing to wear: lounge and work with nothing practical or truly warm for fishing on a lake. Her closet was raided and Teddy slept on the bed. The news said it was supposed to be a whopping forty-five degrees that day, nothing like what it had predicted a week prior. Evie had never handled the cold well since she moved from Alaska.

Well, in Alaska she could be properly dressed for cold weather. Wet snowsuits, rain boots, warm boots, big coats, mittens, scarves. But Missouri was weird. In Missouri, she could wear her big heavy coat in the morning with her mittens and scarves but then be dying of sweat even as she arrived at work. Or it was like trying to guess if it was going to rain or not, and if so, how much rain?

She finally decided on the best thing she could. A pair of comfortable black leggings, a baggy gym shirt, and a pink hoodie. If she zipped the hoodie up and styled it with nice earrings, good hair, and makeup, she wouldn't look so bad. Yet she felt bad. The leggings were stretched out, the shirt hung out lazily below the hoodie, and her shoes were white faux fur-lined boots that made her look like a clown. She opted for a slimmer tank top, but when she went to go check outside for the weather, there was no way in hell that tank top would hold up on a cold lake for hours on end during late winter. And what would Caleb think of her if she showed up wearing earrings and makeup on a day like that?

Evie had to hurry. Rushing around trying to get ready and being picky over her attire drained a lot of time. Not to mention packing up pjs that didn't look too trampy (not that she had any) but didn't make her look like a slob either. And it was almost like another date! She had to look her best, but what the hell would she wear? Once more, she dove into her closet and frantically panicked, throwing everything on the bed. Teddy made the 'mrrp' sound from under a dress. Evie heard his bell jingle when he shook his head out.

As she turned, she saw Teddy crawling out from the dress she wore when Caleb aired up her tire. The dress Pawpaw bought her. Slowly, she left the closet and picked it up, feeling the summery fabric in her hands. It wouldn't fit her now, and the fabric wasn't suitable for the current season or event. However, a smile swept her face, and she thought of Pawpaw.

"I wish you were here, Pawpaw." She turned and sat on the bed, tracing and fumbling the beautiful blue dress with sunflowers on it in between her hands. "You told me to watch out for Caleb. But so far, he's done nothing wrong and has done everything right." She twisted to look out the window, and the pale light washed her body. Soothing. Tranquil.

Peaceful.

"We're dating in a way now, Pawpaw. And he's treated me awfully good. He's helped me with my house, airs up my tires, protects me, open doors for me, cares for me."

And then she broke. She cried, leaning over as the tears dripped onto the dress that lay in her lap. "Saves me."

His truck was coming up the drive, and now it was too late to change. She was going to have to pray that her well-styled hair, cute makeup, and earrings would suffice. Oh, and she grabbed a trendier slouch bag. Evie laid the dress on the bed and hurried to the kitchen to grab some snacks and quickly stuffed them in her purse. She couldn't forget her CBD chews, or her antacids either. She heard Caleb coming up the steps after closing his door and doubt came hard like a tidal wave, crashing into her happy world and destroying it. She felt she looked stupid.

The doorbell rang, and she couldn't turn back now. "Coming!" she called out. Teddy appeared from the bedroom, sat down, and softly closed his eyes up to her. Evie scooped him up and kissed him. "Wish me luck, little man."

She walked to the door, fixed herself once more in the mirror next to it, grabbed her purse, and opened the door. There he was all rugged with his blue jeans, beanie hat and warm sweater. And she felt like she was trying too hard with her makeup, hair, earrings, and beautifully white snow boots.

He smiled underneath his sunglasses with a hand cooly placed on the door frame. He lowered his glasses in a joking fashion. "Hey, cutie. Goin' my way?"

She smirked and checked him up and down. "With you lookin' like that, I'd ride the highway to hell with you."

He gave her a hug, brushed her arms, and looked at her with meaningful eyes.

Once more, he held the truck's door open for her, and she climbed in with a thankful grin. "Thank you."

"You're welcome, princess," he said sweetly. Caleb put her suitcase and bag in the back and laughed, looking at the design on it. "What's with you with cats and flowers?"

"Oh! I actually designed that graphic, and my brother Darren got it turned into a bag for me. Cool, huh?"

"Sounds like you got a nice brother!"

The back door was closed, and he looked, noticing movement out of his peripheral. Sarah was gathering her mail at the end of her driveway but had paused to look at them. He simply waved.

As Caleb got in, he looked in his rearview mirror and started the engine. Evie turned around. "What are you looking at?"

"Sarah was staring at us. Watch what I'm about to do."

He backed up skillfully, turned around, and headed down the driveway. Evie looked forward, seeing that Sarah was still standing there and watching them.

As Caleb pulled down to the end of the road, he took another glance at the broken mail post. "Don't worry. I've still got it in my truck bed, and I'll fix it when we come back tomorrow."

"That doesn't matter to me. I wanna know why you two are having a staring contest."

Before he could even pull out a bit, Sarah started walking over to Evie's side, but Caleb rolled down her window and called, "You're gonna come over here and talk to me."

Evie's body tightened with the thrill of his confidence.

Sarah tried to protest, but Caleb shook his head and beckoned her, "Nope, you're gonna talk to me."

Sarah walked in front of the truck and came to Caleb's side. He rolled down the window. "Evie had a hard week and is not in the mood. What can I do for you?"

"I told her last week that she needs to be careful being seen with you, and she's doing this again."

"Are you her mother?"

"No, but—"

"Are you her boss?"

"No, but—"

Caleb lifted his hand to silence her. "Listen, this poor woman has been through hell these last five months. And I'm the only one making an effort to reach out to her. She fainted from the fucking stress, Sarah. That's some serious shit. She's not eating. Look at her, for fuck's sake!"

Sarah tried to talk, but he sat up right and leaned out his window to her a bit, his deep voice growing in warning, "How would you like it if I told you to stop fucking around with other guys while Joshua is at work?"

Evie clapped her mouth in utter shock. Her eyes went wide.

Sarah tried to answer, but once again Caleb shut her up. "Yeah, thought so. It doesn't feel so good when people know your dirty little secrets and throw them back at your face, does it?"

"You don't know anything about that!" Sarah retaliated.

"Oh yes, I do. You see, I installed a ring camera on Evie's front door while she was at work this week because some fuck head could be stalking her. And I see two different cars pulling up in your driveway, and don't think I don't know who they are, because I do."

Sarah shot back and put her hands on her hips, "That don't mean nothin'!"

"Exactly," he finished.

Sarah withdrew. "People aren't talking about me like they are you guys though."

He raised a brow, the truck's engine still vibrating loudly. "They can, if I tell people. But I'm not gonna, and neither are you, right?"

Sarah sighed.

"RIGHT?"

Evie was completely stunned. Sarah withdrew and agreed not to say anything. Caleb said calmly, "Thank you. I'm tryin' to give this poor girl some company. And so, whatever we do is none of your business. Got it?"

Sarah Jackson had no choice but to agree. Caleb pulled out and began the beautiful drive to Eagle Rock Lake.

Evie slowly pulled her hands away from her mouth, but so many things shocked her. For one, Sarah could be having an affair on such a wonderful man, and two, Caleb installed a camera without her knowing. It could have been considered creepy to some, but not to her. He obviously cared for her safety.

"You installed a ring camera without my knowing?"

"You pissed off?" he said with slight agitation still lingering from confronting Sarah.

"No, not at all. That's insanely nice of you. That actually makes me feel so relieved. Is she really cheating on him?"

Caleb had his eyes fixed on the road. "I don't know and don't care. It's not my business."

They smiled at each other.

"Thank you," Evie said.

He grabbed her hand and kissed it. "You're welcome."

* * *

"Okay, so this is how you hook a live worm."

Evie grimaced but then laughed. "These things smell *so* bad!"

Caleb smiled and began to show her how to hook a worm properly.

The boat was a simple thing, nothing like a speed boat at all, and together they were caught up in the beautiful sounds, smells, colors and life of nature. Eagle Rock Lake brimmed with a subtle fog, just enough to cause a little haze. All around the birds called from the tree lines, and every now and then they would hear the flopping of a fish above the water. That still, lovely, dark water. Evie took the squirmy and slimy thing and laughed.

"Ew! My hands are gonna smell so bad after this."

"That's what washing them in the water is for," Caleb happily replied.

After a few tries, Evie finally got it, and Caleb taught her how to cast a perfect line. She launched it, but it only went about five feet before it slapped in the water. That made Caleb laugh hard, lean over, and slap his leg.

"I suck at this game!" Evie joked.

"You sure do! Try releasing the button a little later."

She reeled it up, and a cold wind made her shiver a bit. Being on the water was much colder than being on land. Once more she cast and onward and outward it sailed, catching the wind before plopping down under. Her anxieties never crossed her mind. She was having too much fun to care.

"I did it! You're a great teacher!"

"Nah." He blushed. "You're a fast learner."

Evie waited. "So now what do we do?"

"Well," he said as he reached for a beer, "we just sit here and wait until the little bobber bobs."

"That's it?"

"More or less, yeah. Want one?"

She shook her head and playfully shoved him. "Oh, that's a *great* idea! Let me just throw myself off the boat right now."

He laughed. "You really are a lightweight, aren't you?"

"Uh, yeah. Embarrassingly so."

He took a swig and then shook the rod. "Nothing embarrassing about that."

Together they sat. And sat. And sat. And just for a little change of pace, they sat some more. Evie smiled at him and scooched closer, in which Caleb then turned and kissed her. "You sure are pretty."

She looked down. "Thanks. I really appreciate that."

He noticed her withdrawing. "You don't think you're pretty?"

"It's not that. I wish I could tell you something that's been on my mind, but I'm afraid you'll think I'm weird."

"I know you're weird. That's why I like you."

She snickered looking up to the sky. "You think I'm weird?"

"Most definitely!" he insisted. He pressed his forehead down to hers, bonking it gently. "I mean, you gotta be some sort of weird to buy that goofy ass funhouse you live in. Buy your cat a whole bed and a laundry basket of toys, read Stephen King books."

Evie held her mouth in amusement.

He encouraged her, "Go ahead. I promise I won't judge. What's up?"

Evie thought and lifted her head to see the pristine view of the lake. Quietly, she began, "A long time ago, well before Pawpaw died, I stopped to pick flowers on the side of 42 for him. He loved those black-eyed Susans. When I got to put them in the back, I got that ad for your company, the one I told you about when you pumped up my tires."

As he looked at her, her face became soft, and her eyes looked downward again. "I thought you were really cute when I saw the ad. And then I saw you again at the general store in town. I didn't put the two faces together because you had a totally different style each time I saw you, but when I saw you at the drugstore, I was really sick with the flu and also missing Pawpaw. Your smile and your kindness were like... I don't know...medicinal."

He listened.

She gave a nervous laugh and continued, "I wanted to ask you out or at least ask your name, but you left before I could get it. I don't think you know how much that simple gesture meant to me. Sure, some people are nice in Laysville, like Hunt, Joey, Myla, and my neighbors. But some can be really judgmental. I was feeling like an outcast because

I was so new. You brought happiness to me when I was at my lowest. I was then going to ask your name and ask you out to say 'thank you', but I saw..."

She looked down.

He asked, "My ring?"

"Yeah. But I was happy for you. It wasn't until I met you at the air pump that everything clicked. And when I saw you didn't have a ring on, I was honestly sad for you. I was worried maybe you were a widower. But when you sent me a friend request that night, I can't lie. I was giddy like a fucking dumb school girl."

He smiled.

"I was so happy that I went into the salon to get my nails done, and that's where I heard from Sandy and Kelly that you were getting divorced." She stopped for a moment, now shifting her glance to the bobber that never bobbed. "I've had a little crush on you for quite a while. So sometimes it's hard and difficult for me to believe when you are around me. I count my blessings with every text, every call, every social media reaction, every kiss, every smile." He rubbed her back and she finished, "Everything."

She had finished talking, and he was without words to say. There was literally nothing he could have said to her that would've sufficed the emotions her confession had stirred within him. "I don't know what to say. I can't believe you've liked me for that long. We're talking almost two years now. What was it that made you like me other than my looks? I don't post much on Facebook, so how did you really start to like me without really knowing me?"

"It was what you posted. The fact you liked the same music I do, how great of a dad you are, how smart you are, the fact you play guitar, how much you get up and go at life despite all the stuff you gotta take care of. Your horses, being a Christian man, and even your job."

"My contracting work gets a lot of girls going," he joked.

"No," she said.

He looked at her.

"Your military work."

Caleb sat upright, rubbed his leg and sighed. "Oh, that thing."

"Is that bad?"

"Kinda. You see, a lot of women have this fantasy about military guys. I get it. A big strong dude going off with a big gun to protect the country. But they don't understand the shit that comes with it. They never do. It's all bells and whistles until the bells crack and the whistling stops. And you being a hopeless romantic Pisces girl, it's a fantasy. I respect it, but it's a fantasy nonetheless. And it's not as glorious as you think it is."

"I never said it was glorious because of it being romantic, Caleb. It's glorious because you're doing something so selfless to protect people like me. You are doing what I can't do. I can't even live on my own without having panic attacks. I get overwhelmed doing a load of dishes. I can't go to the movies anymore because of just being afraid of everything. Hell, I'm surprised I haven't gotten anxious out here on this boat yet. But of course, I'm with you. Yet here you are, leaving your home for up to a year at a time, I'm assuming. You come home and still function."

"Sometimes I don't."

She looked at him firmly. "It's a shame you don't see how amazing you are. I don't give a shit if the bells don't ring and the whistling stops or whatever it is that you said. You're brave. You're selfless. You're strong. You're everything I'm not."

He reeled up his line and cast it again, then took another drink of beer. "You say that until I leave for deployment."

Evie never stopped looking at him as his eyes fixed on the bobber.

"Watch me," she said firmly. That caught his attention. "People get mad at their spouses for the stupidest things because they're selfish. They don't know what they've got, and they take it for granted. They act like everyone is replaceable, and they're not. It's called being faithful, and it's called being proud of someone and loving them regardless."

"Alright. In less than two months, I'm holding you to that," he warned.

"Hold me to it now. I don't care."

They locked eyes and he saw her friendly smile. "If you want me to be, I'll be here when you leave and when you come home."

Evie's bobber went down, and she freaked out, causing Caleb to laugh and urgently tell her what to do.

About five minutes later he took a photo of her holding up a four-pound bass. She was proud of it. The lips felt slimy and weird in her hand, and she felt horrible for holding it out of the water. So, without consulting Caleb, she threw it back.

"Why'd you do that?" he yelled laughing with his arms outstretched. She held her mouth. "Oops! Was I supposed to keep it?"

"What's the point of fishin' if you don't keep what you catch?"

Luckily later on, Caleb caught a nice-sized catfish, and when he taught her how to prep it on land, she didn't like the idea of that one bit. He teased her and went back to scaling it. "I thought you wanted to be brave and strong like me. Afraid of a little ol' fish?"

She whimpered nervously, "I don't like hurting sea life."

He stood up and strutted over to her, leaning his head to the side and then handed her the knife. "It's not sea life. It's lake life." He raised a brow and shrugged. "If I wasn't here and you were starvin', what would you do?"

She did it. And with it she learned how to make a saltwater ice slurry and how to store it properly in the cooler, and even how to bleed it. Afterwards, the cooler was put in the truck bed. He assured Evie that with the cold temperatures, the meat would last until tomorrow easily.

The night carried on with them lying by each other in the motel room, the same one they had previously. While Evie slept on his naked chest after making love, Caleb looked up to the ceiling with his arms behind his head. He couldn't get out of his mind what she had said, how passionate she was towards him. He was unsure if it was even real, for how could anyone, any *human* truly be that invested in someone? It was difficult for him to grasp the concept that a woman had liked him for almost two years, and she had turned down every suitor that came her way. He only knew that because she regularly posted up how frustrated she was that men wouldn't leave her alone on Facebook.

"Evie?" he asked quietly.

"Hmmm?" she cooed with her eyes blissfully closed. Her hand rested lovingly across his heart.

"Why did you always turn down other guys who came after you?"

"Just because there are plenty of fish in the lake, doesn't mean they're all a great catch."

He snickered and smiled, and it made her smile as well.

She fell asleep with her soft snoring. The snoring that he didn't mind. Caleb reached over to his phone on his nightstand and brought up the app for her ring camera to see if there had been any action. There was something two hours ago, but it was Deputy Hunt doing a little look around with his flashlight. Checking on things. Other than that, there was absolutely nothing. Perhaps no one was stalking her, or there were two different people in on it. One could have seen her at O'Malley's, and the other could have seen him kiss her at her house.

He put his cell phone on the nightstand and turned off the lamp to go to sleep.

But his cell phone lit up.

The app detected movement.

He grabbed his phone and opened the app to see a black sedan parked down at her mailbox at the end of her driveway. With the blue light blinding his face, he turned down the brightness not to wake Evie. He narrowed his eyes and studied it. It only stayed for a brief moment before it left.

It could've been someone stopping on the road for a moment.

But that next morning, he saw the car had appeared again at 7:00 a.m. doing the same exact thing.

Chapter Sixteen

The next morning was brisk and chilly, and Caleb woke with Evie snuggled up behind him. She had her arm wrapped around his body and her face smushed into his back. She was still snoring a bit. While she slept, Caleb rolled it over in his mind about what he saw. There was no choice in the matter about telling her, because he knew damn well not to. Evie was anxious enough and telling her that would only build her fears of being alone. Rather, he thought about who it was. He picked up his cell phone and played it multiple times, trying to see the make and model of the car. He was good with cars, having grown up fixing them.

Now with Evie being asleep and the sun shining in, turning up the brightness wouldn't disturb her. He turned up the brightness all the way and saw exactly what it was. It was a 2020 black Nissan Sentra, and only one person he knew drove that car.

Ashley's sister, Breanne.

It infuriated him. He was straight up fucking *pissed off*.

Caleb gently lifted Evie's hand, got dressed, and went outside to get in his truck to make a phone call.

While he sat, a nearby family came out of their room and made their way to their car. Family trip of some sort.

Breanne answered, "What do you want?"

Caleb said calmly, "Hey, there was an accident last night that involved a black Nissan Sentra. I wanted to call and see if you were okay, but I didn't know if that would be appropriate."

"Wasn't me."

"Okay, that's good. I got worried because I know you usually go out to the bar on Saturday nights and drink."

"I was out last night but wasn't drinking."

"Oh, where did you go? Anything fun?"

"Why the fuck are you calling me?"

He smiled and looked out the window. "I wanna know why you're stalking Evelyn Morgan."

"Who?" she snapped back.

"Don't be a bitch, Breanne. I saw your car come by her house *twice*. You stopped down at her driveway once last night and once this morning. I saw you on the Ring camera."

Breanne sighed loudly. "God, you *are* a fucking psychopath! You installed a Ring camera on that poor girl's door? Does she even know? You see, this is exactly why you became a fucking creep with Ashley!"

He stayed calm. "You're not denying it."

"Listen, fuckwit, you can't prove it was me."

"I can by your dashcam. And it's not gonna look good in court if you're stalking her. You're Ashley's sister, you know."

"I ain't givin' you my dashcam. You can go fucking rot and die overseas."

"Is that supposed to make me cry? 'Cause it won't."

"I'm hanging up on you."

"Listen," Caleb interjected, "If you won't give me your dashcam, I'm going to report you to the police as a stalking suspect. Evie's protected under anti-stalking laws, and you were probably the one who followed her and I at O'Malley's. She's deactivated her Facebook page because it turned into harassment. That's some serious shit, Breanne. You're gambling with someone's mental and emotional well-being. Because her mailbox is so far from the house and it's just a side view, I can't get the license plate. So, you better fess up and make it easier on yourself or give me your dash cam footage."

"It won't show nothing."

"Well, good." He smirked. "Because if you delete a sequence of footage that happened around that time, Hunt will be able to detect possible tampering with evidence. And that's a no-no."

She went quiet.

"Be honest with me, Breanne. My life is already fucked up enough. Do you understand that? You are screwing with the *one* good goddam good thing I have now. Do you understand? Do you? Because of this shit that you probably caused, I'm at risk of losing my kids even more than I already have. My case is going to be even harder now because of you and I could lose my kids completely!"

"They shouldn't be with you anyway."

Caleb stopped talking. His body tightened.

"You're a fucking emotional, unstable abusive fuckhead who messed up *my* sister badly. No one cares about you. This isn't about what happened with the chair or you breaking my dad's fucking arm. You got thrown out of the bar because you couldn't handle your alcohol, like you can't handle your emotions."

"What?" he hollered back. "I didn't get thrown out. I left willingly when Hunt showed up!"

"It doesn't matter!" she retaliated. "You did nothing but drink when you got home from your last deployment. You did nothing to help her take care of the kids!"

That was a lie.

"You don't deserve your kids, Caleb. I hope the courts take them away, before Olivia ends up dead in a fucking ditch somewhere and Zack is found choked to death because of your so-called PTSD episodes!"

He went to hang up. He held the phone away and his thumb hovered over that red, circle button. His heart rate was through his head, and his lips were stiff and dry. The anger came in throttles, and he curled his toes inside his shoes.

Evie.

Don't hang up.

Before he acted, he remembered all those beautiful things she had said to him, all those times she faced Sandy and Sarah head on with her concerns and still was a kind soul.

He took a breath and sighed. His hand relaxed on the steering wheel and then rested on his lap. He slowly brought the phone to his ear. He said softly but strongly, "All this shit you're telling me? It doesn't matter. You can tell me all these horrible things, but I can't change your mind. I don't need to change your mind, and I don't care to. You're stuck in your way with your sister, and that's fine. But I'm calling the police and you're going to be investigated for stalking."

He hung up. Caleb leaned over and rubbed his fingers through his hair. He felt utterly alone. Alcohol was his only friend when he had come home that time, other than his children and occasionally his dog and horses. During those times, Ashley had become an absolute nightmare. All of her needs that he could never meet, all of her wants he could never reach, and all the times he overslept but never felt rested at all. One time, she had slammed the door in his face during an argument because he had a moment and blanked out, forgetting where he was.

He had stayed there for an hour staring at the door without knowing it.

When she opened it, he greeted her with a smile and went to hug her, except she had her bags packed and told him she was staying with her parents for the night. She never explained to him why, only that he was a negligent maniac who needed therapy, and it wasn't her responsibility to explain it to him.

Evie.

"Caleb?"

He jerked upright and looked out the window, and there was her sweet face all bundled up in his hoodie. He rolled down the window. She asked, "Hey. Are you... are you...okay?"

"Yeah, I'm fine. Are you?"

"I'm great, but you're not fine. I saw you leaning over with your hands on your head when I came out." He opened the door, and she looked at him seriously. She backed away so he could walk to the room, and she followed.

"Did something happen?" she asked as she closed the door once they were inside.

"I just needed a minute."

Evie quietly folded her arms and her eyes glimmered, and brows raised in worry. "Another episode?"

"Yeah," he stammered. "Yeah, something like that." Then he erected his head and looked at her. "Let's get breakfast."

For once, Evie didn't pry. Although she battled within her heart to ask him about it, she refrained. All she did was approach him and hug him hard. Her body pressed against him, and she nuzzled her face in his strong chest.

Wait.

Her eyes opened wide.

She listened.

His heartbeat was fast and strong.

Evie pulled away and rubbed his arms, looking lovingly into his eyes. He wasn't looking back at her. She smiled with her lips closed. "Come here to the bed with me. I'll order delivery, room service, or something!" she said in a chipper tone.

"Nah, let's go out," he replied.

"Caleb? I want to stay in bed with you."

"But we were supposed to go hiking around the lake today." He pulled away from her and got his wallet. "Get dressed so we can make the breakfast hour at the diner."

"No," she said sternly.

He lifted his body from leaning over the table and turned to her, simply staring in disbelief.

She shook her head. "I'm not leaving."

"Okay, then I'll go and bring you something back."

Evie approached him and he stepped away. She tried to grab his arm. "Caleb, please."

He yanked his arm away, trying to be calm. "Please," he shuddered hotly while holding his head. "Don't fucking touch me."

"Your heart is racing out of your chest. It's okay. We can stay here and be quiet."

"Nope," he said stubbornly.

She watched him try to grab his cell phone, and she had had enough. Evie reached out and grabbed him hard, pulled him around, and forced him to sit on the bed. He tried to stand up but she straddled his lap and hugged him hard. *Very* hard. "I'm here. Rest."

"I've got work to do later. I can't have my neighbor do my work today. You can't call Instacart and have them water your horses."

His body shook. But hers was calm.

She assured sweetly, snuggling into his neck, "But you can rest for five minutes."

He stayed.

Evie felt his arms wrap around her. She smiled in adoration. "You're okay. You don't need to talk. You don't need to explain anything. I can be here and hold you. This is your moment, not mine."

He nearly cried. He nearly broke.

Nearly.

A few minutes later, Caleb was lying on his side with a pillow under his arm, staring at the minutes clicking on by on the clock. Evie turned it around. He tried to pick up his phone, and she took it and hid it under her pillow. Doing things like that was how she coped with her own mania. She stroked his hair and allowed her hand to cherish the beauty of his strong neck, the prickles of the shorter hair at the base of his scalp, and the strong curves of his muscled shoulder.

He was so beautiful to her. She watched with a marveling eye as her fingertips pressed into his muscles, gliding down his tattoos. It was like she did when they first made love.

After ten minutes, she snuggled up behind him, holding him all over again.

He broke the silence with a deep voice, "I've never been held like this until you."

She squeezed harder in an affectionate smile. "You're cuddly. I could do this all day."

Caleb felt his heart slowing down and he closed his eyes. A soft smile crossed his lips. "Thank you."

Evie listened to his breathing. She listened to the depth of his voice. It was rich like a chamber of masculinity that she could lose herself in, but there was so much exhaustion and fatigue sensed in it. She inched closer. "You're welcome. I ordered some delivery for us. Let's rest for a little while. When you're feeling better, we can go to the lake and hike all you want."

"I know you hate hiking. I'm sorry."

"I do," she said with a chuckle. "I'll probably complain a little bit about my legs being sore and my feet hurting. And probably the cold and probably the wind. But I'll try."

He giggled. "That's all I can ask for."

She added, "And I'll probably get afraid of no bathroom access and minimal cell phone service. And worried that if something happens, we're gonna be too far from the exit."

He laughed lowly with his eyes closed. "Wanted to add a case of agoraphobia on top of your claustrophobia as well as your acrophobia and then your misophonia?"

Evie sat straight up. "How do you know about misophonia? Hardly anyone knows about that."

He rolled onto his back and beamed at her. "Do you know how many times I've seen you complain on Facebook about restaurants having TVs AND music going? That's why I offered O'Malley's. It's a bit quieter. Or how much you couldn't stand when your neighbor's dog barked? Or how about the fact that a simple radio playing too loudly overhead at a grocery store will send you flying for the exit?"

Evie frowned.

He elbowed her leg playfully. "You kinda throw out all your stuff on social media."

"In my defense, I've learned to actually feel comforted by Joshua's dogs barking."

He raised a brow at her.

"Okay, I kinda hate it still."

"More like you hate it *sometimes*. Your tolerance for things is very dependent on your mood, I've noticed."

Evie frowned again and regretfully said, "When you listed out all of my things, it made me feel like I'm a head case."

He sighed. "Sudden trauma will do that to you. You've been through that a lot."

Evie looked down at him. Seeing his smile softened her further. "Do you think I'll ever be able to be normal?"

Caleb sat straight up and pulled her close to him. With his head rested on hers, he embraced her gingerly. "Let me tell you something someone told me. And I respect this person a lot." He paused to look up at the ceiling in reflection. "They said, 'but maybe on an emotional or psychological level, we can heal. I think we can. I know we can.'"

He had quoted the very thing she had said to him the night of her anxiety attack when she was massaging his hands.

But it wasn't as easy as she had thought it to be. There was no backing out now. After a good, hearty breakfast, she was strapped up and bundled up for a four-mile hike. How she was going to do it was beyond her. The moment they arrived at the trail head, she had instant regrets. Yet Caleb wasn't going to let her fears pull her away. He could see it in her eyes that her agoraphobia was strong, and every move she made displayed her disdain and regret.

He closed the truck's door. "You know, it's weird to me. You hate excessive noise and chaos, so you avoid going pretty much anywhere these days. But then you get fearful of being alone or trapped where there's quiet."

She met him at the front of the truck with her arms crossed. Nervously, she looked down. "I know. It doesn't make sense, but I can't help it."

He walked back around and got in the back of the truck, messing with something. Evie looked around and slowly turned to the lake. The rocks at the water's edge were white and beautiful, lying in large slats and some boulder shaped. Off further to the right, the edge disappeared beyond wild, wiry shrubs. The local heron and Canadian geese were co-mingling without troubles, and the cool breeze kissed her cheeks. The fog hadn't let up much. He came back to the front and saw her calm face gazing out at the still water.

"Ready?" he asked.

She turned and saw he had a rucksack on. She chirped, "Nice day for ruckin', ain't it?"

"You know it! Come on, pretty. Let's get you lost in nature and back to your roots again."

My roots, Evie thought.

Yes. Memories of Alaska. Memories of exploring the woods across from her home in Anchorage as a little girl and staying out until the aurora came shining. Memories of dog sled rides in rural and desolate mountains just for fun.

They began the trail, and Evie stopped at a wooden sign that read, "Great Missouri Birding Trail."

They continued on the well-paved trail that was immediately swallowed by snow-capped trees and decaying bark from trees that had fallen years ago. She loved how the fiery hue of the sun's rays illuminated the snow on them. Squirrels ran amok every which way, and cardinals called from the canopy above. A woodpecker went berserk against a tree. The gray and dead tone of the forest floor was saddening to look at, but glancing up changed everything.

Evie asked casually, "What's in the sack?"

"Supplies. Food, water, first-aid kit."

"Oh, that's nice," she answered with a smile.

"Guns, ammo, grenade launcher, a few Navy SEALs, a tank."

She busted out laughing. "What? No F-18? I'm disappointed in you."

He smiled at her and chuckled. He said, "Think about nothing at all. If you focus on the beauty around you and the mission at hand, it'll go by faster than you think."

Only in her dreams.

Not even thirty minutes later, she sat down on a mercifully placed bench and Caleb let her rest. He began using his binoculars to look at certain waterfowls that were spotted through the trees and in a little marshland area. The cattails were dried, brown stalks jutting up from the frozen wetlands.

Evie sighed. "I can't do this."

Caleb was apathetic. "Alright. You can walk back on your own and wait for me in the truck."

"What?" she asked. How dare he treat her like that after what she just did for him that morning!

He turned over his shoulder. "Baby, it's fine. Go ahead and walk back and wait for me in the truck. I'll be about thirty-five minutes."

"Walk back...alone?"

"What? Ya afraid of the squirrel gang?"

"N-no, but I can't walk back alone."

"Well," he said, approaching her, "you've got two choices. Either finish this with me or go back without me. I'm sorry, but remember what I said? You can't sit here and fester in your paranoia. At some point, you gotta make a move."

She grew saddened and downtrodden.

Caleb approached and sat next to her and became serious. "Listen Evie, I'm not gonna baby you. That's not how I work. Unfortunately, there's no way to test the waters of embracing and facing your fears without facing them head on."

"What if I get exhausted and can't finish? I'm not athletic like you are," she said in despondency.

"Then I'll carry you."

She laughed. "You can't be-"

She looked at him. He *was* serious.

He rubbed her back. "It's up to you. You're either with me or without. But I'm getting up to go. I want to finish this hike. I love hiking here, so I'm going."

And he stood up and walked away, leaving her behind. She lifted her head and watched him walk, getting smaller in size as he made his way up a gentle curving hill. She looked back to the left where there was emptiness, loneliness, uncertainty. Then back to the right where he was, so sure of the path and the road ahead.

Let him lead you, she thought.

Evie sprung up and ran after him. "Wait! Caleb, I'm coming with you!"

Caleb smiled. Without turning his head, he stood still and called back to her, "I thought you were gonna stay, kitten."

"Well, I thought I'd better come along. Just in case you needed protection."

He nudged her in play. And she did it back.

They ventured off on that long hike. Caleb let her sit and rest when needed, and he would untie his sack to give her water when she thirsted. It amazed her how he never took a drink, not once. Instead, he'd use that time to observe the trees, listen to and watch the birds overhead, take pictures, record videos, and enjoy the silence. Over each old bridge they'd walk, and he noticed that as the time went on, she got a bit more daring with stepping down to the streams to touch the cold water.

To touch the wild waters was precious to her. Savoring each clear droplet in her palms that reflected the canopy above stirred her child-hood up like a hot bowl of chicken noodle soup. Caleb later helped her step onto a larger log and held her hand as she balanced on it, walking the whole thing. He'd pull down a branch for her to pick the prettiest pinecone she saw, and he taught her properly how to climb a different tree, even though she was too weak to do it.

That was until he hoisted her up.

Evie clutched the trunk nervously. But she wasn't that high up. Her nerves eventually melted into childlike laughter, and she asked him to take a picture of her as she sat upon a sturdy branch. Throughout the trail, he pointed out certain birds to her and which ones he had hunted before. While Caleb photographed the birds, he saw the world through God's eyes.

And she saw the world through his.

Memories had been made.

And fears had been conquered.

Evie painfully walked the last leg of the trail to the truck where she rolled onto the concrete to let her back rest. Her back was burning in aching pain, and she twisted this way and that to stretch her lumbar. Her upper back begged for an adjustment, and lying on the pavement gave her as much relief as she could get.

The ride back to Laysville was filled with conversation of all sorts, and Evie completely decided to let it go about asking about his Navy job. It no longer mattered.

The rest of the day was filled with Caleb taking her to the hardware store and teaching her about certain things. He let her pick out paint for her kitchen, and hours were spent tearing down the old wallpaper and putting up that fresh soft and pale green coat of paint. They sat on the floor against the cabinets together, still enjoying each other's company over freshly delivered pizza.

And Caleb didn't care what others thought or what they'd say. He stayed that night.

However, dread and worry forged in Evie's heart as he slept by her.

Her back was burning with pain. Her muscles ached to a point of breaking her emotional threshold. She wanted to cry. Her stomach felt heavy and tired. Her fingers and hands were stiff, and her feet felt like they had been crushed by an anvil. Her head throbbed. Her body craved comfort and relief. All her muscles felt like they were bursting through her skin, and her legs ached so badly that she couldn't keep them still. She longed to stretch them hard but was too tired to do so.

She had been more physically active in one day than she had been in three months. Losing nearly eighty-five pounds didn't mean anything if she wasn't strong or used to moving so much. After he stopped talking to her, she had stopped her Zumba and Pilates work and stopped eating as much. Having a desk job didn't make it easier.

Her heart was tormented. There was no way in hell she was going to be able to keep up with a man who had two young kids, horses, a lot of yard work to do, and who loved to hike and be active like him.

Evie rolled away from him and cried quietly into her pillow, clutching her teddy bear for comfort.

She wasn't built for it. She simply wasn't. No one could help her now. She was in too deep, and there was no way out.

Chapter Seventeen

Evie had kept her concerns to herself, vowing to become stronger. Every day she went to work, she'd get up a little earlier to force herself to make breakfast instead of lazing off with a bowl of cereal. They were hard habits she had to relearn all over again. Life had been a nonstop up and down. One minute she was flying ahead in life with good habits that stuck, and then those manic highs crashed her into a concrete wall with a depressive episode.

Maybe, just maybe, she was in one of those doubtful, depressive plunges.

She perked up. "Get it together!" she said merrily to herself. She jostled her vegetables in the pan before pouring the mixed eggs in. A fresh bowl of fruit was on the table nearby. But her nerves peaked. "It's okay, Evie. Take it one day at a time. You'll get used to it. It's the life you always wanted. You can't get afraid now." She looked at a picture on the fridge of her and Caleb at the lake together. She nodded to affirm herself. "Take the trail one step at a time."

A knock came at her door and Teddy hurried over to it with a meow.

"Coming!" she called as she turned off the burner.

It was Deputy Hunt. Evie tied her robe together a bit more. Not that she was naked, but she wasn't wearing a bra underneath her pajamas. She opened the door excitedly. "Good morning, Hunt! What can I do for you?"

"I was in the area and thought I'd stop by and ask you if you've seen the Sentra out here recently."

Evie shuddered from the nasty cold that came swooping in. She asked in confusion, "Sentra? What's a Sentra?"

"A Nissan Sentra?" he asked.

"Come in."

Evie backed away to let him come in and she offered him coffee, which he declined politely. "Have you noticed the black Nissan Sentra outside your house recently?"

She sighed looking to the left and shrugged her shoulders, then shook her head with her lips tightened. "I literally don't know what you're talking about."

He lifted his head, adjusted his vest, and shifted his weight. "Caleb told me that this specific car was seen numerous times at your house. And he's sent me videos of this car being parked out front. You haven't noticed?"

She shook her head nervously. "N-no. No. I haven't noticed. Caleb doesn't let me have access to the Ring camera because he's worried I'll become anxious or obsessive with it. Maybe he's right."

"And no one's come to your door or anything?"

"No." Evie looked down. "So, someone *is* stalking me?"

"More or less, yes. It seemed so."

Evie grew alert. "*Seemed* so?"

"Yep," he said. "Caleb had a concern that it was Breanne, Ashley's sister. We tried to review the dashcam footage, but since there was so much there, it automatically deleted the footage. Yet after Caleb confronted her, he hasn't seen it appear on the camera since. So, it seems you *were* being stalked."

Evie crossed her arms. "I have no idea why Breanne would want to watch my house. That is some serious crazy-ass shit. Do I have reasons to be concerned?"

"Nah, not now. I noticed you deactivated your Facebook though, and it's still gone. How are you supposed to get local gigs for your work if you're not on there anymore?"

"I couldn't take it any longer. And I don't miss it. I miss seeing Caleb's posts and stuff. But it doesn't matter if I get to see him like I do."

Hunt smiled. "You really love him, don't you?"

She grinned and nodded in reflection, pulling her hair behind her ear sheepishly. "Yeah, I do." They stood in silence with each other. Evie slapped her arms at her sides. "Welp, I gotta get ready for work."

"Yeah, I better get goin' to. It was nice seein' ya again!"

They hugged, and Hunt left.

Evie was on her way to work driving southbound on the interstate. She passed by that little clunky gas station full of wonderful memories, but having to look out the passenger window to see it made her look in her passenger mirror, and she saw a black sedan moving off a bit to the shoulder behind her.

Her heart rate picked up. As she accelerated to the full speed limit, so did the car. For a moment, she slowed down, and the car made a motion like it was going to pass her erratically. It veered off into the left lane without using a signal, gunned up right next to her, and slowed down and got behind her again. Evie turned on her signal and changed lanes, thinking the driver wanted to pass. They mimicked every move.

As panic rose in her throat, she tried to calm down and picked up the phone to dial the highway patrol. But the moment she did, they backed off, slowed down, and signaled they were getting off an exit. She put her phone back down.

It was apparently a stupid driver. Caleb was right. Knowing that someone *was* following her made her more nervous and anxious. She took a deep breath and calmed down.

Until a loud roaring engine came flying up on her left, scaring her half to death. That truck was so fast she didn't even have time to react. She was going to let it pass her, until it swerved directly into her lane. She screamed in fear and moved off the shoulder and felt the bumps rumble loudly under her car. The white truck swerved far off the left shoulder, and the moment she tried to regain her position on the highway, it crossed over into her lane again.

Evie had no choice but to brake, but the truck sped up in front of her without signaling and brake checked her. She tried to calm down. But then, she got pissed. She observed that should she need to, the shoulder would be safe enough to run off onto.

She slowed down and called the highway patrol to report it. While on speaker, she slammed on her brakes when the truck almost came to a complete stop. Evie screamed hard as her stomach went into her throat. She pulled off to the right, but her car skidded due to the gravel. She couldn't stop, and she slid, wavering into the shallow ditch. Luckily, her just car went off the highway. She didn't wreck at all.

The truck was gone.

It was a white Chevy Silverado. And she breathed hard while the troopers had been dispatched both to help her and lead the chase. While she waited for the troopers, she went to call for Caleb until she realized something.

She was fine.

Completely fine.

Evie pulled her fingers through her hair and sighed in a smile. "I did it. I really did it! I handled that like a fucking boss!"

She clapped her hands. She knew the asshole, lunatic driver would be caught. Like Caleb said, everything would be okay. She screamed happily as if she had won the lottery. No longer did she feel like a frightened victim. The relief of playing it cool and keeping her composure was all she had ever needed.

The trooper came to help her within five minutes, and she filed the report on both the black car and the truck.

All signs pointed to Alan Moffet being the culprit, but after the suspect was arrested and the plates were run, she received a call saying that it wasn't who she thought it was. Just a jerk driver.

So much had happened to her in a few short years. At least they felt like they were short years.

It seemed like only yesterday she was picking those flowers on the side of the highway for Pawpaw. She had even fallen in love with a man she believed would never take a chance on her. The long drive to the city left Evie with a lot to ruminate on, and for some strange reason, the situation with the maniac driver left her feeling something strong instead of something frightening.

The lovely Dutch windmill on her right and the rumbling of numerous semis made her think of that cherished day all over again, the day he aired up her tire. It all started with a flyer. The butterfly effect was downright crazy in her life. A while ago, she was being scolded by her boss for not having enough projects done on time. And now she had been a hit with the Laysville residents with all of her local work. Her work at the café with both advertising and menu designing proved to be excellent when Joey's numbers doubled in a month. Not to mention the salon had hired her to redesign their sign as well as their menu, and so many people raved about it on the local discussion page.

That was well before she signed off and things had taken an ugly turn.

But now, with the radio playing and the singing full in her lungs, she thought that maybe she would open her Facebook again. It had been well over a week, and perhaps the mental break was worth it.

Her car stereo buzzed, and her display showed that Caleb texted her a video. There was no way she was going to watch it though. She wasn't that kind of driver. She'd wait until work, but it made the drive all the more annoying with the anticipation.

Evie arrived at work and inched into a parking spot that was barely big enough for her little sedan. She scoffed, "I hate when people can't park within their own lines."

She looked at the time and saw she had fifteen minutes to spare. Glee! She picked up her phone and watched Caleb's video.

He was sitting in a workshop of some sort, and she could see a truck behind him. He had his acoustic guitar on his lap and a nice can of Diet Coke on the table. He was so handsome in his hoodie and sweatpants. He said, "Good mornin', baby! I know you have a long week ahead of you with your presentations and stuff."

Her eyes twinkled.

"I wanted to wish you luck, and in case if you're stressed or anxious, I thought I'd play you a little song."

When he strummed a chord to check the tuning, Evie jumped because a loud howling came from off the camera. She laughed hard!

Caleb reached down and patted something off the camera. "Quiet, Charlie. This is a solo project! There aren't any backup vocals here!"

Evie smiled. Love filled her body as she realized then and there that Charlie had gone everywhere with Caleb. He was in nearly every photo of him, even in his truck, and in every video when he was on work sites.

He must've been a therapy dog.

Caleb began again nervously, yet cutely, "I'm the greatest singer in the world, so you know."

She snickered. He was so damn charming when he was playful. She adored this side of him.

He strummed and sang, Brooks and Dunn's "Brand New Man."

No amount of restraint could contain her laughter. Evie squeezed her face and laughed so hard she about choked! It was one of her favorite songs, and the lyrics were perfect in that moment in their lives. Joy absolutely consumed her as she danced and sang along. It didn't mean anything to her that he was off pitch and a little off time. His deep country accent and darling smile were all that he needed to charm her.

Then she hit the harmonies when they came in on the second verse.

Evie threw her head back and let it all out with happiness. She sang loudly, happily, and giggled with everything he did. There was no way in hell she could possibly be afraid of her presentations now.

Or even life for that matter.

He was in her corner. He was standing behind her, beside her, and leading her all at the same time. Tears came of both delight and comfort.

That dopamine rush hit like a metric ton of cocaine and ecstasy all at once without the lethal effects. Caleb was one intense drug, one that left her with no ill side effects. Just pure good things.

After the song was over, he simply smiled and said, "Love you, baby. You got this."

The video ended, and she giggled. She had tried to control her emotional side a bit since being with him, but no girl in her right mind would've been stoic after that.

She called him, and he answered. She chuckled and said, "You have no idea how much you made me smile! You're an absolute man!"

He laughed and looked at his workers getting the sander ready. "Well, you're an absolute woman! I recorded that a while ago. Normally you jump on my messages in an instant. I started to feel like I was no longer your number one guy."

She laughed at his sarcasm. It was his cute way of flirting. "You're always going to be my number one guy. Especially with those amazing singing skills."

"Yeah, I meant to tell you. I'm leavin' for Nashville next week. Dolly and I got a date planned for a record deal."

Evie snickered, holding her knuckles to her face. "Tell her I said 'hello', I love her music, and that I'll happily share."

He turned and rolled his head in laughter. "Ah, you got me on that one!"

They both laughed. Caleb's workers started looking at him. He had been acting a bit differently those days, and they definitely weren't complaining.

"In all seriousness," Evie said, "thank you. That was so incredibly sweet of you to send me that."

He smiled and put his hand on his hip, looking down at the floor. He idly scooted a paint pan with his foot. "You're welcome. How are you today?"

"I am sorry I didn't respond quicker. I was driving."

"You're alright! Besides, if any other guy messes with you, tell 'em what I do and he'll leave you alone."

"That you're in the Navy?"

He laughed. "Nah, that I'll take a sander to his face."

Her mouth widened and she shouted back with hilarity, "You're a brutal man, Caleb. Can I paint his face with latex-based paint?"

"Oh my God, you're learning! I'm so proud of you!" he laughed back.

"Yep! But back to your question. I got here fine. I think you'd be proud of me."

"I'm always proud of you, but why would you say that?"

"I had a fucked-up altercation with a few weird road ragers on the way to work and ended up having to pull over on the shoulder. I skidded a bit, but I'm okay and handled it like a boss!"

His throat tightened. "What the fuck? I mean, I'm proud of you for handling it, but are you alright? Did you call the cops?"

OUR SMALL TOWN SCARS

"Yeah, I did. Highway patrol got a hold of them. I thought the truck was Alan, but it wasn't."

"What was the other one?"

"A black sedan. They kept wanting to stay behind me but eventually they got off on an exit."

He took a breath on the other side. She heard it.

"Caleb, it's okay. Hunt told me about the black Nissan you've been seeing on the camera."

"I'm sorry. I should've told you."

"It's okay. But...I haven't noticed anything. And I think I'm alright. You having a good day at work?"

"I'm having a great day!" He walked out on the front porch and sat down. "You make my days a bit better. I can't stop thinking about what you did for me at the inn the other night."

He paused. She listened. Then he slowly said, "I never got to thank you for that."

"You actually did. Besides, that little video was all I needed."

He smiled on the other end, and so did she. "I better get goin'," he said. "I got—"

She smiled. "I know. A lot of work to do."

"Yep! You got it, girl."

Her smile never left her lips. "I love you."

He rubbed the back of his neck. He remembered when it came to him that telling her he loved her could've been a bad idea. He had done it so fast and without thinking at all. But maybe he wasn't thinking.

Maybe this time, Caleb was just feeling.

Without any further hesitation, he said, "I love you too, Evie."

* * *

"Good morning, everyone!" Evie announced.

She stood in front of a room of at least twenty people, and they were not going to be an easy crowd. The client of the day was a locally owned fashion brand that touted sustainable fabrics and garment making. The founder and main executive was none other than Bailey Bones, a socialite and debutante of the entire Kansas City Metro with a killer surname moniker. Her rich daddy was investing over a million dollars in her company, and Bailey was looking for a company to not only design their logo and marketing designs, but also host the release party for her debut collection.

This was Evie's biggest client ever. If she played her cards right, her work would be shown on a website that would host hundreds of thousands of visits a month, and her logo would be displayed on the catwalk at KC Fashion Week in which Jamboree was hosting the music and the lighting flair for.

Bailey was a younger woman, about twenty-five years old. As she sat on a chair, she felt her hands up on her slick ponytail. She wore it like Arianna Grande, but her hair was jet-black and glossy like an onyx mirror. Even though Bailey was younger, she dressed like a full-blown businesswoman. With a tangerine sweater dress and large gold hoop earrings, her white boots showed off she was both business and fun. Bailey was about to be the first successful Black fashion designer in Kansas City, and Evie was bound and determined to contribute to that success.

Evie's confidence shone like a diamond. "I'm very honored to have been selected for the opportunity to demonstrate how I can contribute to DVine. I have prepared five samples of the work that I can provide, each with their own style and flair. Given the collection colors, I tried to adhere to those golden and orange tones."

She passed out the folders, and Bailey took one and passed the others along.

Evie clicked to turn on the sleek projector. The lights were dimmed, and she gave a glance to Mr. Perry, who remained expressionless.

Evie couldn't care less. She wasn't trying to impress him. The fashionable Bailey Bones was her goal.

The screen showcased a beautiful logo of a blonde copper palette and abstract leaves with clear lines as the background. The name "DVine" was simply stylized in solid white serif font with the D and V capitalized, and the I was dotted with a beautiful leaf that had another little baby leaf out below it.

Bailey's brows went up, and she gave a surprised nod. "I'm feelin' this, girl. Give me more."

Evie smiled. "I'm very glad to hear that! Every brand needs to have a logo that people can correlate them with. With Chanel, it's the reversed C's. With Dolce and Gabbana, it's the large D and G. Nike has their infamous swoosh. You were very crafty in utilizing a capital D with a simple leaf inside of it, and so I wanted to pay homage and respect to that for brand continuity."

The first presentation carried on, and it stirred numerous murmurs, sounds of pens scribbling, and smiles. Not once did Evie's heart rate elevate. Not once did she panic or feel dizzy. She ignored Mr. Perry and focused straight on her client, her target. Her mission.

After ten minutes, Evie took a breath. "Now, we're going to move on to my second presentation."

Mr. Perry spoke up, "I hope you realized that our client is a *trendy* young girl, not an editorial fashion company."

Evie didn't even need to compose herself this time. She was already calm. "I would appreciate all feedback to be reserved for Jamboree's prospective client and not for anyone else."

But Bailey Bones held her hand up. "I don't wanna see anymore."

Evie breathed calmly.

Mr. Perry shot her a look.

Miss Bones smiled. "I've already made my decision. I'm in love with this first one. You got me hook, line, and sinker."

All the way home, Evie absolutely gushed to Caleb on her car's speaker phone. He was beyond thrilled for her and eagerly took time away from his work to listen. She couldn't stop talking about how she singlehandedly got Jamboree their biggest client to date.

"I mean, I'm so freaking happy!"

"You should be! You did all of this hard work on your own! And you know what you need to do now?"

"Celebrate!" she said.

"Well, yeah! But why don't you go to the salon to let Sandy and Kelly hear *all* about it?"

"You're terrible," she laughed.

"Damn straight! Hell, I'll pay for it. I'll send you some money. Go out and tell the hens at the salon I paid for it."

"Wait, why would you wanna do that?"

"Because if you were to be active on Facebook, you would see that every-body knows. It's no secret anymore, and I'm so damn proud of you and to be *with* you. So go ahead and show the world how much I care about you."

She paused. "Wait, are you serious right now? You really want me to do that?"

"Yep. I'm about as sure as adding an extra block of cream cheese to a casserole dish to make it better."

Evie laughed again.

She looked around at the cars passing her by on the interstate. There was so much goodness in her life now that sometimes it felt overwhelm-ing. She took a deep breath and nodded. "You got it, daddy."

"Hey," he snapped.

Oh shit. I thought he liked that? she thought.

"Don't you be callin' me those sexy things when I'm at work and can't have you." He glanced around to make sure no one was watching him talk outside.

She playfully giggled. "Yes, daddy."

"I hate you," he replied with a laugh.

Within the hour, Evie strutted in to the salon and saw Myla there at her empty station reading a magazine. Kelly and Sandy *were* there. And all of the ladies that were getting their blowouts, pedicures, perms and more, all turned and glared at her.

There Evelyn Morgan stood. Her first time back at the salon in almost four months. She lifted her chin and smiled to everyone. The hum of the dryers continued, but the flipping of pages and filing of nails stopped. She was radiant in her white turtleneck dress with black cowboy boots and a sporty leather jacket. Her light-brown hair was flowing like a crown of wild grasses down her shoulders. Her rosy cheeks had been bitten by the cold, and she pursed her lips in a proud smile.

"Hello, old friends!" she said and waved. Myla looked up to her and put her magazine down. Evie sat right across from her and held her nails out. "Help a girl celebrate?"

Myla grinned deviously as she chewed her bagel from Songbird Café. "Tell me," she said as she shimmied her shoulders, "are we cele-brating something with your job, the fact that you're back, or that tall, cool glass of water Caleb Wright?" She narrowed her eyes when she said the word 'cool'.

"All of it! But Caleb is paying for this, so give me the works, my love, and remember to keep the nails short."

Myla put her bagel down.

All the women stared at her.

Sandy was sitting at the station next to her with her hair up in a wrap to let her highlights set in. She turned to Evie with a dirty look. "Caleb Wright is paying for this?" She threw the magazine down on the workstation. Her tech looked at her. "I knew it. I just fucking knew it. You tried to be all demure about it and-"

"Shut up, Sandy!" Evie snapped. Sandy withdrew. "No one cares about your gossiping antics. You fucked me up real bad with what you said. All I wanted to do was to figure out who tried to ruin Caleb's life, because it was about him, not me. You're an adult, act like one. Caleb is paying for this, and he and I are dating. The whole town knows it so..." She sat upright proudly before glaring at her again. "Why don't you tell the town something they don't know about me and go spit your daggers elsewhere?"

Every woman came over in a cackling frenzy of a hurry to talk to Evie. Sandy and Kelly sat dumbfounded. The women wanted to know what he was like, how she was handling his PTSD, and some even pulled up chairs to indulge themselves.

But Myla shooed them off. "Leave this girl be! This ain't about none of y'all."

"Yeah," Evie groaned.

There came the banker, Miss Margie Atwood. She shooed all the girls away with her magazine. "Don't y'all have a spice rack to rearrange or something? A casserole to go burn?"

The women left in a drone of disappointment. Myla giggled and went to work. "Pink?"

"You know it."

Myla smiled and let her pick out her color. "Mmmm, let's go with peach. I want pink, but not too pink, you know?"

"That's my little graphic designer."

As she began, Myla smiled. "I'm so proud of you to see you back. I've missed you."

"Thank you for always being so nice to me."

Myla grinned and tilted her head. "So, you want the works today?"

"Yep! Caleb's paying for it."

"As a good man should. One trip around the world, comin' up!"

Myla got up to get her a glass of wine, and together they sat down to catch up. "Now, darlin', tell me everything."

Chapter Eighteen

The town knew. Everyone knew. Instead of hiding away and being fearful of what people would say about her, Evie opened her Facebook page back up and saw hundreds of comments, friend requests, messages, and the like. These were ones that had been leftover that she never looked at prior to deactivating her page.

Stay away from him. He's a drunk.

Have fun getting beaten.

I fucked him in high school. He's good, ain't he? Too bad he's washed up.

Watch it. He can't even take care of his own kids.

He's Navy. He'll fuck you up big time.

You're after his money.

Grow up.

Slut.

Whore.

I hope you get shot.

Wait until he rapes you. He's military. Never fall for a military guy.

I knew him. You should date me instead. I'll treat you good.

Valentine's Day was close, and that meant Caleb's deployment was drawing closer. It was a miracle how she had grown so much with him at her side, but she began to worry how she was going to manage without him. Once again, she would be alone.

There were numerous times she had visited Pawpaw's grave, and now with her growth at work and other projects going on locally, perhaps she'd be too preoccupied with things to notice. Yeah right. She couldn't lie to herself. Caleb was leaving soon.

In six weeks.

It would be a long spring without him, and an even longer six months or heaven knew how long. The cold rain was nasty outside her bedroom window, and there she sat upright with her knees bent and her arms gently wrapped around them. That week, she had spent a lot of time at the gym and hiking, trying her hardest to get in better shape to be a better woman for him and for herself. And if she was lucky, for his family.

Caleb didn't post anything at all. She had missed seeing his posts, but he had only posted a few photos of himself with his kids and his horses just once in that time period.

She couldn't stop the hands of time if she tried. She was going to be forty-one soon.

In her black leggings and baggy sweater, Evie's face was pale as she looked out at the cloudy and dreary day. Teddy purred next to her, and all around her house had slowly become a better reflection of her. Luckily, the foundation wasn't bad. But many things were still in need of repair.

She reached for her guitar and tuned it. Then, she sang deeply with profound emotion, closing her eyes to the rain, Leona Lewis's "Bleeding Love."

What a beautiful trip down memory lane. She kept her eyes closed and sang.

The late winter days grew even wetter, and so many things felt unsolved. She still didn't know who was in the black sedan or who had actually told Sandy. But now, it seemed not to matter at all. Time flew by faster than she could grab hold of, and each day as the weather got warmer, it felt like some sort of impending doom was lingering in her home's air, the very air she breathed.

She had to keep on top of her tasks. She couldn't let herself fall behind. Hunt still never found out whose black sedan it was because it had stopped coming by altogether. And as she and Caleb casually dated, she should have been satisfied. But she wasn't. She still wanted to know if it was Alan, Kelly, Breanne, anyone. Caleb had another custody hearing in a few days, and he informed her that he wouldn't be coming over or really talking to her because he needed to prepare for it mentally. As hard as it was to respect his boundaries, she had no choice but to let it go.

She didn't understand. He had already had four since the divorce started. But this time, this was on Ashley's request. And it worried her that Ashley was going to fight for full custody, and the divorce probably wouldn't even be settled until he came back from deployment. It was all such an ugly mess.

Poor Caleb.

A Facebook notification popped up, and it was a message from Sandy above all people. She thought Sandy had blocked her. It read, "How much would you charge to design t-shirts for our girls' basketball team?"

Flowers could have bloomed, and they would weave their illustrious petals within the vines of her heart. She smiled and wrote back, "I won't charge anything if you tell me who told you that Caleb and I were seeing each other."

"Would you trust me that soon the actual person will confront you? I feel like the talkin' in this town has gone far enough."

Evie believed her. It could've been stupid, but she did. "If I don't get a sign in two weeks' time I'm coming after you for $300." She ended it with a laughing emoji.

Sandy loved the message and replied, "It's a deal." There was a smiley emoji at the end.

Evie smiled. Perhaps that was one bag of trash taken out. Maybe Sandy wasn't so bad after all.

That night as she got ready for bed, she texted Caleb, "I hope you have all the luck in the world with your custody hearing. I'll be rooting for you."

On the other end, Caleb was staring out the window of his back porch. There wasn't a drop of alcohol in him at all, only a long hard stare. His phone was in his jeans' pocket, and it did buzz, but he didn't notice it.

"Daddy? Dad?"

He suddenly felt a little hand touch his leg. He jerked and looked down. He saw his little girl Olivia looking up to him. He sighed deeply and fast before noticing Zack came in with his mom. Ashley was there inside his house. She brought them over to stay on a random Saturday because Caleb had plans to take them to the football game the next day.

He pulled his head back. "How did you get in here?"

She tilted her head. "They do have keys, you know."

She pulled Olivia and asked her, "Can you go play in your room with your big brother?"

The little girl nodded.

The two children were scooted off to Zack's room, and Ashley and Caleb looked at each other in silence.

Caleb firmly asked with his arms crossed, "What do you want?"

"Don't get all tough with me. Chill."

"I'm not getting tough with you, Ashley. This is awkward for me as much as it is for you. First, you accuse me of throwing a chair at you, then people in town think I cheated on you, which was never fucking true, and you *know* it—"

He had more to say, but Ashley quieted him rudely. "Look, do you want me to be nice or not? I wanted to discuss our separation agreement. I had my lawyer redraft our documents to state that I was okay with you dating Evie. I have them right here. That way, when the judge hears our case, it won't matter if you've been dating her or doing whatever it is you're doing with her."

Caleb glanced at her with hesitation and disbelief before taking the documents and looking them over. He skimmed through. She wasn't lying. For some odd reason, Ashley went through the extra trouble to tell him that things could be okay. He looked up at her from the papers. But it wasn't just that. She had ruined his partial custody arrangements, and he wasn't getting to see his kids as often. He wanted to yell at her and throw the papers at the wall. She had destroyed his life. But now... his heart was steady. He was trying to see the good things with it.

"Wait, are you saying..."

"I know this shit going on for over a year now has done a great deal to you and that innocent girl. I hated her guts at first, but that's all behind me now." She shook her head hard with her eyes closed, her emotions being wrought out. "I was angry." Then she dropped the ball, "And I want you to have your custody arrangements back. I want you to have them back during the week. Every week. They miss you terribly. And it's about them, not us."

Caleb felt his whole heart shatter, and tears welled in his eyes. The love of a good father showed strong. It took all of his efforts not to crumble and hug her. His large and empty house would have that warm laughter and sense of family all over again. He stood upright to gain his composure.

Ashley looked down. "I won't tell anyone if you cry."

He *was* happy inside, because the divorce had been going on for longer than two years, and it was the worst time of his life. To have some sort of peace of mind, even if it meant for her to treat him better, it would have been the biggest blessing of all. However, he put himself back in military mode, as Ashley could be cunning and sometimes use his emotions against him. If he cried, she might yell and call him unstable, and everything would be ruined again. He lifted his dark eyes to her and held the papers up. "You think this is gonna erase everything?"

Ashley clenched.

He looked around and spoke curtly, "This whole damn town hates me now. People think I'm taking medication for God's sake! Do you know what that feels like?"

"Well, you're *supposed* to be."

"I don't *have* to! It's anti-depressants! But they don't do no good if the whole town won't shut their mouths!"

She lifted her hands. "Keep your voice down. You know Olivia doesn't like it when you yell."

He wasn't actually yelling at all, but he was about to. His voice was just more serious in tone. His body crawled with fury, and confusion. One minute she was trying to legally encourage him to date, therefore settling partial custody rights of his kids, but then pulling these weird gaslighting moves. This was the exact thing Ashley always did to him. The blood within his muscles boiled over, spilling all out into his skin.

And then he breathed.

For some reason, the warmth of Evie's personality came back, the personality rich with love and peace.

Caleb let it go. Even if he didn't feel like he was in the wrong, he said, "I'm sorry. I'm just upset. Thank you for doing this. This really means a lot to me."

She crossed her arms rudely. "I didn't do it for you. I did it for her. You don't deserve good things."

He snickered and looked down at the papers. The comment didn't anger him at all. He smiled. "Apparently, I do. Because I've got Evie now." He raised his brows lightheartedly. "Thank you. I do appreciate it."

The children said loving goodbyes to their mother, and Caleb walked her to her car.

He even opened the door for Ashley, who was taken aback by the gesture. "What the hell are you doing?"

He smiled. "Being a gentleman. I've always been this way. You've been too blind to care."

She sat in the car and ignored him. But before he closed the door, he said to her leaning over, "Oh, and one more thing. In all honesty, Ashley? I hope you're happy in the end. And for what it's worth..."

She stared at him.

He swallowed hard. *Tell her the truth.* "You really did a wonderful thing for me. Thank you so much." He looked down for a moment as they both softened in their demeanors. "Thank you for caring, for coming by, and letting me take them to the game tomorrow. You don't know what that means to me. Thank you." He flashed her an honest, heartfelt smile, then closed the door.

He closed the door on his past.

Almost.

He watched that little sedan car drive off down his long gravel drive off of Highway 42. A place where the horses could roam freely on his forty-acre lot. A place where the sun rose on the eastern front porch and settled in the western back porch. A place where it was serene at all times of the day. A place where black-eyed Susans grew on the shoulder line during the appropriate seasons.

He looked at the papers in his hand. She had signed her side, and all he needed to do was sign his. Standing alone at the front of the house, Caleb let a tear roll down his cheek but quickly wiped it away and went back inside. He had work to do.

Dinner sizzled on the stove while his beloved children watched *Home Alone* for the third time that season, even though it was almost time for the Superbowl. He made a palette for them on the floor with loads of blankets and pillows, snacks and one cuddly and lovable bloodhound. Olivia settled against Charlie, and Zack was on his belly with his chin rested on his hands. Caleb was sitting at his island counter on his laptop and signed the documents, took a picture of them with his phone, and sent them to his lawyer.

He called out really quickly, "Don't forget, we gotta get some good sleep tonight, guys. We're going to the game tomorrow!"

He texted Evie, but Zack suddenly appeared out of nowhere with an innocent smile across his sweet face. His hair was messy, and Caleb smashed it down in a grin. "You look like Albert Einstein."

"Like whooooo?" Zack asked in a kiddish tone.

Caleb laughed and pulled Zack in to give him a hug, but Olivia immediately came running over and wanted one too. He grabbed her arm easily with one hand and yanked her on his lap, hugging them both. He kissed their heads. "I got a question for you guys."

Olivia squeaked, "We can have ice cream now?"

"No, no, no," Caleb laughed. It stirred a giggle in them all.

Zack asked eagerly, "You wanna know if we wanna go to Disneyland or Universal?"

Caleb looked at him with a playful threatening look. "You know it'll always be Universal."

He calmed them down and served dinner, trying to get them to be serious. After grace was said, Caleb placed a napkin on his lap. "Okay, kids, Dad's gotta ask you something serious. What would you say if I brought a lady with us to the game tomorrow?"

Olivia slowly asked with a fry held to her lip, "Like a girlfriend?"

Caleb folded his fingers on the table. "Yes, like a girlfriend."

Zack asked, "Dad, you've been seeing a girl who's not Mom?"

This wasn't going to be an easy conversation. He spoke calmly to his son, "Yes, but I wanna see if you guys like her."

Olivia, being a sweet and innocent age of five now, asked, "Is she pretty?"

Caleb smiled. "Yes, she's pretty, but that's not the point. I'm asking if you'd both be okay with it. Olivia, she's really good at art. Maybe she can draw with you sometime?"

His daughter gave an approving smile. He then looked to Zack, who seemed withdrawn. "Buddy? What about you?"

Zack got up and ran into his room.

Immediately, Caleb got up and told Olivia to stay seated. He walked fast down the hall to Zack's room and called, "What's going on? Come on Zack, talk to me bud." He opened the door and saw Zack crying on the bed. "Hey," Caleb began curtly, "I thought I told you that crying doesn't solve anything. You can't run away and not tell me what's on your mind."

Zack cried quietly, "I love Mom though, Dad. I don't want a new mom."

Caleb heard his son's tears and immediately settled down his stringent ways. He always tried to teach Zack to be strong, but it wasn't a time for that. His son needed a caring and patient father, not a drill sergeant. He sat on the bed and patted his son's back. He encouraged him, "Buddy, you're not getting a new mom. Your mom will always be your mom." He smiled.

Zack's eyes peered over as he turned. "Then why do you want a new girl? Isn't Mom enough?"

What a horrible conversation to have all over again. Caleb had learned how to deal with his kids ever since the divorce, but this was something new. He wanted to be respectful of his kids' needs, but at the same time he himself was a man with his *own* needs. he reached over and picked up the Batman action figure on Zack's nightstand and handed it to him. His son slowly took it. Then he pulled his son up and held him close.

"Remember what I taught you? Things happen in life that we can't change. Your mother and I aren't together anymore. At some point in your life, you're gonna have to accept that. I know it's hard. Believe me,

I know. But that doesn't mean we can't all still get along, be a family, and have fun and love each other, right? And that's why I asked you. I want to make sure you're comfortable with it. So, let's talk about this. Father to son."

Zack looked up to him, feeling his toy with his fingers. "But I don't want you to have another lady. I want you and Mom to get back together."

Caleb sighed and smiled affectionately. "I know you may want that, bud, but we can't always get want we want. Your mom and I don't get along like we used to, and we're trying to do what's best for not only us, but you and Olivia as well. But we can learn to be happy with what we're given. And right now, I believe the Lord has given me Evie to help me. She's done a lot of really good things for me."

Zack sat up. "She has?"

Caleb rubbed his son's head. "She sure has, bud."

"Like what?"

He grabbed his son to lure him out of the bedroom back to the dinner table. He brushed his son's back with a comforting hand. "You'll see tomorrow. How about it?"

Zack smiled and nodded.

The only thing Caleb could do now was find solace in his workshop with Charlie. The kids had been put to bed with full bellies, and once outside he picked up his guitar and tuned it. He tried to find peace within the night, but he was still in heavy thought about when he was going to tell Evie about what happened overseas. He almost felt obligated to tell her, but he was worried that if he did, she would never look at him the same way again. He took a hard swallow of whiskey to ease his nerves.

He picked up his phone and texted her, "Would you like to go to the Chiefs' game with my kids and I tomorrow?"

On the other end, Evie was relaxing in a hot bubble bath reading her favorite Stephen King book again. Teddy was next to her, sleeping on the faux fur rug and letting his gentle purrs rumble. When the notification went off on her phone, she sat up so fast and hard that the water gushed out and plopped on Teddy. He didn't like it one bit! She petted him to apologize but frantically read the message and replied, "I thought you needed time with your kids? What about Ashley?"

"Let me send you something."

Evie waited and looked at the photo of documents he sent. "What is this?"

Caleb felt a smile taking over his whole soul. "Ashley brought over the amendment papers, and we signed them today. Legally, I can date you now without issues. And she's giving me back my old custody rights, so my lawyer will be presenting all of this to the judge on Monday. Then, when we have our *final* hearing, it won't look bad to the judge that we've been dating."

Her fingers crept to her lips, and she touched them in awe. "Are you serious right now? Caleb I'm literally screaming in happiness for you!" She actually was. Teddy hated that, too.

"Yep. Pick you up at seven? It's gonna be an early morning!"

Evie held her chest. "I would love that! Do the kids know?"

"Yep! They know. But I promised Olivia you'd help her with art."

She reclined gently in the tub and felt love consume her again. Nothing mattered anymore except this moment. To make it right. To make his children happy. If Caleb was asking her to meet his kids, she was definitely not a fling. He had divorce papers amended for her. There was no doubt now. "You've got it. It's a deal."

He smiled cutely. "Love you, baby."

Her jaw tightened in profound joy. "I love you too. Sleep well."

She could hardly sleep that night. It was going to be another moment of getting out of her comfort zone.

The following morning found her confused about what to wear. With losing all the weight she did, she didn't have much to choose from that would be practical for being outdoors for so long in such dreadful weather. The only thing she could gather was a pair of gray sweatpants and a Chiefs' hoodie that she had bought just to try to impress him last year. Now it was time for hair and makeup.

Or should she even bother wear makeup and do her hair?

There were way too many choices! The thought of meeting his kids that day meant she needed to leave a lasting impression. And now suddenly, she felt her outfit looked like crap. One more closet raid left her throwing all sorts of clothes on to the bed until Teddy meowed. She turned around and saw he had moved to lay by the beautiful blue sunflower dress that Pawpaw had bought her. She had thrown it on Teddy again. Everything in her life slowed as she approached it, smiling wide in blissful memory. She picked it up and examined it. Even though she couldn't fit into it anymore, she kept it.

Evie clutched it close and closed her eyes. "Oh, Pawpaw. I wish you were here. I promise I met someone good. You're never gonna believe who it is."

Her thoughts were interrupted by the sound of Caleb's truck pulling up the driveway. She had no choice but to be satisfied with what she wore and how she looked.

The doorbell rang and she went flying in a mad rush to grab snacks to put in her purse for the kids and gave one final look at herself in the mirror by the door.

She answered it and saw his handsome face sporting a Chiefs' hoodie and gray sweatpants. She smiled and they kissed.

"Damn," he said smiling. "You look hot in that stuff."

She raised a brow playfully. "I wonder why."

He grabbed her hand and led her down the stairs. "I know this has gotta be hard for you, but...it'll be okay." He smirked and said sarcastically, "I'll whoop their butts if they get outta line."

She laughed. "Sure, you will."

"Oh no, I'm serious." His playful antics kept making her laugh. He smiled looking away. "I'll make them do ten hours of horse lunging. Especially little Olivia. She'll do it for twelve."

Evie grinned up to him. "Poor horses."

"Not the horses. For a few hours, Zack will be on the lead and Olivia can lunge him and then they'll switch."

Evie laughed again and playfully slapped his chest. As they walked to the truck, Caleb warned with a grin, looking at the yard, "Don't get outta line with me either young lady, or you'll do the weed-eatin'."

"Gotta teach me first. Unless you want a ruined weed eater," she taunted.

They smiled at each other.

Caleb took her around to the side where Olivia was and ordered

Zack to get out of the back. He unlatched his little girl from the child seat. "Alright, lil' Liv. Time to meet Evelyn!"

He whistled for Zack who replied sluggishly, "I'm coming."

Evie could hear him kicking the gravel as he came around the truck. Caleb ordered in a nervous smile, "Hey, don't be givin' that 'tude little dude. Evelyn is a really nice lady, okay? I promise you'll love her! Remember how we act in the presence of a lady?"

He put Olivia down who just looked up at Evie, who was vibrating with nerves. Olivia *stared* at up at her, and it made Evie uncomfortable. She took a deep breath and casually offered her hand. "Hey, Olivia! I like your name. It's really pretty! It's nice to meet you."

Olivia smiled with a missing tooth and shook Evie's hand hard with both of hers. It jostled her when the kid hopped up and down. "Wanna see my drawlings?"

"*Drawings,* baby girl," Caleb corrected.

Olivia asked again, "Drawlings? They're in the back in my book bag!"

Evie snickered, "Of course! I'd love to see them!"

But Caleb's masculine dad voice came in, "In a minute, sweetie. Let Zack meet her." He then put his hand around his son's back. "Zack bud, this is Evelyn, but you can call her Evie."

She could tell he didn't like her at all, but Evie knew damn well that with her brother's kids, that kids could take a bit of warming up to someone. She smiled and pulled a few stray hairs behind her ears. That damn Midwest wind. "Hi, Zack. I hear you like Batman a lot. I love Catwoman! Your dad has told me a lot about you," she said in a quiet and tender voice.

"He hasn't told me anything about you."

"That's okay. I understand." Evie paused for a moment. "But I'd like a chance to be friends with you. Is that okay?"

"You don't need to talk to me like I'm five."

Caleb rubbed Zack's back. "Be nice. She's done nothin' wrong."

But Evie looked at Caleb with an encouraging smile. "It's not a problem for me if he has boundaries or preferences."

"It bothers me. I taught him to be respectful to *all* people."

She withdrew respectfully. Zack was Caleb's child, not hers. "I appreciate that. But, Zack? I do hope we can have fun today. Your dad tells me you're doing great at sports! Hopefully I can come and watch you play sometime?"

The conversation was interrupted when Deputy Hunt's cruiser pulled up the driveway. Caleb groaned with a laugh, "Oh boy. Is this gonna be another one of his three-hour talks he has with you?"

Evie held her mouth in laughter. "I'll try to keep it short." Then she looked to the kids. "Do you guys wanna see a really cool dog that can do some really cool tricks?"

Hunt got out of his vehicle, and Caleb shook his hand, and Evie gave him a hard hug. "How are you today, Hunt?" she asked.

"Oh, ya know. Livin' the dream!"

Caleb said, "Can't complain?"

"Nope! No siree."

"Hey, Hunt," Evie began, "we're in a little bit of a hurry for the game. But while we chatted, do you think you could earn me some brownie points and bring Atlas out for the kids to see him?"

"Well, sure! But brownie points? For what?"

Caleb pulled Evie close and wrapped his arm around her shoulder. She snuggled into him a bit and smiled at Hunt, whose face was as surprised as seeing a squirrel shit gold. His shocked look faded into a wide smile. "Well color me stupid. I can't believe it! You two are officially together now?"

Caleb flashed a wide smile. "We sure are."

Hunt rested his hands on his vest straps and rocked on his heels. "Evie, I'm damn happy for you. Caleb, you ought to know that this little feline has been hotblooded for you for a long time now."

Caleb kissed her cheek. "I've kinda gathered that."

Evie didn't want the conversation to get too uncomfortable, and so she asked him quickly to bring Atlas out. Within a minute, Atlas's door was opened. Evie coaxed Zack and Olivia over, and she smiled mostly to Zack. "He's really cool and super friendly!"

When that big German Shepherd came out, both kids were stunned in excitement. Olivia awed out loud, and Zack laughed at how hyper the dog was, loving to pet his fur.

While the kids entertained themselves with the dog, the three adults chatted until Evie ran inside to get an extra scarf.

Hunt smiled to Caleb and kept an eye on the dog and kids. "Going to the Chiefs' game?"

"Yes, sir, we sure are!"

Hunt smiled. "I hope you two have fun. So damn proud that our boys got to the Superbowl again!"

Evie came back out. "Was there something you needed, Dan?"

"Oh, nah. I just wanted to stop by and see how everything was doing and to make sure you haven't noticed any weird activity lately."

Caleb spoke, "I haven't seen anything on the ring camera." He looked at Evie.

She said, "I haven't noticed anything, either."

"Well," Hunt began, "that's good then. I'll head on out. Have fun at the game!"

Later on, the drive to the stadium was a weird one. Because Evie and Olivia liked the same exact Spice Girls songs, and Caleb and Zack were trapped against their wills to hear and endure the girliest renditions ever known to them. Yet it didn't actually bother Caleb at all. He groaned in play as a dad would, but it made him happy to see Evie doing the arm moves of certain dance routines in the passenger seat, and hearing Olivia singing off key in the back trying to mimic the dance moves.

It was breakfast at McDonald's for the kids, and a special stop at Starbucks for Evie. She assured Caleb he didn't have to do it, but he knew McDonald's didn't settle well in her stomach. And on that day, Zack had his first taste of coffee. On Caleb's request, Evie recorded the reaction by twisting over in her seat to film him with Caleb's phone, and the reaction left the whole truck roaring in laughter that reached Heaven. He *hated* coffee.

They yelled over each other, teased each other, jested at each other in good humor, and all decided to leave it on the country station to sing songs they all knew. Until on a commercial, Caleb asked Evie to switch the station to station that played a variety of genres. As she flipped through the channels, a song came on.

A song that made them both focus on what they were each looking at. Caleb on the road, and Evie at the interface.

Evie looked at him as Caleb lowly sang, still focused on the road.

She rubbed his leg, and they looked at one another. As if they knew each other's very thought patterns, needs, wishes, and dreams, they both sang softly along.

Caleb removed a hand from the steering wheel and rested it on hers. Their fingers slowly curled into one another.

* * *

Hot dogs, sodas, nachos, oh my! Evie thought. She huddled against Caleb, as the game was loud, busy, chaotic, and hectic. People were everywhere, and the echoing of the announcers and music that played during the breaks were loud. Everything was loud. There was movement everywhere, and Olivia had a tenacity to be hyperactive, and Zack was demanding of his dad. She didn't know how he did it.

Already before halftime, she wanted to go home where it was quiet, calm, peaceful, and easy. She was having a good time in a way, but she had been so depressed and ridden with her manic episodes that she didn't know how to function in a situation like that anymore.

She reached for her phone to have some sort of an escape from the noise and chaos of the stadium with people stomping, smoking, whistling, screaming, yelling, spilling popcorn. It was all nuts to her. Over the last six years, her tolerance for football games vanished. As she looked at her phone, she was desperate for someone to text with to take her mind out of it. And it hit her how alone she was. Even with Caleb, she felt alone all over again. Evie rubbed her face in frustration at herself. Was that not enough for her?

No. She needed something quiet then. A friend that she could tell how stressful that situation was. How badly she wanted to go home but felt awful about it. As she scrolled through her contacts, she had no one.

Being with Caleb, Evie was going to have to become a part of a life that wasn't hers and meet new people she didn't know and build new friendships. She didn't have a problem making new friends, but it all was just too much to handle that she was truly alone. Who would she have to gush to about Caleb? They were dating, and she didn't have anyone at all to giggle about it to. No girlfriend, no family member, nothing. Not even a coworker. She got to talk to Myla about it, but Myla and her hadn't grown that close yet.

Telling Caleb she needed to use the bathroom, she went out somewhere quieter and composed herself near the concessions.

She hated herself. When was her mind going to finally be satisfied with something and not find something *new* to be upset about? She hated the women in town. They were so loud, conniving, untrustworthy, and bitchy. Sarah was nice, but Sarah and Evie weren't really that close. They'd only known each other for two years, and they only met about a handful of times. Not to mention, Sarah could be a little bit conservative, even more so than Evie. How she wished she and Missy didn't go their separate ways. If Missy were to have ever straightened up or grown up, it wouldn't't've been a problem.

The Chiefs won, and the drive back home was as loud as it was on the way there. Yes, it was great on the way *there*, but on the way back, Olivia had started to get fussy, Zack started to get moody with wanting to eat somewhere when Caleb wanted to wait until they got home, and Evie...

She wanted to *go* home.

The din of the stadium had exhausted her mental threshold, and fatigue seeped into her body, marinating her bones with a toxic sludge. All she wanted to do was go home and be warm and quiet in her bed with a good book, and it broke her apart.

Caleb never took her home. He took a different exit to Highway 42 and Evie didn't even want to *dare* ask him to take her home.

You can do this, Evie. Fight through it. You're new to this. It's like the first day on the job. You'll be okay. Take the trail one step at a time.

As the truck rode up the long gravel driveway however, Evie slowly pulled herself forward and looked. She saw the horses.

Coming up a hill where pastures were wet and dead, the beautiful sunset cast a fiery halo behind a large and beautiful home. Wood fencing trailed all over, and to the right she saw the small herd of horses grazing. Trees of glimmering wet bark birthed their wiry branches high into the sky in several random areas, and a dog rose to its paws on the front porch.

Evie's breath left her body as she gasped, "Caleb..."

"Do you like it?"

"This is," she stammered looking at the horses again, "your house?"

"Yep! It's beautiful at night. Wait till you see the big pond in the back!"

"You have a pond, too? It's beautiful!"

"Sure do!"

Olivia chirped, "Daddy, when we come home from school tomorrow, can I go riding with Evie?"

Evie smiled. She sat back and relaxed. It was her paradise. And to hear that little girl wanting to spend time with her? Double paradise.

Caleb looked in his review mirror to his little girl. "Absolutely!"

Then it all hit her so hard that it heightened her senses, and she could've screamed. Inside, she screamed as hard as she could.

Evie realized how much she had been stuck in the past. She never healed from her parents' death, her pawpaw's, in a way losing her brothers, and moving all over the place trying to find where she belonged.

Maybe she could belong there.

She wanted change but was afraid of it. Afraid of a new norm because she longed for things in her life to be the way they were before her family fell apart. But perhaps God had sent her a new family. A new home. A new place to belong. It obviously wasn't going to be easy to adapt, but she had to try. She wanted to try.

Throughout the time of making dinner with Caleb for all of them, Evie had been welcomed into a house that was clean, comfortable, open, and quiet. The only real sound was the sound of company. Perhaps, she had thought to herself, that the only reason she had wanted to go back home earlier was because that was what she had been *used* to for all those years.

But it wasn't what she had *wanted*.

After the kids were put to bed, Caleb and Evie went to sleep in separate rooms out of respect for his kids, but he didn't go to sleep with a clear mind.

The next morning, before the kids woke up, he took her hand and led her outside to the front pasture. The fields were small patches of white snow and dark earth from the wakening of dawn, and the trees had lost their brilliant sparkles, but the tall grasses swayed in their blond tones. The snow had melted enough for them to sprout and grow. And the horses nickered at each other while they grazed. She knew it was something serious.

He stood on the hill with her and wrapped his arms around her. Their embrace was tight and full of intent, and she grazed her loving hands along his side to his back. Caleb's face snuggled down into her hair.

"What's wrong?" she asked.

"I gotta tell you what you've been waiting for for over a year, and I'm worried you're going to leave me after this."

"I won't," she urged. "I can't. I'm in love with you. People don't leave people they love."

Evie's eyes soared into his, her beautiful dark jewels glittering as the pinks of the sky washed her cheeks. It was easy to see that Caleb was hurting. She held his cheek. He had shaved that morning.

"What is it? I'm here. Lay it all on me, please."

He began lowly, "I've not had a good past. And because I don't talk about it, it makes people angry at me."

She listened, bracing for something devastating. She ignored the nipping cold of the early hour.

"I'm in the Navy, as you know."

Here it is. Be patient. Be calm. "I do, but I never knew what you did."

"I'm an SWCC. Please don't ask what that means. It's too much to explain right now."

She let him gather his breath. Her eyes never left him even though he was now looking down. Their arms hung down between them and they held their hands with each other.

He hesitated and breathed rapidly. He almost gripped her hands too tight. He began, "I've seen things I can't forget, but I want to. It doesn't matter what I do. It's been hard. Everyone always sees me, and they think I just shoot guns because of the marksmen awards I've gotten, or that I kill people. But they don't know what kind of rescue and humanitarian things I've done, too."

Evie felt her blood go cold. Yet it wasn't for the reason one would believe. She already knew it was a hard thing to talk about, but her blood went cold because she couldn't imagine holding something that fucking heavy. With a tilt of her head, the center of her brows rose upwards in compassion, listening deeper. She had no clue what an SWCC was, but apparently, they did both risky things and also helped people.

He was getting uneasy, and she rubbed the top of his hands with her thumbs.

He shook his head. "All I want to say is that when the War on Terror started, things went from bad to worse. There was an accident with a friend of mine, and that's really all I wanna say." Caleb clenched his jaw and licked his lips. The memory was ripping his heart out, and he felt the tragedy was all his fault. But he would never disclose that to her.

Evie saw his shoulders rise and tense. She yearned to touch him and soothe his nerves, but she refrained, knowing it wasn't the best thing to do at the moment. She started to lose feeling in her fingers from how hard he held her hands. She didn't care.

Once more, he aggressively licked his lips and forced a smile. "Please don't ask me any further details. It is what it is."

"I won't," she cooed affectionately.

And Evelyn Morgan grew up in that moment. Two years ago, that response wouldn't've satisfied her. Now, it did. Because he was there with her, trying to open up.

She grew up. And she felt she grew up *with* him.

The winds came gliding across their faces. He managed to conjure the strength to continue, "When I came back, people in town thought everything was a joke. They made horrible jokes about how proud they were that I served but then others hated me for it, and all sorts of fucked up shit."

His lips trembled. "Ashley was seeing shit on the news, believing one way while I was living it and believing another. It started to be too much to take, so I stopped associating with people in town so much. Every time I tried to stick up for myself, they only would say stupid shit like, 'Oh come on, it ain't that bad.' I couldn't deal with it anymore. Now that I'm gone, I don't associate hardly at all. People took me as wigging out and having psychotic breakdowns every time I got angry. If I had a fight with Ashley, my PTSD was to blame for it. It didn't matter if it was because she did something to upset me, no. It was always because I was acting out and needed therapy.

"I ended up getting on medications that didn't help. The VA here is a fucking joke, as everyone knows. But I had an incident with Ashley's dad where I ended up fighting him and breaking his arm, and that was blamed on my unstable mental state, and I almost lost my kids."

Evie was about ready to completely, utterly, totally, and viscerally cry. No. She swallowed and stood strong for him. She fought back those tears with a strong heart. His tears that began to pool in his eyes were damaging to her heart to see. She wanted to kiss them away, erase his pain, and hold him close.

"There's more to that story, but I'll save that for a rainy day."

"I understand," she managed to say.

"Before I filed for divorce, I had a fight with Ashley. I tried to stay as calm as possible. But I had simply said, 'If you don't settle down, I don't know what I'm gonna do, but it ain't gonna be pretty.' I didn't mean that as a threat to her or anyone. I meant like I was gonna leave her. But she took it seriously and called the cops on me and reported me for suicidal attempts. I was taken up north to Bridgerton Hospital. I went willingly, trying to appease her, and was stuck there for a week. That was one brick in the wall that made me wanna file for divorce. All I wanted was to be left with my kids and to have someone listen to me."

He paused and as the tears finally fell, so did those shackles that kept him for so long. "Someone like you."

No longer could Evie refrain. She lifted his hand to her lips and kissed his knuckles. Instead of letting their hands hang back at rest, she kept them clutched to her chest and looked at him like her life depended on it, because his life *did*.

He chuckled sheepishly and shifted his stance. "You can imagine what went on in the town after that. Everything I did was wrong." His head was downturned, and she watched his handsome face tighten. He sniffled.

Silence.

More silence.

Apparently, he was finished.

Evie let his hands go, stroked his face and looked up to him.

"Caleb," she said with a breath of feminine care. As their eyes met, Caleb was losing the battle of controlling his feelings. Evie's expression pulled every fiber of emotions to the surface, and he was struggling to hold on. He jerked, and then he fully let go and cried.

Evie held him immediately and pulled his face to her shoulder to cradle him as best as her shorter height could allow. "It's okay. Nothing is your fault," she soothingly whispered.

A knotting was felt in his body, and he squeezed his arms around her so hard he could've broken her back. Evie embraced it as best as she could despite her breath being difficult to take. Louder she heard his cries, and slowly they turned into screams that were quieted by his face into her neck.

His fingers dug into her. He gasped.

She wanted to assure him everything was okay, but she refrained from talking. She didn't dare to interrupt it. After a minute, they turned into blood-curdling screams, and her eyes winced in sadness for him. The nape of her neck was wet with his tears, and he pressed his face harder into her.

Let him cry.

Although he never mentioned it, she gathered he lost a friend and probably had survivor's guilt. Something dreadful happened overseas. Maybe one day she would know, but maybe she would never know. And she was okay with that.

After a few more minutes, she reached up to use her sweater's sleeve to dry his pretty eyes. She whispered, "I don't care what they say about you, because you're the only peace I've ever known."

Caleb let it go. He placed his past within her palms then and there. It was no longer his to hold on to. He had to let it go.

She welcomed it.

He cried hard into her cheek then, squeezing her soft body with his strong arms.

"It's okay. I'm here for you. You're safe," she whispered with her eyes closed and her arms tight around him. His fingers pressed into every place they touched.

Evie lifted her hands to his upper back to calm him. It was a beautiful thing to feel his tall and muscled body give out the way it did, fracturing into tiny pebbles of pain that her hands would hold. No matter how many pebbles fell into her palms, the load would never make her falter.

He sniffed a bit, "Thank you. But I have to also say, I leave for deployment soon, and I'll be gone for almost eight months."

"And I will be here when you come home."

"Everyone says that."

She assured, "But some keep their promises. You're not a difficult man to love, Caleb. I've been around men who are truly abusive, and that's not you. And what happened with your friend, it's not your fault. None of this is your fault. I know that doesn't make it better, but it's the truth. Go on your deployment, work your twelve-hour shifts here at home, spend hours in your garage working on your truck or yard or horses or whatever. I truly don't care. Because that's what I always found attractive about you. You do things I can't, and you know things I've wanted to know but don't. But above all else..."

He looked at her anxiously.

She smiled up to him. "I'm proud of you."

Chapter Nineteen

The truck was warm with heat and basking love as they all were together, taking the kids to school the next morning. All was peaceful in the stillness of the moment. Evie turned around and looked at Olivia sleeping with a teddy bear on her lap, too tired to really care that she was on her way to school. Zack had respectfully kept his tablet off and looked out the window. She looked at him and saw him entrenched in his thoughts. She was still brimming with elation and gladness from the early morning situation with Caleb, and so she wanted to help his son, too. "You okay, buddy?"

"Yeah," Zack answered slowly.

"What's the matter?"

"I didn't remember my lines for my play."

Caleb looked in his rearview mirror as his son looked down.

Evie asked, "How many lines is it?"

"Five."

"Oh, that's not bad! Get your paper out and write them down until we get to your school. That helped me a lot. Then, we can rehearse them together here in the car."

Caleb looked at her and chuckled with a smile.

Zack lifted his head and pursed his brows. "You'd do that for me?"

"Well sure! And if you're alright with it, I'll come and watch it. If you forget your lines, I'll mouth them to you."

Caleb about put a stop to that. He always taught his children to stay strong and be independent, but it was Evie's way of trying to bond with his son. And so, he tried to take a back seat as hard as it was.

Evie looked at Caleb with a smile. "That's if it's alright with your daddy. Don't wanna make him madder than a wet hen."

Caleb chuckled and held her hand. "It's alright with me."

Zack scribbled his lines down and began practicing them with her. Caleb looked out at winter's presence with the gray skies and wet roads. Somewhere the little critters of the wild countryside would be burrowed and warm. The cows they passed by lay down like large lumps of coal. A minute later, the windshield wipers came on for the little drops that started to fall.

They dropped off his children and, on the way out, he was quiet.

Evie wasn't even worried that he was mad. He was deep in thought. That handsome face leaned on his knuckles with his elbow resting on the door. His adorably warm company sweater that she helped him find that morning was snuggly looking on his tight muscles.

But instead of going to drop her off at home, Caleb took a left turn and headed straight into Laysville town center.

Evie panicked a bit and sat forward. "Where are we going?"

"The Songbird Café."

She looked around, perplexed. "Why?"

"Because," he began in that thick honey accent, glancing at her, "I want people to see us together."

She leaned over and kissed his cheek, stroking it lovingly. Even though he kept looking at the road, fixed in thoughts and emotions, he could see her gazing into his eyes out of his peripheral vision.

The way she always looked at him burned his roots to the ground. She turned his rotten roots into beautiful fruit. Ashes to ashes he fell into her love. He couldn't stand properly when she looked at him, so passionate and focused, as if her looking at him gave him the very breath he needed to breathe. Caleb couldn't understand how she was so satisfied with him. And perhaps, he never would. But she would remind him every day. He hadn't had a quiet ride to his kids' school in ages. And just like that, Evie had brought within their family a quiet and calmness they all so desperately needed.

They reached the café and parked, but before Evie could get out, Caleb told her to wait. He leapt out of his truck and grabbed an umbrella in the back, opened her door, offered his hand, and shielded her from the rain.

He was covered in true and unbound happiness, and no one could come into his world but her because of it.

Her pale face glistened as she looked up to him. And they kissed with her hands to his stomach. Caleb pulled her by the waist closer to him and pressed her against the truck while trying to shield them both from the rain.

If the world would burn, let it.

If the sky would fall, let it.

If a wave crashed through the town, they wouldn't even know.

She whimpered as she was pressed against that big pickup truck and reached up to pull him closer. She lifted her leg to his hip. He let go of the truck and grabbed her leg to hold it for her. The rain fell hard and racked against the umbrella in percussive notes, drumming in rhythm with their hearts.

The people inside the café all stared outside the window, but that didn't stop Evie or Caleb.

They were in love.

Falling deeper into more passionate kisses, Caleb dropped the umbrella in the rolling stream of the side street and clutched her with both arms; his right arm around her neck and the left around her lower back. Their lips were wetter than before, but their heat kept them warm. Evie's hair clung to her face, and the brief shock of the cold rain made her gasp a bit, but Caleb crept his large hand on top of her head as if still trying to shield her. She squeezed her eyes tighter together and could *feel* in his kisses that his eyes were tightly closed as well. They were.

She let out a gasp and clutched his wet sweater sleeve and for a moment, they stopped to look at each other. He saw the rain glistening against her full lips, and her large eyes expressive as if in sadness, but she was simply moved. He whispered to her, "I love you, Evie."

Her jaw shook from the cold and the emotions, the muscles in her temples tight. "Caleb," she stuttered looking at him.

I'm here. What is it? he thought, never looking away. He cradled her face and watched her lips, then gazed into her eyes.

The words tumbled out of her mouth in one breath of longing, "I love you."

He pulled her in hard and kept her warm.

And the patrons inside watched.

Joey had stopped pouring a cup of coffee for the local Navy veteran Donald Eaton, who was smiling at the young couple. He nodded. Another veteran stopped plucking at his old acoustic guitar on the comfortable chair by the window to look.

Sandy and Kelly stopped in mid-gossip and stared as their pastry flakes fell from the pastries in their hands. Sandy tried not to grin.

Myla Marr smiled and took a sip of hot cider.

Deputy Hunt, Hawkins, and Martin tried not to look.

Sarah watched.

Joey finally walked over and threw open the door. "Hey, you two lovebirds! Get yer asses in here where it's warm before I get a switch on ya!"

Caleb and Evie laughed with all of their hearts. He picked up the umbrella and held Evie's hand to walk inside. Joey held the door open for them as they walked by her old iron bistro tables outside. "I was gonna say! Take any longer and I'll pull your britches down and embarrass y'all further in front of your friends!"

Upon getting inside, Sandy sneered in playful jest, "Y'all looked like two rats in a sock out there."

Evie raised her brows and flashed a smile.

Kelly gawked.

Sandy winked.

The sound of the café was still quiet as Caleb and Evie walked in between the motley of tables and people staring at them. Donald Eaton stood up and saluted Caleb with a weak smile. "Good to see you back in town, Mr. Wright."

Evie stopped and watched him salute Mr. Eaton back, smiling. They shook hands and then Evie and Caleb heard Joey call from behind the counter, "C'mon, you guys! Y'all are off like a herd of turtles! Evie, I only got one bagel left and it's got your name on it!"

She giggled, and they made their way to the front. Joey asked while she frantically began preparing Evie's go-to order, "If you can see, I used your designs, and people love them, but I hate them."

Evie laughed and tilted her head in a good-humor smile, knowing Joey's behavior. "Why is that?"

"Because it's not mine, and I can't take credit for it. Y'all's breakfast is on me today. I never got to pay ya for it."

"Don't worry about it, Joey. You've been nothing but nice to me."

Joey said loudly in her normal voice, "What? You were mad at me the last time you saw me!"

"I know, but please understand why. It's all water under the bridge now, right?"

Brooks and Dunn's "Brand New Man" played on the radio suddenly.

How fitting, Caleb thought with a smile.

Joey gave Evie a high-five. "You know it, girl. But look!" She pointed to her fun and trendy spring menu up on the board behind her and added the lighting Evie recommended. There were photos by the local photographer that showcased an aerial view of a rustic country table setting with a closeup of little flowers, strawberries, leaves, pineapple, a bowl of honey, a blue ceramic coffee pot, and the main attraction was a pie done in three segments showing off her three seasonal pies of strawberry, apple, and lemon custard.

The actual café menu had been switched over to a tone of faded yellows, soft greens, and subtle blues for a softer feel. The font had been designed to be more legible and simpler.

"Aw, Evie babe." Caleb smiled, looking up. "You designed all of this?"

"I did! And you encouraged me."

Joey cocked her hip with her hand on the counter and the other on her hip. She sarcastically and spiritedly said, "Thanks, Caleb, for encouraging someone to point out how much I suck at things."

"Oh, no one need that to be pointed out. They already know how much you suck at things," he teased.

Together, they placed their orders and went to sit down on the brown sofa and listened to the rain outside the window. Caleb made small talk with the veteran with the guitar and politely asked if he could use it. The two gathered to talk happily while Caleb tuned it. Evie looked over as Mr. Eaton came to sit and she and Caleb scooted over to give him room. As she smiled, she looked over and noticed that Sarah looked unwell. It was like she was hiding her face.

Why, she seemed like she was dying inside of something. And then she got up and left. Evie tried to greet her before she left, but Sarah seemed like she was in a bad mood, and so she refrained.

The whole café lit up when Caleb turned to Evie and sang the song to her, Lady A's "Need You Now."

She absolutely blushed, laughing like a lovestruck little girl all over again. She was proud of him. He was singing without needing the whiskey!

And then they left, passed his exit, and carried on to Maple Street.

Evie's heart radiated happiness. The rain came harder as Caleb slowed down, and Evie enjoyed looking out the window at all of the winter decorations at the end of people's driveways and even up on their porches.

She felt colorblind to the world of pain and heartache now, but her heart could color all of those sepias and grays with the joy she felt.

They got closer to her house, and she began planning in her quiet mind what food she would cook for him after they made love. She imagined cuddling up on the couch with a banquet of anything she could throw together, or maybe he was gonna drop her off and leave. That didn't happen either. At that point, even if she never got her Valentine's date, it wouldn't matter. Every day was like that with him.

As they walked inside, Evie saw a note wedged into her mums' pot. She let Caleb go inside, but she picked it up and opened it up. It read...

"I guess I should've told you sooner. I'm sorry. I won't bother you anymore, but I didn't mean for it to get this far. I guess I should be brave like you and go after what I want and not settle for less than what I deserve. Can we please leave this alone and have you forgive me for what I did? I didn't mean to ruin your life. You deserve him. You really do. I hope you're happy, my friend. Love..."

Joshua Jackson.

Evie gasped and felt her head overcome with a crushing sensation. She looked across the road and could barely see Joshua sitting on his porch way up in the drive.

Joshua brought out his phone and texted her, "Are you going to report me to the cops?"

She gasped in shock and wrote back, "It was *you* who did all of this?"

He wrote back, "Yes. I'm so sorry."

She swallowed hard and settled down. Joshua would never have done anything like that unless he was inclined to. Something was wrong. She wrote, "It takes a hell of a lot of a man to admit this. No, your secret is safe with me. But why would you do that to me? You almost ruined my life and his." She ended it with a sad emoji. It really crushed her.

Across the street, Joshua clutched his face. Sarah had cheated on him with Alan Moffet of all people, and no one knew. Sarah didn't even know that he knew, and when he had found out Caleb was tailing Evie, he was looking for a hot recovery, and she was the best thing he could try to go after. He was hoping he would have gotten to her first, but he didn't. And he tried to break them apart.

He wrote back to Evie, "I don't wanna say because as you have said, the talking has gone far enough. I'll deal with it. Let's just say I was jealous. Caleb was a tough case that you broke. I hope the best for you and him."

"Evie!" Caleb called.

"Coming!" she answered. Evie texted, "What happened? Why did you do what you did? Why did you tell Sandy?"

Joshua thought sadly about his wife and his situation. "Like I said, I have my reasons, but I now know what can happen to someone's life if they gossip too much. I'd rather keep that between my wife and I."

"Whose car was the black sedan?"

"It was Breanne."

"Let me guess. You slept with her?"

Joshua frowned in shame on the other end. "Things get nasty in a small town. I'm sorry I got so jealous over Caleb having you. I know none of this probably makes sense, I just wasn't thinking."

Evie sighed and wrote, "Yeah, but sometimes we gotta try to stick together and be honest with people about who we are, what we need, and why we're hurting."

Joshua let it sink in.

Then she wrote, "It's the only way we can heal our small-town scars."

It was Joshua Jackson all along. But it no longer mattered. Evie forgave him. She knew what it felt like to be in that position a little bit.

Inside, Caleb was sitting on the couch and looked worried. He patted the couch, and she sat next to him. His voice spoke dryly and slowly, "Sit next to me, I gotta talk to you about something."

Evie drafted up all sorts of miserable scenarios and reluctantly sat next to him. "What is it?"

He shook, his nerves unsettled. The low light was ominous, and the rain came hard. The lights cast a shadow on his eyes as he looked downward. The house was quiet. "I have to confess something to you. I was gonna wait until Valentine's Day, but I can't."

She steadied herself, but it was hard. "It's alright. Whatever it is, we can get through it."

"I'm in love with someone." He still held his hands, leaning over on his knees in thought.

Her whole head felt like it was going to burst, and her lips went numb and cold.

"And I can't hide it anymore. My past is healed, but this woman also feels like she can mend my future."

The knife twisted, and she felt like she was going to choke. Internally, she was. Her heartbeat hit the floor, or so it felt.

And with that, Caleb scooted off the couch, turned to her, and got down on one knee. Evie felt the tidal wave coming into her chest, for she didn't know what was going on.

Until he pulled a small black jewelry box from his pocket.

She absolutely burst into tears.

He gently grabbed her hand and spoke to her tenderly, "That woman is you."

She covered her face with her hands. All over her body shook.

"Evelyn Marie Morgan, I know I leave soon for deployment, but...

when I come back, will you marry me?" He opened the box to show her a beautiful gold band with a ruby surrounded by diamonds. She had never wanted a diamond. A ruby with gold was her dream ring.

Evie's emotions crashed as she fell on top of him, knocking him over. Together, they held each other and rolled over on their sides. She bawled and clutched into his chest with reckless abandon, and she was stuttering the word "yes" over and over again. She cried harder, "Yes!"

Caleb lifted her hand and helped her sit up. She was shaken to the core. He had to steady her hand with his. He lifted the ring from the box then lifted her chin. As he kissed her, he delicately slipped the ring on. Through broken lips and breath, she returned that sweet kiss.

He *was* worth waiting for.

Epilogue

March 4th

Evie was kneeling in the rain, but she never felt the wet ground. She set a pot of flowers next to a gravestone. She lowered her head and wept, touching the stone that read "George 'Pawpaw' Morgan. 1940-2023. USN Fighter Pilot. Beloved husband, father, and grandfather. Forever soaring the eternal patrol."

She lowered her head and pressed her forehead to the stone and rested her left hand on it. The rain still didn't touch her, and neither did the wet grass. "Pawpaw, I've met someone. He's a damn good man."

She felt herself breaking. Her face twisted and she choked, rubbing her forehead against it. "I've got my pretty ruby ring I've always wanted. And you'd love him. He's in the Navy, like you. He fixed up my house, and we're gonna get married when he comes back. He leaves for deployment in two days, and I'm praying that you keep him safe. Let him come home to his children and I."

She shook her head, forcing her emotions deeper into the ground. "I wish you or Daddy could be here to walk me down the aisle."

A warm hand came to her shoulder.

She cried silently for her pawpaw, for her daddy, for her mama.

Sniffling, she composed herself and looked down at the sweater that someone had given her to kneel on. It was utterly cold. "You'd love him, Pawpaw. And I can finally tell you his name."

She chuckled. "His name is Caleb Wright. You'd love him. He's gonna take good care of me."

A quiet and deep voice came from above her, "Yes, sir, I am."

"Tell Daddy and Mama that, would you?"

She looked up to her right and saw Caleb smiling, holding the umbrella for her. He was simply sparkling in his service uniform to show his respects. Behind her, she could hear Olivia sniffling and Zack being patient and kind. Evie laid another bouquet on the grave and kissed it.

Evie was right. No matter how deep scars ran, they could heal.

No, she wasn't alone.

Not anymore.

About the Author

~~~

Jak Angelescu, born Lindsay Hoffman, is a musician and author. Her early life was marked by adventure, moving from Florida to Alaska, where her imagination flourished.

After her family settled in Missouri, Jak faced challenges, including the loss of her sister in a car accident. She found solace in music and poetry, eventually becoming a guitarist and forming several bands. Jak's passion for music led her to Los Angeles, where she worked at a rehearsal studio, rubbed elbows with famous musicians, and joined a Judas Priest tribute band.

Her debut fantasy novel, A Promise Kept: A Guardian's Travail, ended up on the #18 spot on Amazon for the category of women's action adventure. She has hosted several events where she shares her insights on being an author, as well as numerous successful conventions where she enjoys meeting new people and connecting with her readers.

Jak is currently a guitarist for the heavy metal band Unknown, performs country songs locally, and resides in Kansas City, Missouri. She is a devout Methodist Christian, supports animal rescues, and she enjoys chocolate and Italian culture. She is also a proud supporter of our military and law enforcement.

List of Other Books by the Author

A Promise Kept – A Guardian's Travail. An epic fantasy story about a blind girl who joins the elite village Guardians in hopes of bringing her lost friend home.

www.jakangelescu.com

www.facebook.com/missjakangelescu

www.instagram.com/missjakangelescu